"You have two weeks left in Glendovia, and I fully intend to enjoy them. To enjoy you."

Nicolas moved closer, his arms drawing her into his embrace. "I know that you'll need to spend your days working. But your evenings will be free. And I'll expect you to spend them with me, in my bed."

"Absolutely not." Alandra shook her head and took a step back, breaking away from his touch.

As much as he wanted to close the distance between them and kiss the quarrel from her lips, he remained where he was, allowing her to believe a few inches of space would keep her safe from him.

Rossellini's Revenge Affair
by Yvonne Lindsay

ᛒ ⌘ ᛒ

Raffaele despised her with every breath in his body.

Lana was widowed, when she should have been a divorcée. Tall, elegant, unnaturally composed. Had she even loved her dead husband? He doubted it. If she'd loved him, she would have let him go. Let him go to Maria, Raffaele's sister, instead of clinging to a marriage long dead.

Would his treasured sister be lying in a hospital bed right now, supported only by life-giving machinery, if Lana had only given in to her husband's repeated requests to be set free? Set free before the birth of a child who would now never know its father or its mother.

He'd failed to protect his sister but he would *not* fail her unborn child.

Raffaele Rossellini never made the same mistake twice.

Christmas in His Royal Bed
HEIDI BETTS

Rossellini's Revenge Affair
YVONNE LINDSAY

MILLS & BOON®
Pure reading pleasure™

First published in Great Britain 2008
by Harlequin Mills & Boon Limited,
Eton House, 18-24 Paradise Road, Richmond, Surrey TW9 1SR

The publisher acknowledges the copyright holders of the
individual works as follows:

Christmas in His Royal Bed © Heidi Betts 2007
Rossellini's Revenge Affair © Dolce Vita Trust 2007

ISBN: 978 0 263 85922 5

51-1208

Printed and bound in Spain
by Litografia Rosés S.A., Barcelona

CHRISTMAS IN HIS ROYAL BED

by
Heidi Betts

Dear Reader,

I've always wanted to write a story involving some type of royalty…a prince hero or princess heroine. I also knew that I wanted to give Alandra Sanchez, whom I introduced in my April 2008 Desire™ book, *Blackmailed into Bed*, a very special hero of her own. Well, what could be more special than a prince, right? Putting them both together seemed like the perfect solution. Add to that the opportunity I was given to set this story during the holidays, and I was one happy camper!

I hope you enjoy *Christmas in His Royal Bed* and this little jaunt through the island kingdom of Glendovia.

And don't forget to visit my website, www. HeidiBetts.com, as often as you like for information about all of my books!

Happy holidays!

Heidi Betts

HEIDI BETTS

An avid romance reader since school, Heidi knew early on that she wanted to write these wonderful stories of love and adventure. It wasn't until her first year of college, however, when she spent the entire night reading a romance novel instead of studying for finals, that she decided to take the road less travelled and follow her dream. As well as devoting her time to reading, writing and creating romance, she is the founder of her local Romance Writers of America chapter. She also has a tendency to take injured and homeless animals of every species into her Central Pennsylvania home.

Heidi loves to hear from readers. You can write to her at PO Box 99, Kylertown, PA 16847, USA (an SAE with return posatge is appreciated, but not necessary) or e-mail heidi@heidibetts.com. And be sure to visit www.heidibetts.com for news and information about new books.

In loving memory of Helen Brown. When she passed away this time last year after a long and valiant battle with breast cancer, I lost a friend, and the romance world lost a dedicated fan. We miss you, Helen. And if Heaven is any kind of Heaven at all, it will be filled with romance novels for you to enjoy.

And with much appreciation to loyal reader Jennifer Yates, who, when I challenged readers to help me out, came up with many of the names used in this story. Thanks, Jennifer!

One

*O*nly she would do.

Prince Stephan Nicolas Braedon of Glendovia watched the ebony-haired beauty from afar. Tall and lithe, with an hourglass figure, she had silky black hair that fell in a straight curtain to her hips. He was too far away to know the color of her eyes or see the full pout of her lips, but he trusted the feeling in his gut that told him both would be just as alluring as the rest of her.

Cocking his head toward the tall, suited man

at his side, he said in a low voice, "Find out her name."

His bodyguard followed the direction of his gaze, then gave a stiff nod before moving away. Nicolas didn't need to ask how Osric intended to get the information, nor did he care.

A few minutes later, his bodyguard returned, standing at attention at Nicolas's side.

"Her name is Alandra Sanchez, Your Highness. She is in charge of the organization of this evening's event."

Alandra. A beautiful name for a beautiful woman.

She floated around the large, crowded ballroom, smiling, chatting with guests, making sure everything was running smoothly. The full-length lavender gown she wore shimmered in the muted lighting every time she moved, and fit her perfect feminine curves like a glove.

Nicolas hadn't attended this fund-raising dinner in hopes of finding a lover, but now that he'd seen her, he knew he wouldn't be leaving the United States without making arrangements for her to become his next mistress.

It was true that he was the member of the royal

family in charge of overseeing Glendovia's charitable organizations, but his duties did not extend to attending charitable events outside of his own country. That, he usually left to his sister or one of his two brothers.

But though his sister, Mia, had been scheduled to make the trip to the States and attend this dinner to raise funds for a new children's wing at a central Texas hospital, she'd had to cancel at the last minute. Since Nicolas was to meet with very wealthy oilmen to discuss fuel for his country, he decided to attend.

Until a few minutes ago, he had been resenting the interruption of his own life and plans, and all but cursing his sister for being the cause. Now, however, he was considering sending Mia a bouquet of flowers or a box of her favorite truffles. He wanted to thank her for putting him on a path to what could turn out to be an extremely pleasurable experience.

Smiling so brightly the muscles in her cheeks ached, Alandra Sanchez moved around the room, making sure everything was running smoothly. She'd been working to set up this gala for months now, in hopes of raising both awareness and money for the new children's hospital wing.

Unfortunately, things weren't going quite as well as she'd hoped, and Alandra knew she had only herself to blame.

Everyone in the room seemed to be watching her. She could see their curiosity. Sense their condemnation.

All because she'd had the dreadful misfortune to get mixed up with the wrong man.

Of all the things that could have happened to put a damper on this evening's event, this was the worst. A hurricane, a flash flood, even the hotel catching on fire…

Those were all disasters she could have handled. They barely would have caused a blip on her radar. But instead, she was being personally attacked, her reputation besmirched.

It served her right for ever getting involved with Blake Winters in the first place. She should have known the minute she met him that he would end up causing her nothing but trouble.

And now everyone in this room—everyone in Gabriel's Crossing, the great state of Texas and possibly the entire United States of America—thought she was a home-wrecking adulteress.

That's what the newspaper gossip columns were saying about her. Her picture, along with Blake's and that of his wife and two children, had been plastered everywhere, with glaring, slanderous headlines.

Ignoring the stares and whispers she knew were aimed in her direction, Alandra held her head high and continued wending her way through the ballroom, acting as though nothing was wrong. As though her heart wasn't racing, her face wasn't flushed with humiliation and her palms weren't damp with anxiety.

Nothing that had happened in the week since the story of her affair with Blake Winters broke had led her to believe the fund-raising dinner wouldn't still be a complete success. None of the invited guests had cancelled, making excuses for why they couldn't attend. No one from the hospital benevolence society had called to complain about the scandal she found herself suddenly embroiled in, or to voice concerns about her name being linked to the organization.

All of which led her to believe everything would be fine. That even though reporters were camped out on her front lawn, the rest of her life continued to run smoothly.

Now, though, she wasn't so sure. Now, she thought perhaps every seat in the room was filled because the cream of central Texas high society wanted an up-close-and-personal glimpse of one of their own who had so recently fallen from grace.

She might as well have a scarlet letter pinned to her chest or a piece of spinach stuck in her teeth, for all the attention being focused on her every move.

The attention—even negative attention—she could handle. What concerned her more than the stares and whispers was the impact her newly sullied reputation might have on the amount of money collected this evening.

She'd worked so hard to put this event together, was so passionate about her philanthropy, giving of both her time and money to support the causes she felt most strongly about. And she had always been quite successful in convincing others to give to those causes, too.

Usually, by this point in the evening, she would

already have collected a dozen extremely generous checks slipped to her by those in attendance, with more to follow at the end of the night. Tonight, however, her hands—and the hospital's coffers—were still empty.

Because she'd had the misfortune of meeting Blake Winters at another fund-raiser last year, and hadn't been wise enough to turn him away when he'd started asking her out, those who were most in need could very well end up going without.

The prospect broke her heart, and she pressed a hand to the snug satin stays sewn into the lining of her gown in an attempt to settle the nervous caterpillars squirming and wiggling in her belly.

She would act as though nothing was wrong, nothing was out of the ordinary—and pray like the dickens that the crowd got over their curiosity and remembered their true purpose for being here before the evening was over. Otherwise, she had a sneaking suspicion her personal bank account would be taking a hard hit when she attempted to single-handedly make up for what the children's wing fund should have earned tonight. And probably would have, if not for her bad luck and some of the poor decisions she'd made recently.

Once she'd made her loop through the crowd to be sure every seat was filled, every guest served and everything was running as smoothly as possible, she returned to her own place at the front of the room, where a raised dais had been set up for the event's organizers. She made small talk with the women on either side of her and choked down her meal, barely tasting a bite.

Next came a speech from the organization's president, and a short ceremony where plaques were given to several members who had gone above and beyond in the past year. Even Alandra received one, for her continued dedication to raising money for the hospital.

Finally, the evening drew to an end, and she breathed a sigh of relief. She was now holding a few generous checks, and had received promises for more. Not as many as she'd collected in the past, and she had definitely noticed a distinct difference in the way people had treated her throughout the evening. But at least things were looking a bit brighter than they had when the night began.

She made a final round of the room, nodding farewells to guests as they exited the ballroom, and making sure no one left anything behind before the hotel staff started cleaning up.

Gathering her own small, beaded clutch and shawl from her seat, she found her mind racing ahead to what she needed to do the next day— thoughts that were interrupted when she heard a low, masculine voice call her name.

"Miss Sanchez?"

Turning, she found herself dwarfed by a wide-shouldered, dark-haired mountain of a man.

She swallowed once before pasting a smile on her face and tipping her head up, up, up to meet his gaze.

"Yes?"

"If you have a minute, my employer would like to speak with you."

He inclined his head, drawing her attention to the back of the room, where a lone gentleman sat at one of the now-cleared round tables.

From what she could see at this distance, he was quite handsome.

He was also staring at her.

"Your employer?" she asked.

"Yes, miss."

So much for gaining more information about who, exactly, the mountain's employer was.

But if he had attended tonight's dinner, then he was likely a current or potential donor, and she always had time to speak with a contributor. Especially one who could afford his own bodyguard, or CIA agent, or professional wrestler....

"Of course," she said, maintaining her bright, upbeat demeanor.

Turning sideways, the giant gestured for her to move ahead of him, and then escorted her across the nearly empty room. Around them, dishes clinked and stacked chairs clattered as the kitchen and cleaning staff worked to disassemble what had taken all day to set up.

As she approached the man who wished to speak with her, he lifted a flute of champagne and took a long sip.

He wore a smartly tailored jacket of navy blue, cut quite differently than most of those she'd seen throughout the night. He definitely was not a local.

She also noticed that her earlier perception of

him being "quite handsome" was a gross inaccuracy. He was movie-star gorgeous, with dark hair and startling blue eyes that seemed to bore into her like laser beams.

Holding out her hand, she introduced herself. "Hello, I'm Alandra Sanchez."

"I know," he replied, taking her hand and refusing to let it go as he tugged her gently forward. "Have a seat, won't you, please."

Letting her shawl fall lower on her bare back, she slid onto the chair beside him. "Your…employee said you wanted to speak to me."

"Yes," he replied slowly. "May I offer you a glass of champagne?"

She opened her mouth to refuse, but the hulk was already pouring and setting a glass in front of her.

"Thank you."

Though they both had drinks now, and the evening's event was clearly over, the man seated beside her still didn't speak. The silence made Alandra shift uncomfortably, and caused gooseflesh to break out along her arms.

"What did you need to speak with me about,

Mr...." she finally pressed, careful to remain as polite as possible.

"You may call me Nicolas," he replied.

His voice carried a slight accent. Perhaps the hint of a British lilt, but Alandra couldn't place it.

"Nicolas," she repeated, because he seemed to expect it. Then she continued in her attempts to get to his reason for wanting to speak with her.

"Were you interested in making a donation to the fund for the new children's cancer wing of the hospital?" she asked. "If so, I would be happy to accept a check tonight. Or if you'd prefer, I can put you in touch with someone from the organization you can speak with, to make your contribution personally."

For a moment after she finished, he simply continued to study her, his lapis-blue eyes sharp and commandingly intense.

After taking another sip of the expensive champagne, he slowly said, "I would be happy to give to your little...cause. However, that is not why I invited you over here."

Alandra's eyes widened fractionally at that, but she did her best to hide her consternation.

"I am staying in a suite of rooms here in this hotel," he informed her. "I'd like for you to return there with me. Spend the rest of the evening in my bed. If things go well and we are…compatible, perhaps we can discuss further arrangements."

Alandra blinked, but otherwise remained frozen in place, her entire body mannequin-stiff and unmoving. She couldn't have been more stunned if he'd lifted a hand and slapped her across the face.

She didn't know what to say. Didn't know what she *should* say.

This certainly wasn't the first time she'd been propositioned. Young or old, rich or poor, men had always been attracted to her, and she'd had more than her share of invitations to dinner, the theater, even romantic jaunts to private island hideaways.

And, yes, she was well aware that every single one of those men had hopes that dinner, the theater and tropical getaways would help him to seduce her into his bed.

But never—*never*—had any of them been so bold, so brash, as to flat-out ask her to sleep with him.

This was all because of the scandal, she realized

suddenly, her spine snapping straight with offense. Those bloody articles had labeled her an immoral home wrecker. And this man had obviously gotten wind of that and decided she wouldn't be averse to an indecent proposal.

Well, she was averse. She was disgusted and thoroughly insulted.

Pushing her chair back, she rose to her feet, rearranged her shawl across her back and arms, and tightened her fingers on her small clutch purse. Concentrating on her breathing, she stood perfectly rigid, looking down at him.

"I don't know what kind of woman you think I am. But I can assure you I'm *not* the kind to go to bed with a man I've just met."

She cut a quick glance at the bear standing at attention a yard or two away. "Maybe your bodyguard can find someone a little more willing and a lot less discriminating to go back to your room with you tonight. That is, if you're utterly incapable of finding her on your own."

With that, Alandra turned on her heel and marched out of the ballroom to the elevator.

Just who the hell did the man think he was?

Two

Who did she think she was to speak to him in such a manner?

Nicolas had never been turned down like that before.

He blinked once, slowly, searching his memory for a similar incident that might have taken place during his lifetime.

No, he didn't think he'd been turned down *ever*.

Had she actually implied that he was incapable of finding his own female companionship? Or that he had to order Osric to *pay* a woman to spend time with him?

He shook his head, still not quite believing what had just taken place. Behind him, Osric shuffled closer, looming over his right shoulder.

"Your Highness, shall I go after her and bring her back so that you may finish your conversation?"

Nicolas could picture his oversize bodyguard, who closely resembled a brick wall, tackling Miss Sanchez to the ground and carting her back to him…and the fuss the lady would kick up if he so much as tried.

"No, thank you, Osric," he replied. "I believe I'll be returning to the suite alone this evening."

Placing his hands on the tabletop in front of him, he stood and straightened the front of his jacket, then started out of the ballroom, with his trusty security guard close on his heels.

He should be upset, Nicolas thought, as they made their way through the hotel to his private, luxurious suite on the thirty-third floor.

Ironically, he was more intrigued than ever by the ebony-haired beauty. It was her face and figure that had first caught his attention, and seeing her up close hadn't changed his mind about having her in his bed.

He would have expected a dressing-down such as she'd given him to turn him off, to make him realize he didn't want to sleep with a woman who possessed such a sharp tongue. Instead, her spirit fired his blood.

If anything, he found himself wanting her more. She was lovely and fierce, and he could only imagine how passionately those qualities would translate between the sheets.

Alandra Sanchez might think she'd gotten in the last word downstairs, when she'd all but told him to take his offer and go straight to the devil. But Prince Stephan Nicolas Braedon was used to getting his way, getting what he wanted.

And he wanted *her.*

So he would have her. He only had to figure out how.

One week later...

"Pop? Alandra? Is anybody here?"

Alandra heard her sister calling from downstairs,

and was more than happy to take a break from the event plans she'd been working on all afternoon.

Since Elena had moved out of their father's house and into her own with her new husband, Chase, Alandra didn't get to see her as often as she used to.

Abandoning her desk, she found her sister looking slightly frazzled as she flipped through a pile of mail stacked beside a large arrangement of fresh flowers on the round table in the center of the foyer. When she heard Alandra's approach, Elena raised her head and rolled her eyes.

"A reporter tried to follow my car through the security gate," she snapped, waving a hand over her shoulder in the direction of the front door. "He was camped out front, waiting."

Alandra frowned, moving closer to give her sister a gentle squeeze. "I'm so sorry. I really thought they'd have lost interest by now and moved on to something else."

"It's not your fault," Elena said with a sigh, returning Alandra's hug. "And eventually they *will* lose interest and move on."

"So what are you doing here?" she asked distractedly, her mind still on the reporter. It was one thing for *her* to be harassed and annoyed because of her own foolish actions, but it was another for her family to be dragged into this mess.

"Since Chase won't be home for dinner because of a late meeting, I thought I'd stop by to say hello, see how you and Pop are doing, and grab a bite to eat. Not to mention picking up any stray mail," she added, stuffing a few letters into the side pocket of her handbag.

Her sister had married and moved out last year, but the change-of-address process took time, and the odd letter or piece of mail showed up for her occasionally.

"Well, dinner will be served at seven, as usual, and as far as I know, everything is fine around here. Pop is still at the office, and I've just been working on the plans for that fund-raiser for the animal shelters."

"Will Chase and I be invited?" Elena asked.

"Of course."

"Looks like you got something important," her sister said, nodding toward the letter left on top of the stack.

Alandra picked up the thick envelope and read the return address, which was embossed in dark blue, fancy raised script on parchment-quality stationery. "H.R.H. Prince Stephan Nicolas Braedon, Kingdom of Glendovia."

"His Royal Highness?" Elena asked. "Really? You got a letter from a prince?"

"It appears so." She opened the envelope and skimmed the official-looking letterhead and neatly typed text of the top page. Then, heart stuttering, she read it again. "Oh, my God," she breathed.

"What?"

"This Prince Stephan wants me to come to his kingdom and oversee all of their fund-raising organizations."

Both sisters scanned the letter. It touched on Alandra's past fund-raising accomplishments, which the prince claimed were very impressive, and stressed how much Glendovia could use her assistance. He even went so far as to enclose copies of a contract for her employment that he hoped she would peruse and strongly consider signing.

Lifting the cover sheet, Alandra read the one-page agreement. It briefly outlined her duties and obligations, if she chose to accept the royal family's offer, as well as their obligations to her.

"Do you think this is legitimate?" Elena demanded.

The Braedon name did ring some bells. "I guess it would be easy enough to check out," she replied.

The two of them went into Alandra's office, where she started going through her guest lists, and her sister did a quick search on the Internet.

"Huh," Elena said when they discovered at almost the same moment that Stephan Nicolas Braedon was, indeed, a bona fide prince, and the island of Glendovia really did exist. According to Alandra's records, another member of the Braedon royal family—a Princess Mia—had attended one of her recent fund-raisers.

"What are you going to do?" Elena asked.

"Well, I'll reply, of course, and thank him for the generous offer, but I can't possibly accept. I'm already knee-deep in organizing my next event, and Christmas is a month off. I don't want to be away from my family over the holidays."

"I don't blame you, but you have to admit it's a flattering offer."

Extremely flattering, Alandra thought, glancing once again at the raised script of the letterhead. She almost wanted to reach out and run her fingertips over the prince's name. Her letter of refusal definitely wouldn't be an easy one to write.

"But maybe…"

Alandra glanced at her sister. "What?"

"I was just thinking that maybe this position in Glendovia is exactly what you need."

Alandra frowned. "What?"

"Well, things are anything but simple around here for you right now. You've got a reporter camped outside the house, that jerk Winters still calling you, and…well…" Her gaze skittered away and her voice softened slightly. "I heard that last week's fund-raiser didn't go as well as your events usually do."

Alandra took a breath, trying not to let the pain of having her shortcomings pointed out by her own flesh and blood overwhelm her.

Running a supportive hand down her arm, Elena continued. "I was just thinking that if you got away for a while, where no one could find you, this would all blow over. And when you came back, you could get on with your life as though none of it had ever happened."

"But I would be away from you guys," Alandra murmured. "Over Christmas."

"You could come back before then. But even if you didn't, it's only one holiday. There's always next year." Wrapping an arm around her shoulders, her sister added, "I don't necessarily *want* you to go, I'm just saying that maybe you should think it over and do what's best for you. I think Pop would agree."

"I'll consider it," Alandra said, realizing her sister was making a good point. Perhaps the best way to leave all this scandal behind *was* to fly off to a foreign country.

Three

Less than a week later, the Saturday after Thanksgiving, Alandra arrived on the island of Glendovia, hoping against hope that she'd made the right decision.

Her flight had been uneventful. And a limousine had been waiting at the airport for her, as promised in the itinerary that had been faxed to her as soon as she'd accepted Prince Stephan's offer.

Staring out the window as the car sped through the countryside, Alandra was swept away by the beauty of the tiny island country. Located in a northern area of the Mediterranean, it was postcard perfect, with a clear azure sky, rolling emerald hills, and the sprawling blue-green of the sea visible in the distance.

Even what she assumed to be the center of the capital seemed more quaint and clean than anywhere she'd traveled in America or Europe. The buildings were tall, but not mammoth. The streets were busy, but not crowded and harried.

Things seemed more tranquil here, and for the first time since scrawling her name across the bottom of that employment contract, she thought she might actually be glad she'd agreed to come.

Her family had supported the decision wholeheartedly, wanting her to be happy and get away from the scandal they knew was causing her such pain. She had accepted the position in order to protect them from a part of her life that had gotten ugly, in hope it would not spill over onto them.

The limousine slowed and waited for a tall, antique iron gate to slide open. They drove up a long, winding lane that ran among pristine, well-manicured lawns and gardens.

The house—*palace* was a better word—was somewhat historical in design, but looked updated and modern. Eggshell-white, with pillars and balconies and a myriad of floor-to-ceiling windows, it stood atop a small rise overlooking the splashing waves of the Mediterranean.

As the driver opened the door and helped her out of the vehicle, she couldn't tear her eyes away from the breathtaking view. Alandra continued to gawk while the driver removed her bags from the trunk and escorted her to the front door.

A butler opened it and invited her inside, where a handful of maids dressed in matching gray uniforms collected her luggage and trotted off with it.

The butler said, "The prince has requested you be brought to him immediately upon your arrival, Miss Sanchez. If you'll follow me."

Feeling as though she'd just stepped into a fairy tale, Alandra did just that, taking in every detail of the foyer as they passed.

The floor was of highly polished marble in squares of black and a mottled gray-white. A chandelier the size of a small bus hung overhead, with thousands of dangling crystals twinkling in the natural light. Directly across from the front entrance stood a wide staircase leading halfway to the second level before branching off to either side.

The butler led her to the right of the foyer and down a carpeted corridor lined with priceless artwork. He paused at one of the closed doors and knocked. When a low, muffled voice bade him enter, he stepped inside, announced Alandra's presence and then moved aside for her to pass.

The personal office was decidedly masculine, with a dark area rug, built-in bookshelves lining three of the four walls, and a large cherrywood desk taking up a good portion of the room.

Dragging her gaze from the impressive surroundings, Alandra turned her attention to the man sitting behind that desk…only to feel her eyes go wide and her mouth fall open.

"You."

"Miss Sanchez." He rose and regally rounded the desk until he stood directly in front of her. "How good of you to accept my offer and come to work for our family."

"You're Prince Stephan—"

"Nicolas Braedon of Glendovia, yes. You may call me Nicolas."

Nicolas. The same Nicolas who had asked her over for a glass of champagne and then invited her to sleep with him.

Her mouth went dry with shock, her stomach clenching and her pulse kicking as though she'd just run a marathon.

How could this be happening?

"I don't understand," she said, her voice faint as she struggled to put her thoughts into words. "Why would you invite me to work for you after the way we parted? All you wanted from me then was…"

Realization dawned.

"You did this on purpose. You lured me here under false pretenses so that I would sleep with you."

"My dear Miss Sanchez," he replied, standing straight as a sword, with his hands clasped behind his back, "Glendovia is very much in need of someone to organize its charitable foundations. And, after seeing you in action, I decided you would be the perfect person for the job."

"And you've changed your mind about wanting me in your bed?" she challenged.

Nicolas studied the woman in front of him, struggling not to smile at her forthright manner and the fury snapping in her brown, almond-shaped eyes. It was a sight to behold, and only made him more certain of the wisdom of the campaign he'd put in motion.

Her rejection of him during his stay in America hadn't dulled his desire for her at all. He had decided, not long after, that since the direct approach hadn't worked, perhaps he needed to go about attaining his goal in a more subtle way.

When it came to Alandra Sanchez, it seemed a bit of seduction was in order.

It had taken him a few days after returning home to land on the idea of asking her to his country for an extended stay. He knew she wouldn't accept if he merely invited her…or if she knew he was extending the invitation, for that matter.

But because they had philanthropy in common, he knew that was the one motive that had a chance of catching her attention. There was also the rather generous bonus he'd included in the employment contract as an added incentive—two hundred and fifty thousand dollars to be donated by him to a charity of her choosing once she'd fulfilled her part of the bargain.

And now she was here, exactly where he wanted her.

Not that she looked even remotely willing to jump into bed with him at the moment. But as with everything else, that would come.

He would see to it.

"I wouldn't say that," he murmured, replying to her question about whether or not he'd changed his mind about wanting her in his bed. "But I am certainly capable of separating business from pleasure."

Without giving her a chance to argue, he continued. "Come. I'll show you to your room, where you can unpack and perhaps rest before supper."

Dropping his arms to his sides, he stepped around her and crossed the room to open the door.

"Don't bother," she replied curtly behind his back. "I'm not staying."

Half turning to face her once again, he maintained a neutral expression. "Don't be ridiculous. Of course you are. You signed a contract."

"Contract be damned." She started for the door, her demeanor icy.

He waited for her to pass, then caught her arm as she marched down the empty hallway. "Are you really willing to deprive one of your favorite charities of a quarter of a million dollars?"

The reminder stopped her in her tracks, and he pressed his advantage. "If you leave, reneging on the agreement, you forfeit the bonus. Stay through the month of December and you will not only be paid the agreed-upon wage, but will also earn a hefty sum to bestow as you see fit."

He could almost hear the gears turning in her head as she weighed her options. Leave, and she would be safe from him; he would have no opportunity to try to lure her into his bed. Stay, and she would be all but walking into the lion's den, but would also end up earning a quarter of a million dollars to fund one of her pet projects. It was a compelling enticement.

The seconds ticked by while she stood in the middle of the hall, wracked with indecision. Once again, he chose to give her a small nudge in the direction he wished her to go.

Moving closer, he placed a hand at the small of her back. She stiffened and pulled away just enough to break the contact.

"Please," he said diplomatically, "allow me to show you where you'll be staying if you elect to remain and fulfill your contract. The family will gather in the dining room for dinner at eight o'clock. I'd like you to be there, if you would, to meet everyone. After that, if you still wish to return to the United States…"

He paused, choosing his words carefully. "I won't say I'll let you go without penalty, but I will be willing to discuss the situation further."

For a moment, he thought she would continue her retreat. And then the rigid line of her spine relaxed slightly and her shoulders lifted as she inhaled a deep breath.

Without turning around, she said, "Fine. I'll stay through dinner."

"Excellent. Come along, then," he replied, careful not to let his satisfaction show as he stepped around her and walked the rest of the way down the hall.

He led her through the foyer and up the curved staircase, toward the west wing. There were more hallways and a second set of stairs before they reached the suites of rooms reserved for guests.

The royal family's quarters were located in the east wing, on the opposite end of the palace. But that was for the best. If his plan to seduce Alandra succeeded, their relationship could be kept almost completely secret, thanks to the relative privacy of the west wing and the fact that she would be the only person in residence there for the next month.

Reaching her suite, he opened the heavy, carved mahogany door, standing just inside to allow her to enter ahead of him. Briefly, he showed her the sprawling sitting room, with its large-screen plasma television and DVD library. Nicolas hadn't known her personal tastes, so he'd ordered the room to be stocked with a variety of choices, any of which she could exchange in the family's entertainment room whenever she liked.

Glancing through the bedroom door, Nicolas was happy to note that Alandra's things had already been unpacked and put away. She was carefully observing her surroundings, and if she was offended that the palace staff had handled her belongings, she didn't say so. She looked pleased with the accommodations, her expressive eyes taking in every detail of the beautifully decorated rooms.

"I'll leave you alone now, to rest or take a tour of the grounds, whatever you like. One of the staff can show you to the dining room when you're ready."

Turning on his heel, he left her standing in the middle of the bedroom.

Alandra watched him go, still seething at his manipulation, and yet not so angry that she failed to notice the handsome, regal picture he made as he exited.

She supposed she should be flattered that a prince wanted her in his bed. Most women would be, she imagined.

The problem was that he hadn't seemed interested in *her*, in getting to know her or starting a relationship with her. His request when they'd met in Texas was to take her to bed for a night—or perhaps a handful of nights. And because of who he was, he expected her to simply acquiesce.

Even if she might have been attracted to him otherwise, that fact turned her off entirely. She didn't want to be some playboy prince's temporary intimate diversion.

With a sigh, she began to explore her rooms,

checking to see where all her things had been stored. Dresses, blouses and slacks hung in the wardrobe. More casual tops and pants had been folded and stacked in the dresser, along with her underthings. And her toiletries had been lined up on the bathroom counter or tucked into the available drawers. Even the books and folders she'd brought, for work and for leisure, had been neatly stacked on a small desk set before one of the windows overlooking the balcony.

She hadn't made up her mind yet about whether she planned to stay, but had to admit that if she *did* decide to fulfill her bargain with the Prince of Lies, the view alone would make her visit feel less like manipulation and more like a paid vacation.

Stepping onto the wide stone balcony, she moved to the railing and gazed out at the ocean beyond. Waves rolled to the shore, bringing with them a gentle lulling sound that could soothe even the most restless soul.

Glancing at her watch, Alandra saw that she still had a couple of hours before she needed to start getting ready for dinner with the royal family. The thought of meeting them caused her stomach to dip dizzily.

But she would deal with that when she had to. For now, she would call home to let her father and sister know she'd arrived safely, and to maybe get Elena's advice about her current situation.

Should she stay or should she go? Should she tell the prince just what he could do with his devious, conniving contract, and walk away from the chance to gift a quarter of a million dollars to a charity that could dearly use the money? Or should she swallow her pride and do what she had to to get through the month?

Four

At five minutes to eight that evening, Alandra followed the maze of hallways on the palace's second floor and found her way to the main staircase. The maid who had come to check up on her earlier had given her general directions to the dining room, and Alandra thought she could find it on her own.

But she needn't have worried. As soon as she reached the stairs, she found Nicolas standing at the bottom, waiting for her.

He was dressed in a dark suit, which made her feel better about her own outfit. She hadn't known quite what to wear to her first dinner with a royal family, so had opted for a simple blue silk dress.

"Good evening," Nicolas said in greeting, watching her intently as she descended the stairs.

Alandra felt a skittering of awareness as his gaze swept her from head to toe. No doubt about it, this man was dangerous. If she decided to stay, she would have to be very careful not to let those blue eyes and his handsome face lure her in and make her do something she wouldn't normally do.

"Good evening," she replied, pausing at the bottom of the stairs.

"May I?" he asked, offering his arm.

She hesitated only a second before accepting, lightly slipping her hand around his elbow.

"You look lovely," he told her as they crossed the marble floor. The chandelier had been turned on, sending bright, twinkling light throughout the foyer and beyond.

"Thank you."

She was saved from having to make further con-

versation as they reached the dining room. Nicolas opened one of the tall double doors, ushering
her inside.

The room was as opulent as the rest of the palace. A long, narrow trestle table ran the length of
it, surrounded by heavy, high-backed chairs with
seats embroidered with what must be the Braedon
family crest. Light trickled down from another
chandelier hanging over the table, and glowed
from many wall sconces.

The queen and king were already seated at the
table, which held intricate place settings laid out
for six guests. Nicolas guided her forward, stopping near what she assumed would be her seat.

"Mother, Father, I'd like you to meet Alandra
Sanchez. She's from the United States and will be
our guest for the next month while she works to
help us better organize Glendovia's charitable
foundations. And hopefully increase their profit
margin. Alandra, this is my father, King Halden,
and my mother, Queen Eleanor."

The older man rose and came halfway around
the table, taking her hand and pressing a soft kiss
to her knuckles. "Welcome to Glendovia, my dear.

We appreciate the work you'll be doing on behalf of our country."

"Thank you, Your Highness," she replied, only slightly intimidated by meeting and speaking with a real live king. "It's a pleasure to meet you."

Turning toward the queen, Alandra noticed that she'd remained seated. And when Alandra approached, she didn't offer to shake her hand.

"Your Highness," Alandra murmured politely and respectfully, pausing before the older woman.

She was greeted with a rather stiff nod, giving her the uncomfortable feeling that she wasn't as welcome as Nicolas and his father would have her believe.

"Please be seated," the queen told her. "Dinner will be served soon."

Returning to Nicolas's side, Alandra allowed him to hold her chair for her before he made his way around the table to the place directly across from her.

A second later, the dining room doors opened again and another couple swept in. It was obvious to Alandra that the gentleman, at least, was related to Nicolas. He had the same build, coloring and facial structure as Nicolas and the king.

The woman had similar physical traits, but Alandra didn't want to assume anything for fear she was a wife or girlfriend rather than a sister.

"Good evening, everyone," the man boomed, smiling easily.

"Mother, Father," the young woman intoned, removing any doubt of her relation to the others. "Nicolas," she added, laying her hands on his shoulders and leaning in to press a kiss to his cheek.

"Menace," he replied, one corner of his mouth quirking up in a grin before he shifted his attention back to Alandra. "I'd like you to meet my younger brother, Sebastian, and my sister, Mia, the baby of the family."

Princess Mia gave a short, harried sigh. "I hate it when you introduce me that way," she told him.

"I know. That's why I do it," he countered. Alandra didn't miss the affectionate sparkle in his eyes or the amusement that lingered on his sister's face as she strolled around the table to take the seat to Alandra's left.

"Our eldest brother, Dominick, is out of the country right now, but hopefully you'll meet him before you leave."

Shaking out the napkin on her plate and placing it neatly in her lap, Mia said, "It's nice to meet you, Alandra. Nicolas mentioned that you would be coming. He says you have brilliant ideas about increasing the amount of funds taken in by non-profit organizations."

Alandra's gaze flashed to Nicolas, flattered by his indirect praise, but he was looking at his sister.

"She's done terrific work with several charities back in the States," he announced.

From his seat across the table, Sebastian said, "That's good. We certainly have our share of worthy causes here on the island that could use a bit of a boost. And it helps that she's quite the beauty." Glancing in her direction, Sebastian winked.

For a moment, Alandra was startled by his brash behavior—in front of his family, no less. Then she realized this must simply be his personality. He was the youngest son, the one furthest in line from taking over the throne, and from the looks of it, a bit of a playboy, to boot.

She returned his good-natured smile before noticing the scowl on Nicolas's face. Her enjoyment fled immediately, replaced by a strange sensation in the pit of her belly. She didn't know whether to be concerned or intimidated, or even amused.

He had brought her here to be his mistress; she knew that. Under the pretense of working for his family, perhaps, but that didn't change the fact that he wanted her in his bed.

However, that didn't explain why he would look so cross at his brother's harmless comment and teasing.

Unless Nicolas and Sebastian had fought over— or perhaps shared—women before. Was Nicolas concerned that his brother would catch her eye before he'd had a chance to seduce her himself?

Oh, that was an interesting twist. And it would serve him right for spinning such a web of deceit to bring her here in the first place.

Servants arrived then to pour glasses of water and rich red wine. When the salad course was served, conversation turned to family and Glendovian affairs. Alandra ate in relative silence, finding the topics interesting, but having few comments of her own to add.

During dessert, Mia and Sebastian asked her about her own family and life back in Texas. She was only too happy to answer, but avoided any mention of the scandal that had driven her away.

"And what are your plans now that you're here?" Mia inquired. "Where do you think you'll begin with the charities?"

Before Alandra could answer, Nicolas interrupted. "That's something I intend to discuss with her at great length, but she's just arrived and I haven't had the chance to fill her in yet on everything she'll need to know." Pushing back his chair, he rose to his feet. "In fact, if you'll excuse us, I'd like to get started on that now."

He came around to her side of the table, taking her arm and giving her little choice but to leave with him. She said her good-nights and followed him across the room.

"Nicolas," the queen called out as he reached the door. "I'd like a word with you."

"Certainly, Mother," he replied in a respectful tone. "As soon as I see Alandra to her rooms, I'll return to the library. We can speak there."

His mother offered an almost imperceptible nod and they left.

With his hand once again at the small of her

back, he guided Alandra to the main stairwell, and they started slowly up the steps. She didn't miss his continued attempts at familiarity. And while his fingertips warmed her through the material of her dress, sending tiny shocks of desire through her system, she had to wonder if it was merely the first phase of his orchestrated attempts at seduction.

Even if it was, it wouldn't work.

She was stronger than that. Nicolas might be charming and gorgeous, his status as a prince alluring, but he had brought her here under false pretenses, and she was not going to be won over.

"So," he began, his voice low and persuasive, "have you had a chance to look over the files I left in your room?"

He had, indeed. A pile of colored folders had been left on the desk, each summarizing a different Glendovian charity she assumed she would be working with if she decided to stay.

"I glanced at them," she said.

"And…"

"You have some interesting organizations set up."

"They're not running as well as they should," he said.

"I noticed."

"Do you think you can fix them?"

That was the problem—she did. Even looking over the files for a few minutes before she'd started getting ready for dinner, she'd had a dozen ideas for improvements. Not to mention raising awareness and drawing in larger amounts of funding.

They were concepts she was excited about and eager to put into effect. But in order to do that, she would have to remain in Glendovia and fulfill the terms of her contract.

"I have some ideas," she replied guardedly, as they turned down the hall that led to her suite.

"Excellent." He waited a beat before continuing. "Does this mean you've decided to stay and work here?"

"I'll stay," she told him. "I'll stay through the month, as agreed in the contract, and at the end of the month you'll give me the bonus you promised."

"Of course."

He might have said more at that point, but she cut him off. "And no matter what your reason for bringing me here, no matter what you expected to happen, I will *not* be sleeping with you. You can cross that little item right off your Christmas wish list."

At that, she turned the knob, spun on her heel and disappeared into the suite.

Five

The door to the library was open when Nicolas arrived. His mother was sitting in one of the armchairs before the fireplace, sipping a glass of sherry and staring at the flames leaping in the hearth. Closing the door behind him, he moved to the sideboard and poured himself a drink before joining her.

"You wanted to speak with me?" he asked, leaning back.

Typical of his mother, she got right to the point. "What is she doing here, Nicolas?"

He didn't pretend to misunderstand the question. "As I told you at dinner, I hired her to help with our charities. She's very good at what she does. I think she'll be a boon to the organizations."

"And that's the only reason," his mother said shortly, eyeing him over the rim of her glass. "Nothing else?"

He took a sip of his brandy. "What other reason would there be?"

"Come now, Nicolas. I may be your mother, and therefore not your first choice of confidante about your love life, but I'm well aware of your… leisure pursuits. Are you sure you didn't bring her here to be your next conquest?"

While his personal relationships were no one's concern but his own, it was hard—not to mention foolish—to tell the queen to mind her own business. Even if she was his mother.

So he did what he and his siblings had done many times while growing up. He looked her straight in the eye and lied.

"Of course not. I take my responsibilities to our country very seriously. As soon as I saw what Alandra had done with the event I attended in

America, I knew she would be a great benefit to our own charitable causes."

His mother narrowed her gaze momentarily, as though gauging the truthfulness of his statement. "I'm glad to hear that. You understand, I'm sure, that it wouldn't do for your little associations to become public this close to announcing your engagement. We both know that you haven't been celibate since you agreed to wed Princess Lisette, but it's important that you keep up pretenses and do nothing to upset her or her family. This marriage will create a very important bond between her country and ours."

A brief second passed, and when she spoke again, both her tone and expression were sharper. "We can't jeopardize that association simply because you can't keep your hands off some American commoner."

Letting another swallow of brandy warm its way through his system, Nicolas consciously unclenched his jaw and forced himself to remain respectful.

"I know my duties, Mother. You needn't worry about me causing any problems with Lisette.

Alandra is a lovely woman, but she's no threat to my engagement, believe me."

"That's good to hear. But just in case you change your mind, or Miss Sanchez suddenly begins to look like an amusing diversion while she's visiting, I have something I think you should see."

With that, she reached between the side of her chair and the cushion and removed a folded piece of paper. She handed it to Nicolas and then sat back, every inch the queen as she awaited his reaction.

Unfolding the page, he found himself staring at a printout of a newspaper article with Alandra's picture. On either side of her photo were two others with jagged edges.

The headline accused Alandra of coming between the man and woman depicted, of being the ruin of a happy home and marriage. He scanned the write-up, which made Alandra sound like a selfish, devious trollop with no compunction about carrying on a torrid affair with a married father of two.

"She isn't one of us, Nicolas," his mother intoned. "She created a scandal in the States and brought shame upon her own family with her promiscuousness. We don't need her here, doing the same to us."

Nicolas tensed in response to both the content of the article and his mother's high-handed warning, then relaxed. This revelation about Alandra surprised him, but didn't concern him. And it certainly didn't change his mind about wanting her in his bed, despite his mother's cautionary warning.

"I appreciate your trepidation, Mother, but I think you're making too much of Alandra's visit. She's only here for a month, and only to help with the charities. Nothing more."

The queen arched a brow, but remained silent, making it clear she doubted his claims. But his life was still his own, and until he had actually taken his wedding vows with Princess Lisette, he owed no explanation to anyone.

Refolding the printout and slipping it into the front pocket of his jacket, he pushed himself to his feet and returned his empty glass to the sideboard before crossing to his mother's chair and leaning down to press a kiss to her cheek. "Good night, Mother. I'll see you in the morning."

* * *

Alandra was up early the next day, ready to get to work and start putting some of her strategies into action.

She also hoped to see more of the island and get *away* from Nicolas. He was dangerous to her peace of mind, and the less time they spent together during her stay, the better.

Carrying a briefcase stuffed with papers, she arrived in the dining room. The family was already gathered and eating. A plate was quickly set before her, and Alandra enjoyed her breakfast until the queen inquired about her plans for the day. Alandra still had the distinct feeling Nicolas's mother didn't like her.

"After studying the notes Nicolas gave me, I thought the local orphanage would be the best place to start," she answered. "I've got an idea directly connected to the holidays that I think will be quite successful, but since Christmas is right around the corner, it's important to get things moving as soon as possible."

If the queen was pleased with Alandra's response, she didn't show it. Instead, Nicolas replied. "I'll have a car brought around to take us to the children's home," he said, pushing back his chair and moving toward the dining room's double doors.

"You're…coming along?" Alandra asked, her words stumbling over themselves as her heart thudded. She really, *really* didn't want to spend the day with him.

He stopped at the door and turned back to face her. "Of course."

Swallowing past the lump in her throat, she tried to ignore the heat suddenly licking its way through her insides. "That isn't necessary."

"But it is," he replied softly. "Glendovia's national charities are my responsibility. I take that duty seriously and intend to work quite closely with you over the next month. I hope you don't mind."

He added the last, she was sure, for the benefit of his family, all of whom were watching and listening attentively. Because it was clear that even if she did mind—which she did—it would make absolutely no difference.

If they had been alone, she might have argued,

but she certainly wasn't going to put up a fuss in front of the royal family.

Forcing the words past her tight throat, she said, "No, I don't mind at all."

His lips curved in a smile that told her he knew exactly how much it had pained her to acquiesce. "I'll meet you at the car, then," he murmured, before walking out of the room.

Ten minutes later, they were seated in the back of a luxurious black sedan, driving away from the palace. According to the map of the island she'd studied the night before, the orphanage was nearby.

She was happy to simply gaze out the window at the passing scenery and mentally review what she hoped to accomplish at the children's home. But she should have known Nicolas would never allow her to keep to herself for long.

"So tell me about this holiday idea you have for the orphanage. I'm surprised you've begun to devise a plan already, without even having visited."

Keeping her fingers tightly wrapped around the folders on her lap, she tore her gaze away from the view and turned to face him.

"The files you supplied gave me a general impression of the home, and the type of event I have in mind is something I've been a part of before. It seems to go over well and is usually successful in getting the community involved."

"Sounds promising," he intoned. "What is it?"

"Basically, we throw a small party where Santa Claus visits the children and hands out gifts, and we invite the press and locals to attend. The goal is to draw attention to the orphanage, reminding people that the children are alone and in need not only over the holidays, but year-round."

Nicolas nodded, his mouth pursed in thought. "Interesting. And who provides the presents for the children, given that your fund-raising efforts haven't yet been put into effect?"

She smiled. "You do."

He raised a brow, and she hurried to elaborate. "Or rather, the royal family does. We'll be sure to mention that to the press, throwing your family into a very positive light. In fact, if this goes over as well as I think it will, you may want to consider sponsoring the event every year. Back home, we've made the visit from Santa an annual event, and it goes over extremely well."

Inclining his head, he said, "I'm sure that's something my family would be willing to consider."

The car eased to a stop in front of the children's home. A second later the driver came around to open Nicolas's door. He stepped out, and a bevy of flashbulbs immediately began going off in his face.

Alandra had slid across the seat to exit behind him, but rather than reaching for his hand, which he held out to her, she lifted an arm to shield her eyes from the blinding onslaught.

"Who are all these people?" she called to him.

He leaned in a bit closer to keep from having to raise his voice. "Just members of the press you were speaking of. They tend to follow members of the royal family wherever we go."

Reaching for her hand again, he said, "Come along. It's time to go in, and you'll get used to the attention."

She wasn't so sure of that. Where she had been happy a moment ago, and eager to get to work, she now dreaded having to step outside the vehicle into the crowd of photographers circling like vultures. She'd had quite enough of that back in Texas.

She'd come to Glendovia to get away from the

media. Now here she was, smack in the middle of the frenzy once again.

Of course, she wasn't the center of their attention this time, which she considered a blessing. But that didn't mean she appreciated having her picture taken without her permission here any more than she had back home.

Drawing a breath, she pushed aside the anxieties swirling in her chest as best she could, then placed her hand in Nicolas's and let him help her from the car.

She stared straight ahead, at the redbrick building they were about to enter. The fingers of her left hand tightened almost desperately on the handle of her briefcase, while she concentrated on keeping those of her right loose and relaxed. She didn't want to give Nicolas a single sign of just how disturbed she was by the reporters crowding around, still snapping pictures and calling out to the prince.

Nicolas smiled and gave a polite wave, but otherwise ignored them as he led her forward. The sea of photographers parted at his approach, and finally they were inside.

Releasing her pent-up breath, she let go of his

hand and stepped away, leaving a safer distance between them. When she lifted her gaze to his, she found him watching her, an amused glint in his eyes.

The move had been an act of self-preservation, and he knew it.

Dammit, he must sense that she was attracted to him, and he probably took it as a sign that he was that much closer to his objective: seducing her into his bed.

"Your Highness," a voice called, and footsteps clacked as an older woman came forward to greet them.

She offered him a small curtsy and smiled at Alandra. "I'm Mrs. Vincenza, administrator of the children's home. We're delighted to have you visit us. I hope you'll find everything to your liking, and we'll happily do everything we can to help you with your efforts."

"Thank you, Mrs. Vincenza," Nicolas replied with a small bow. "This is Alandra Sanchez. She'll be handling the fund-raising plans."

"Where *are* the children?" Alandra asked, scanning the open space, with its center stairwell leading to the upper floor.

"The older ones are in school, of course, and the younger ones are upstairs in the nursery. Would you like to meet them?"

"I'd love to," she answered.

She followed Mrs. Vincenza up to the second floor, with Nicolas behind them.

They toured the nursery, where Alandra played with the babies and toddlers for a bit, then met a few other members of the staff. From there, Mrs. Vincenza showed them the children's bedrooms, dining hall, playroom and reception area.

The reception area, Alandra realized as soon as she saw it, would be the perfect place to set up the Santa Claus event. It was large enough for all the children, the media and any number of guests they might invite. There was even a lovely tree already set up and decorated in the far corner.

She jotted down notes as fast as she could, her mind racing ahead to everything that would need to be done. At the same time, she shared her plans with Mrs. Vincenza, whose eyes lit up at the prospect.

Behind them, standing tall and straight in the doorway, Nicolas listened silently. Alandra assumed that meant he approved of the project so far. She was certain he'd let her know if he objected to anything.

An hour later, she'd finalized the initial plans with the administrator and had a list of tasks to deal with herself. After thanking the woman for her time and enthusiasm, she and Nicolas made their way back outside, through the throng of reporters still hovering on the sidewalk, and into the back-seat of the waiting car.

The vehicle had barely started rolling away from the curb before Nicolas faced her and asked, "How do you feel it went?"

"Very well," she answered, flipping through the pages of her spiral pad and reviewing some of the notations she'd made. "Mrs. Vincenza is eager to help us because she knows it will ultimately help *her,* and even though there's a lot of work to do, I think we've got enough time to set everything up so it goes smoothly."

A small smile touched his lips. "I have to admit, I was quite impressed with what you said to her. You're very good at describing your visions so that others can see them clearly."

Her cheeks flushed with pleasure at his compliment and she nodded a silent thank-you.

"Allow me to buy you lunch at one of our local eateries to show my appreciation for all your hard work. We can discuss what else needs to be done to have everything ready by the week before Christmas."

Although she was starting to feel hungry and certainly could have used a bite to eat, she didn't think it was a good idea to spend any more time with him than absolutely necessary. It would be better to go back to the palace and ask for something to be sent to her rooms, where she could hide out and get some work done *away* from Nicolas.

Without meeting his gaze, she said, "Thank you, but no. I'd prefer to go back and get straight to work."

His eyes narrowed slightly at her refusal, and she almost expected him to argue. But then he turned to look forward and said, "Very well. You should remember one thing, however."

"What's that?"

His eyes returned to hers, bright blue and blazing. "You can't avoid me forever."

Six

For the third time in ten minutes, Nicolas checked his watch. He was standing at the bottom of the main stairwell, awaiting Alandra's arrival, while everyone else was gathered in the dining room, ready for dinner.

But the minutes continued to tick by, and still there was no sign of her.

Spotting a maid leaving the dining room, he motioned her over. "Would you please run up to

Miss Sanchez's room and find out why she's running late for dinner?"

"I'm sorry, sir, but she called down earlier to make her excuses and ask for a tray to be brought to her room."

"Is she ill?" he asked, his brows knitting with genuine concern.

"I'm not sure, sir. She didn't say so."

"Thank you," he said, nodding to dismiss the maid.

As soon as the maid disappeared around the corner, he turned and started up the stairs. Minutes later, he was knocking on Alandra's door.

He heard her call that she was coming, and then the door swung open. She was standing there in a short, turquoise-blue nightgown and a matching robe in some slinky material that made his mouth go instantly dry. Her hair was pulled up and twisted into a loose knot at the crown of her head.

Her lovely chocolate-brown eyes went wide with surprise for a second before narrowing with annoyance.

Noticing that his gaze was inexorably drawn to

the shadowed valley between her breasts, she raised a hand to close the edges of her robe.

"May I help you?" she asked in a tone that surely wasn't often directed toward someone of royal lineage.

Biting back his amusement, he kept a straight face and linked his hands behind him. "I heard you weren't coming down to dinner and wanted to make sure you were feeling well. Is everything all right?"

Her expression softened at his inquiry. "I'm fine, thank you. I just decided to have my meal in my room so I could continue to work."

"You've been working since we returned from the children's home," he said, more of a statement than a question.

"That *is* why you hired me," she replied with a tiny smile.

Her grip on the front of her robe loosened and he caught another quick glimpse of cleavage. His body immediately went tight and hot.

Clearing his throat, he struggled to make his brain work past the thought of stripping her bare and having her writhing beneath him. When he couldn't seem to manage that, he gave a curt nod and headed back the way he'd come.

It took him the full length of both hallways and the staircase to regain his reason and decide on a course of action.

First, he strode into the dining room, where the rest of the family had already been served, and told them he wouldn't be sharing dinner with them. Then he went to the rear of the palace and entered the kitchens, asking that two trays be made up and taken to Alandra's suite rather than only one.

He waited while that was done, and then accompanied the servant as the young man delivered the cart. Alandra answered the door when he knocked, a frown marring her brow when she noticed Nicolas trailing behind. To her credit, she held her tongue as the cart was wheeled into the center of the sitting room.

Glancing toward Nicolas, the servant waited to be told where they wished their meals to be served.

"That's fine, Franc. I'll take it from here. Thank you."

The young man inclined his head and quickly

made his way from the room, closing the door behind him and leaving Nicolas and Alandra alone.

Her gaze skated from the cart, with its silver-
domed platters and bottle of wine, to him. "You're
not planning on eating with me?" she asked, not
bothering with even a modicum of civility as she
crossed her arms beneath her breasts and tapped
the red-tipped toes of one bare foot impatiently.

"We have a lot to do, as you've said, and I agree
that taking dinner in your rooms is a good way to
make rapid progress. We'll eat on the balcony," he
added, pulling the cart out onto the terrace. "You'll
like it out there. Bring some of your files, if you
like, and we can discuss them while we eat."

She didn't say anything, but he wouldn't have
stopped if she had. Giving her the chance to respond was only inviting a refusal, and he had no
intention of being put off.

She followed him to the French doors, still without uttering a word, but stopped before actually
stepping onto the balcony.

It was still light outside, edging into dusk, and
the bright shades of sunset could be seen on the far
horizon. The temperature, normally quite com-

fortable at this time of year, was even warmer than usual, giving him no qualms about inviting her out in little more than a thin slip of satiny material.

And if she got cold…well, he could think of several ways to heat things up quickly enough.

He moved to the round, glass-topped table outside, and pretended not to be watching her as he transferred their dinner from the cart. In reality, however, he kept track of her in his peripheral view. He saw her fingers twisting nervously on the frame of the open double doors, and her bare toes curling on the threshold rather than taking the step that would bring her out onto the balcony.

"Maybe I should change," she said in a soft voice.

Though he was careful not to let it show, he felt a flash of triumph. She had apparently accepted that arguing or asking him to leave was futile. He was here for dinner, and he meant to stay.

Raising his head, he once again looked directly at her. He wanted her sitting across from him just like that, with her legs bare and the turquoise fabric bringing out the sparkle in her dark eyes.

"What you're wearing is fine," he replied. "This is a casual meal, and we'll be talking about the charities most of the time. In fact, I'll join you in getting more comfortable."

Shrugging out of his suit jacket, he hung it neatly over the back of his chair, removed his tie and rolled up his shirtsleeves. "How's that?" he asked, giving her a moment to study his appearance. "I can remove more of my clothing if you like, but I have a feeling you would consider that a bit *too* casual. Am I right?"

He cocked a brow, silently challenging her to deny it. If he had his way, they would both be naked before the night was over.

For a second, she returned his look with a steady, rebellious one of her own, then spun around and disappeared into the bedroom.

At first, he thought she'd gone to cover herself in battle armor. But she reappeared a moment later, still wearing the same nightgown and robe, and not a stitch more. She was also carrying a legal pad and small stack of folders.

She took a seat and pulled her chair closer to the table, acting as though she was sitting down to a business lunch in a full business suit. But he certainly wasn't going to complain now that he had her exactly where he wanted her.

Following her lead, he lifted the silver covers from both plates and set them aside, then took his own seat across from her. He uncorked the bottle of wine, from one of Glendovia's own vineyards, and poured a healthy portion for each of them.

Nicolas made small talk while they ate. And though Alandra's side of the conversation was stilted at first, eventually she relaxed and spoke to him as easily as she would anyone else.

They'd just begun discussing the plans for the children's home when a knock sounded at the sitting room door.

"That will be dessert," Nicolas announced. Rising to his feet, he slung his jacket over his arm. "Let's move things into the other room, shall we?"

He strolled in that direction, leaving her to follow with her stack of files.

Before the waiting servant had a chance to knock a second time, Nicolas pulled the door open, gestured for him to enter and instructed him to serve the coffee and dessert at the low, square table in front of the fireplace.

While that was being taken care of, Nicolas

lowered the lights, then proceeded to build a small fire in the hearth.

Alandra watched from the bedroom doorway, chagrined to find herself admiring the broad expanse of the prince's back. The narrow span of his waist. The ripple of muscles beneath his crisp white shirt and dark trousers as he moved.

She swallowed hard, feeling a flush of heat flow over her chest, up her neck and into her cheeks.

Noticing Nicolas's considerable physical attributes was the last thing she should be doing. Finding him attractive at all, in any way, would be the kiss of death. A risk she could not afford.

And yet she couldn't seem to tear her eyes away from him.

"Isn't it a little warm for a fire?" she asked as the servant finished his task and slipped silently from the room.

"I thought you might be chilly," the prince replied, turning from the flickering flames and glancing in her direction.

His attention lingered on her bare legs, she noticed, and it took all her willpower not to shift uncomfortably or attempt to cover herself. The only thing that kept her from doing either was the knowledge that he'd noticed the tiny goose bumps beginning to break out on her arms and legs earlier. She was unaccountably touched by his consideration, which was *not* what she wanted to be feeling.

"We won't get too close," he said, dragging the table back from the hearth a few more inches before taking two cushions from the sofa. "Come, have a seat."

He lowered himself onto one of the cushions on the floor and sat cross-legged, leaving the other for her. Instead of sitting across from each other, they would now be much closer, with only one small corner of a rather small table between them.

It wasn't the typical setup for a business meeting. But then, her attire wasn't exactly typical, either. None of this was.

Striding across the room in her bare feet, she set her files aside and curled her legs beneath her as she sat down.

Nicolas poured coffee from a brightly polished silver carafe while Alandra studied the dessert. A fluffy, golden pastry was sliced into layers and

filled with large, juicy strawberries and a deca-
dent amount of rich cream. Her mouth watered
just looking at it.

Because this situation could easily begin to take
on a romantic feel, Alandra immediately started
back on the topic of Christmas at the orphanage,
and didn't stop until they'd made it through the
pastries and a cup of coffee each. To his credit,
Nicolas stuck with the conversation, never trying
to change the subject or insert a level of intimacy
that didn't belong.

His enthusiasm and participation delighted her.
She'd expected him to put in only a minimum
amount of effort, to convince her he'd brought her
to his country for legitimate reasons rather than
simply to become the latest in what she was sure
was a string of lovers.

But he was taking their conversations and the
business of organizing these fund-raisers seriously.
Taking *her* seriously.

It was a welcome change after being made the
butt of any number of jokes and cruel jibes back
home once the rumors had spread that she'd been
sleeping with a married man.

Despite the cup of coffee she'd just consumed, Alandra found herself blinking tired eyes and covering her mouth to stifle a yawn. And maybe she was off her game, maybe her defenses were down, because it seemed sensible, almost natural, to join Nicolas when he moved closer to the fire.

She reclined beside him, letting the flickering flames and the opulence of her surroundings lull her. Keeping company with a gorgeous prince didn't hurt, either, even if she had to steel herself against his charms, his looks, the spicy scent of his cologne.

And he was about as handsome as a man could be. If he weren't already a prince, she would think he should be. A prince or perhaps a movie star.

"What are you thinking?" he asked softly from only inches away.

He had a nice voice, too. Low and slightly husky, it rumbled up from his chest and straight down her spine, causing her bare toes to curl.

If he wasn't a royal, constantly being followed by paparazzi, and if she hadn't recently been slandered and torn apart by vicious rumor and innuendo, she might just be willing to throw caution to the wind and sleep with him, after all. Not become his mistress—that was a bit beyond even her—but spend one passionate, sure-to-be-glorious evening making love with a man who had the power to turn her knees to jelly.

Thank goodness he didn't know that. Thank goodness he couldn't tell exactly what she *was* thinking. Otherwise all her good intentions, her insistence that her presence here was purely business, with no possibility of pleasure being thrown into the mix, would drift away like a wisp of fog on the ocean breeze.

Thank goodness.

"Only that this is nice," she replied. "Relaxing. I should still be working, but I think I'm too tired."

He turned, and she found her own shimmery image reflected in his pupils.

"Would you like to go to bed?"

It was on the tip of her tongue to say, "Yes, very much," before her hazy brain identified the danger his question posed.

"Clever," she said with a chuckle, feeling just tranquil enough to find his attempt to trap her amusing. "But while I would like to go to bed… eventually…I won't be doing it with you."

"What a shame. Although there's always to-morrow."

There it was again, that calm, cajoling tone. The voice that thickened her blood and sent warm, tingling sensations to areas she'd rather not have tingling in his presence.

"I didn't come here for that," she replied quietly.

He was only an inch away now, his heated breath dancing over her cheeks and eyelashes. His mouth looked incredibly inviting, sexy and about seven kinds of sinful.

Surely one little kiss wouldn't hurt anything. One tiny peck to satisfy an overwhelming curiosity.

It wasn't smart. Was, in fact, ludicrous.

Before she had a chance to decide if she could afford a momentary lapse of sanity, Nicolas made the decision for her.

Seven

*O*h, my.

He tasted of wine and the strawberries and cream that had been part of their dessert, with a hint of the coffee he'd sipped afterward. Sweet and tart and smoky all at the same time.

It was a heady mixture, but nothing compared to the feel of his tongue sweeping into her mouth, tasting, stroking, claiming.

His hands gripped her shoulder and the side of her face, gently pulling her up. She wasn't sure how it happened, had no conscious memory of moving, but suddenly she was on her knees, pressed chest to chest with Nicolas and kissing him back with equal vigor.

While his hands kneaded and caressed her upper arms, hers clutched at his shirt, desperately holding on and pulling him closer. Her breasts were squashed between them, but she could still feel her nipples beading. Heat gathered and pooled low in her belly, and her heartbeat was a thunderbolt blasting in her ears.

She'd been wrong about keeping her distance, wrong about trying to convince herself she wasn't interested in this man. He was hard and strong and self-assured, and brought to life emotions she'd never felt before, at least not to this degree.

Her fingers trailed upward to tangle in the short strands of his silky hair. The two of them were already mouth to mouth, body to body, as close as they could be while still clothed, but that didn't keep her from exerting a small amount of pressure at the back of his skull and—if it was possible—taking the kiss even deeper.

With a groan, Nicolas moved his hands to skim

the undersides of her breasts. He cupped them in his palms, measuring their fullness and weight before letting his thumbs slide up and over the tight peaks of her nipples.

The caress, made even more erotic by the thin layer of cool, slick material between her flesh and his fingers, gave her shivers.

As she wriggled in his grasp, her knee bumped into the coffee cup she'd set aside earlier. The rattle of the porcelain on the saucer startled her out of the haze of passion and arousal she'd been lost in.

She pulled back slightly, breaking the kiss even though her body cried out for more. Her lungs heaved, straining for breath. Her arms and legs quivered, overcome with a lassitude she couldn't remember ever feeling before.

Good Lord, what had she almost done? How could she have gotten so wrapped up, so swept away by a single kiss?

His hands remained at her breasts, his fingers lightly brushing the rigid peaks. His eyes blazed a deep, dark sapphire in the firelight, no less heated than a moment ago.

Did he not realize she'd pulled away, or was he as blinded by desire as she'd been?

Regardless, she had to stop this, had to make it clear to him that what had just taken place between them was a mistake. A mistake of monumental proportions that could not, *would* not happen again.

"Stop," she gasped.

"What's wrong?" he asked in a ragged voice. Though he dropped his arms to his sides, he clenched his hands, betraying the tension vibrating through him.

"This is not going to happen," she said, though her tone was less firm than she'd have liked. Still on her knees, she inched away, afraid that he might reach for her again and she wouldn't have the conviction to fend him off.

One dark eyebrow hitched upward. "I thought we were off to a fairly adequate start," he replied.

Without looking at Nicolas, she rose to her feet. "I told you before that I didn't come to Glendovia to become your latest conquest. I'm here strictly for business purposes. That kiss was a mistake. It never should have happened, and it won't happen again. Things only got as far as they did because I'm tired and let my guard down."

But Nicolas wasn't ready to walk away, not quite yet.

He also got to his feet, then touched her elbow, stroking the satin fabric of her sleeve. "I could stay," he whispered smoothly, seductively. "Make sure the rest of your evening is both restful and enjoyable. Infinitely enjoyable."

The spark in her eyes let him know he'd overstepped his bounds. She shrugged out of his hold and moved passed him. Wrenching open the door, she stood back, body rigid, and glared.

"Good night, Your Highness," she said, her tone only a shade shy of disrespectful.

If he weren't such a patient man, intent on his goal, he might have taken exception.

But he *was* a patient man, and he knew that pushing Alandra was not the way to win her over, not the way to lure her into his bed. Better to take things slowly, to woo and seduce her properly.

"I'll see you in the morning, then," he said politely, moving to stand before her, giving no indication that her attitude or demands disturbed him in the least.

Though she remained stiff, he took her hand and lifted it to his mouth, pressing a soft kiss to the back of it.

"Thank you for being such a lovely dinner companion, and for all of your hard work on behalf of the children's home. I knew bringing you here was the right thing to do."

With a swift grin, he left the room and strode casually down the hall. A few seconds later, he heard her door close with a slam, and his smile widened.

Alandra Sanchez was a fiery, passionate woman with a temper to match. She thought she was brushing him off, holding him at bay, but her reluctance merely intrigued him all the more.

For the next two weeks, Alandra did her best to avoid Nicolas whenever she could, and treat him with cool professionalism whenever she couldn't.

Nicolas, meanwhile, did *his* best to get her alone as often as possible, to touch her hand, her arm, her cheek on a regular basis, and to romance her into letting down her guard and inviting him into her bed.

So far, she'd remained firm in her commitment

not to be seduced. But she had to admit, at least to herself, that it had been no simple feat.

Nicolas was nearly irresistible. He was attractive and charming, and if he hadn't approached her to sleep with him before getting to know her—which she found gallingly arrogant—she very well might have fallen into bed with him by now.

Sad but true, and rather ironic. If he'd gone about courting her in a more traditional manner, he'd have likely gotten lucky.

Alandra might be considered beautiful by many—a fact of life that was sometimes a blessing and sometimes a curse for her—but she was anything but compliant.

And then there was the continued guilt and humiliation over the scandal that still clung to her name back in Texas.

She'd phoned home numerous times since arriving in Glendovia, and each time she'd asked her sister about the scandal she'd been running away from. Elena had admitted that people were still talking, but the reporters had finally stopped camping out at the house.

But even though the attention had died down,

Alandra knew she'd been right to leave town when she had. She was also even more determined never to leave herself open to disgrace again.

She reminded herself of this, firmly and repeatedly, as she made her way down to the foyer.

In the time she'd been a guest of the royal family, the palace's decor had gone from tidily opulent to brimming with holiday cheer.

The banister had been strung with long, twisting garlands of holly and ivy. Giant wreaths hung on both the outside and inside of all the main doors. And in the center of the foyer was a towering evergreen tree, covered with gold ornaments. A golden angel perched gloriously at the very top.

The holiday decorations were helping Alandra feel more at home. She missed her family terribly, and it broke her heart to think that she wouldn't be spending Christmas with them. But she found it soothing to be surrounded by all this cheer.

She was smiling when she reached the front door, where Nicolas was waiting. Tonight was the Evening with Santa event at the children's home, and he had insisted on accompanying her, despite the fact that she had to be there early. The rest of the royal family would arrive later.

Even Nicolas's mother, Queen Eleanor, had reluctantly approved of Alandra's efforts to aid the local orphanage. She hadn't come right out and complimented her on all of her hard work, or changed her attitude, but the few remarks she'd made about tonight's event had been mainly positive.

Alandra didn't let it go to her head. She knew the queen still disapproved of her.

As soon as she drew close, Nicolas took her elbow, offering a small smile. He was dressed in his princely finery, complete with a red sash running from shoulder to hip, and a number of important-looking medals pinned to his chest.

Alandra's dress was a sumptuous red velvet gown that hugged her curves and left her shoulders and arms bare. She wore classic, understated diamonds at her ears and throat.

"Shall we go?" Nicolas asked, and escorted her out of the palace into the slightly chilly evening air. It wasn't yet dark, but the sun was setting and dusk was well under way.

She had purposely scheduled tonight's affair so

that it could be both a fun party for the children and an opportunity for the adult guests to mingle. Especially since she had invited some very wealthy, influential individuals, whom she hoped would make generous donations.

When Alandra and Nicolas arrived, a crowd of photographers was already gathered outside the orphanage, snapping pictures. Inside, the home was decorated festively. There was a tree in the main entranceway, covered with ornaments handmade by the children. Holiday music filled the air.

After Alandra settled a few last-minute issues, she started mingling with the arriving guests.

The appearance of the rest of the royal family caused quite a stir. Voices hushed, heads turned and people stood frozen as they watched the king and queen.

Leaving Nicolas with his family, Alandra made her way to the other rooms. She began wandering around, double-checking that everything was running properly.

All in all, it looked as though the evening was progressing perfectly. She released a sigh, praying no accidents or crises cropped up to mar an otherwise successful occasion.

Turning back to survey the reception area, she immediately spotted Nicolas striding toward her. Tall and imposing, he seemed to tower over the crowd.

The air caught in her chest. She would have liked to blame her sudden inability to breathe on the tightness of her form-fitting dress, but knew it was all due to Nicolas.

Nicolas, who could stop her heart with a glance.

Nicolas, who made her palms damp and her stomach quiver.

Nicolas, who made her want to rethink her decision not to get any closer to him than necessary during her stay.

Be strong, she told herself, swallowing hard and making a concerted effort to keep her knees from quaking as he came closer.

When he reached her, he gave a small bow and took her hand, his eyes holding hers the entire time.

"Dance with me," he murmured softly.

His tone and princely manner made it more of a command than a request, but she did her best to argue. "I don't think Christmas music is exactly conducive to dancing," she said, glancing about the room. Although there were several couples taking the floor.

"Of course it is."

He tipped his head, as though paying extra attention to the slow strains of a holiday classic. Tightening his grasp, he tugged her behind him as he headed to the clear space at the center.

"Besides, it's my royal duty to set a good example for others, and we want everyone to enjoy themselves, don't we? Isn't that your goal, so that guests will feel more generous when it comes time to start writing checks?"

She could tell from his expression that he was taking pleasure in teasing her, tossing her own ambition back at her in an attempt to get what he wanted. His lips twitched and the corners of his eyes crinkled as he tried to keep his amusement in check.

She might have continued protesting, but it was too late. They had reached a small empty stretch of the hardwood floor, and Nicolas had his arm around her waist, pulling her against him.

He splayed his fingers at the small of her back, holding her in place and guiding her as they swayed in small circles. And just as he'd predicted, others began to follow their lead and joined them, dancing to the holiday carols being piped through the building.

This hadn't been part of her plans for the evening, but it did seem to be having a positive effect. Alandra hoped Nicolas didn't notice, or she might have to swallow her pride and tell him he'd been right.

The song came to an end and they stopped moving, but instead of releasing her, he continued to hold her, staring down into her eyes until her mouth went dry and butterflies decided to take up tap dancing in her belly. Her chest was too tight to draw a full breath, which made her head begin to spin.

She thought, for a brief moment, that he was going to kiss her. Right there, in the middle of a roomful of people.

And she was chagrined to realize that her mouth had opened slightly, that she was both anticipating the kiss and looking forward to it. Yearning for it, even.

With his gaze still locked on hers, he leaned in another inch, until she could feel his warm breath dancing across her skin.

"I can't kiss you here and now, the way I'd like, but I promise to rectify that before the night is through." His voice was low and mesmerizing, washing over her.

Dropping his hand from her waist, he smiled, gave a small bow and then turned and walked away, as though he hadn't just set every nerve ending in her body on high alert.

She watched him go, trying to regain control of her senses. And control of her limbs, which seemed incapable of movement, even as she struggled to get her brain to send the correct signals.

It wasn't until she noticed people beginning to stare that she shook off whatever spell had overtaken her, and was able to take step after measured step to the refreshment table. She poured herself a glass of punch and drank it down in nearly a single gulp.

This was bad, so very bad. He was wearing her down, eroding the last of her defenses.

She was very much afraid that she wouldn't be able to evade him for much longer.

Eight

It was late by the time the evening wound to a close, but as Alandra watched the guests filing out, she was delighted to see that the majority of them had smiles on their faces. Better yet, Mrs. Vincenza had happily reported that she'd received several generous contributions throughout the night, with promises of more to come.

Watching Santa Claus hand out presents to the children had obviously turned a number of hearts—exactly what Alandra had been hoping for. She'd seen more than a few eyes turn misty during the gift-giving ceremony, and many follow the children out of the room and up the stairs at bedtime.

While it hadn't been her main goal, Alandra hoped that tonight's event would result in some much-needed adoptions, as well as added donations.

Stifling a yawn behind her small clutch purse, she watched the door close behind the last guest a moment before she felt Nicolas come to stand beside her.

Although she wasn't surprised that she could sense his presence even before she saw him, it did disturb her. She didn't *want* to sense him. Didn't want to believe that they might be growing that close in such a short time, especially when she'd spent most of the last three weeks avoiding him.

Not that she'd been terribly successful. Nicolas, she was learning, had a way of being everywhere she was, whether she wanted him there or not.

She had to admit, though, that he'd been a definite asset this evening. Not only had he gotten everyone in the room to relax enough to dance to Christmas music, but he'd spent the rest of the night circulating through the crowd to shake hands, kiss cheeks and talk up the orphanage as an extremely worthy charity—or write-off, depending on who he was conversing with.

And she admired him for it. For caring about the children's home and about what he could do to make the fund-raiser a success.

Glendovia was his country, and she had been hired to do a job for it. But he seemed to know that she took her work of organizing charitable events and raising funds for worthy causes very, very seriously. Seemed to know…and in his own way, care.

That touched Alandra more than a dozen roses, a hundred glasses of champagne or a thousand romantic dates ever could have.

He might have taken a wrong first step with her by inviting her into his bed before even getting to know her, but he had taken a few right steps since. Redeeming right steps.

When he took her elbow now, she felt a familiar tingle in every millimeter of skin his fingers came in contact with.

"Ready to go?" he asked.

She nodded and let Nicolas adjust her wrap

around her shoulders before guiding her outside
and into the waiting limousine.

Despite the late hour, there were still plenty of
paparazzi gathered to snap more pictures upon the
royal family's departure. The camera flashes
burned her eyes and blinded her vision. She was
only too happy to have the car door slam behind
her, blocking out the pesky photographers.

When they arrived home, the family said their
good-nights before heading for their respective bed-
chambers. Alandra wished them all a good night,
as well, before turning toward her own rooms.

"I'll walk with you," Nicolas said, catching up
with her and once again slipping her arm through his.

She started to tell him it wasn't necessary, but
thought better of it with his parents and siblings
still within earshot. Instead, she inclined her head,
tightened her hold on his arm and murmured,
"Thank you."

They walked to her suite without speaking, and
she was surprised to find it a comfortable silence.
Perhaps because it had been such a long and busy
day, and she was too tired to worry about what she
should be saying or doing. She couldn't find it in

her to be concerned about what Nicolas might say or do, either.

When they arrived, he opened the door, then stood back for her to enter. Crossing the dark sitting room, she turned on a small table lamp, which bathed the space in a yellow-gold light.

Alandra straightened and turned, and nearly bumped into Nicolas, who had followed her silently and was standing mere inches away. For a moment, her mind went blank. Her breath hitched and her heart leaped at finding him so near.

She swallowed nervously and opened her mouth to speak, though she didn't have a clue what she planned to say.

Not that it mattered. Before she could utter a sound or get her brain to function properly, Nicolas had lifted a hand to the back of her neck and threaded his fingers into the loose hair at her nape. He tugged her forward, and she went easily, willingly, like a puppet on a string.

Their eyes met, and in that brief second, she saw passion and fire and desire. Those same emotions caused her stomach to tumble to her toes, and made her feel suddenly light-headed.

Then he bent and lowered his mouth to hers.

The minute their lips met the earth seemed to rock on its axis. Alandra had never felt such heat, such electricity, such an amazing and overwhelming need.

Nicolas's fingers at her nape tightened, while his other hand grasped her hip. Her own hands were on his shoulders, gripping and clawing. She couldn't seem to get close enough.

His scent filled her nostrils, spicy and masculine. As his tongue swept through her mouth, he tasted the same.

She kissed him back with equal fervor, delighting in the way contact with him flooded her senses.

Just when she thought she might expire from pleasure, Nicolas broke the kiss. "Say no," he whispered raggedly against her lips. "Tell me to go. Tell me you don't want this."

He kissed her again, hard and swiftly. "Go ahead, Alandra," he taunted softly, "tell me."

She knew what he was doing. He was challenging her to stick to her declaration that she wouldn't sleep with him during her visit. That she wouldn't allow herself to be seduced.

But, God help her, she couldn't. She wanted him too much to deny it any longer.

To deny him.

Wrapping her arms around his neck, she pressed her mouth to his. The same smoldering heat washed over her again and, with a sigh, she whispered, "Don't stop. Don't go. I do want this."

She expected him to smile—a cocky, self-important response to show her he'd known all along he would win their little cat-and-mouse game.

But he didn't smile. Instead, his eyes flashed with fire, a second before narrowing dangerously.

Bending slightly, he scooped her up, ball gown, high heels and all. His determined strides carried them to her bedroom, where he kicked the door closed and crossed to the wide, four-poster bed.

The room was dark, with only a hint of moonlight shining through the diaphanous curtains on the French doors. It took a moment for her eyes to adjust, but as Nicolas deposited her on the mattress, then stood back to unbutton his jacket, she decided it didn't matter. She could see him just well enough, and in a few minutes she would be touching him everywhere. Feeling him everywhere.

He stripped off his jacket and kicked off his shoes, then loosened the first few buttons of his shirt, keeping his gaze locked on her the entire time.

Not wanting to be a mere bystander, Alandra rose to her knees and pulled off her strappy heels, tossing them aside. She reached behind her for the zipper of her dress.

"No."

Nicolas's low, stern voice stopped her. He took two steps forward to the edge of the bed and ran his hands seductively down her bare arms.

"Let me."

Her stomach muscles clenched as his fingers ran over her abdomen and around her sides, to her lower back. Slowly, he slid his palms up the line of her spine.

His touch burned through the velvet of her gown as his hands trailed upward, and then drew the zipper down. The quiet rasp of the tiny metal teeth parting accompanied their harsh breathing.

When the zipper was lowered, her dress fell open, helped along by Nicolas's large, strong hands. She shrugged and shifted slightly; he pulled it away and dropped it unceremoniously at his feet.

Alandra knelt at the edge of the king-size mattress in her cherry-red bra and panties, and a pair of sheer, thigh-high stockings. Her heart was racing out of control, her nerves skittering like a million angry ants. Licking her dry lips, she remained perfectly still, watching Nicolas and waiting.

He stood equally still, his blue eyes riveted on her face. And then he reached for his shirt, undoing the buttons and pulling the tail from his slacks.

His movements weren't hurried, but they weren't patient, either. He made short work of removing the garment, letting it flutter to the floor while he reached for the front of his pants. There was no belt to slow him down, and with a flick of his wrist, he released both the catch and zipper.

Half-naked, he was impressive enough. But fully naked, he was the stuff of dreams and naughty female fantasies. His arms and chest were beautifully sculpted. A tight, flat abdomen flowed to narrow hips and long legs corded with muscle.

Alandra's pulse skittered and her mouth went dry as she focused her gaze to the area between his thighs. He was impressive there, too.

She didn't know what to say or how to act, so

merely sat where she was and waited for him to make the first move.

It didn't take long. With a single stride, he was with her, cradling her in his arms, while his mouth devoured hers.

Their lips meshed. Their tongues tangled. And everywhere their skin touched, she sizzled.

Alandra curled her fingers into his shoulders, her nails gently scraping. Behind her, she felt him fiddling with the clasp of her bra, and then it came free. She released him long enough to allow him to remove the garment.

Rather than wrapping his arms around her again, Nicolas reached for her breasts, cupping them in his palms, toying with the tight, beaded nipples. All without breaking their kiss.

She moaned into his mouth, pressing even closer. Her own hands roamed over every inch of hot, hard flesh she could reach—his arms, his back, his pectorals and the slim, sensitive sides of his waist.

It was his turn to make a ragged sound of longing when she ran her fingertips over the taut twin globes of his rear, then raked her nails back up to the base of his spine.

She almost smiled. She could feel the desperation rippling through him as he tightened his grasp on her breasts, deepening their kiss, pressing himself against her belly.

Without warning, he tugged her legs out from under her, so that she fell flat on her back on the bed. He followed her down, covering her completely as he trailed his lips across her cheeks, over her eyelids, along her jaw and behind her ear.

At the same time, his hands worked to remove her stockings, rolling them slowly down her thighs and calves, and over her feet. Next went her panties, and she lifted her hips to help him, until she was blessedly naked, rubbing against him in all the best places.

His mouth was at her throat now, licking and sucking and humming, sending little trills of sensation straight to her core. He cupped her buttocks, bringing her flush with his arousal and turning her insides liquid with longing.

"You're so beautiful," he murmured, still kissing everywhere he could reach. "Lovelier than I imagined. And much better than anything I've dreamed of these past weeks."

She smiled, running her fingers through his hair and enjoying his husky declaration, even if he'd said it to a million other women before. This wasn't about commitment or honesty. It was about lust and desire and untold pleasures, fleeting though they might be.

"You're not so bad yourself," she replied, remembering the multitude of erotic dreams that had revolved around him since she'd moved into the palace.

Grinning, he raised his head to gaze down at her. He leaned in to kiss her, hard and fast, then pulled back, his expression serious. "Tell me you want me," he demanded.

She studied him for a long moment, her eyes locked with his. He was more handsome than any man deserved to be, and when he focused his attentions on her, she felt like the only woman in the world. The only woman he was interested in, at any rate.

And right now, that was all that mattered.

"I want you," she whispered, wrapping her arms and legs around him and holding him tight. "Make love to me, Prince Stephan Nicolas Braedon."

No one had called him by his first name in years, not since he decided to go by Nicolas, after years of his sister referring to him as Nico. He held her gaze for another split second, then pressed his lips to hers. The kiss was hot enough to suck all the air from her lungs and from the room, and she kissed him back with equal enthusiasm.

His hands raked her sides. Then he was caressing her thighs, both outside and in.

His knuckles brushed the triangle of curls between her legs as he began to explore. He stroked and teased, groaning when he found her already damp.

She writhed beneath him as he used two fingers to plumb her depths. She was panting now, and her breathing grew more shallow as he traced his fingertips over the tiny nub of pleasure hidden within her folds.

He touched her there, and she exploded. The orgasm washed over her like a wave of heat.

His smug, satisfied smile greeted her when she opened her eyes. Her cheeks heated at his close scrutiny, and she felt suddenly self-conscious about her wanton response to his touch.

"You blush beautifully," he told her, kissing the corner of her mouth.

He didn't give her a chance to respond, but immediately began caressing her again, his hands filled with magic as they danced across her flesh, leaving no part of her unsatisfied.

The tip of his erection pressed against her opening, and she spread her legs wider, inviting him in. Little by little, he entered her, his heat and hardness filling her. The deeper he went, the more she responded, any signs of discomfort overpowered by the delight shivering through her.

But when he thrust forward in one powerful motion, what had been a minor tenderness turned to a sharp stab of pain that had her gasping aloud.

Nicolas jerked back, brows knit and eyes narrowed as he scowled down at her.

"Alandra," he said, his breathing slightly labored as he held himself perfectly still. "You're a *virgin?*"

Nine

She was a *virgin?*

How in the name of all that was holy could she be inexperienced?

Nicolas's mind raced back over everything he knew about Alandra. All the times he'd been with her, spoken with her, observed her from across a room without her knowledge. Nothing in her demeanor so much as *hinted* that she was an innocent.

And what about the scandal she'd been involved in back in the States? His mother had been only too pleased to share the details of Alandra's indiscretion—a love affair with a married man.

A love affair with a married man that had left her a *virgin?* Nicolas could feel his brow furrowing, the skin of his face tightening as he continued to study her. And all the while he was powerfully aware of their physical connection, of the fact that he still ached and throbbed inside of her.

"How can you be a virgin?" he demanded, his tone brittle and more accusing than he'd intended.

Alandra's eyes grew wider, but passion still filled them. "Forget about my virginity and finish what you started."

To drive home her point, she wrapped her arms around his neck and tilted her hips just enough to send lightning bolts of sensation through his rigid length. He sucked in a harsh breath, using every ounce of willpower he possessed not to start moving, and thrust himself to a glorious but premature end.

His nostrils flared as he took several measured breaths, counting to ten, then twenty. When he could finally speak without groaning or sweating too profusely, he said, "I'm all for carrying on, but as soon as we're done, I *will* want to talk about this."

She rolled her eyes. "Fine. I fully expect you to make my first time memorable, though."

A grin flashed across his face and the mood in the room instantly shifted to a less intense level. There must be traces of royal blood somewhere in Alandra's ancestry. She had the imperial air down pat.

"Oh, darling," he murmured, leaning in to cover her mouth with his, "you can rely on it."

He occupied her with kisses and featherlight touches on her breasts and abdomen. And at the same time, he began to move his hips, slowly and carefully.

By now, her body had adjusted to his size and invasion. Her muscles were relaxed, warm and silky smooth with arousal.

He used long, gentle strokes to start, not wanting to do anything that would hurt or startle her. He hadn't been with a virgin since he himself had been one, and he wasn't sure exactly how to act. How fast might be too fast. How much might be too much.

But Alandra seemed far from intimidated. Her arms and legs were in constant motion, shamelessly exploring his naked body. And she wiggled beneath him, making it difficult for him to hold on to his resolve.

He locked his jaw and concentrated on breathing. His body was alive with sensation, his nerve endings electrified with need and lust and desperation.

"Can't you move any faster?" she panted at last, her back arching and nails raking his damp flesh.

He raised his head to look down at her. Her face was flushed, her hair spread out in a gleaming mass on the pale satin sheets.

"Is that an order?" he retorted, torn between amusement and disbelief.

Her lips curved slightly. "A request. You're treating me like I'm made of glass," she told him, "and I most certainly am not. I may be inexperienced at this sort of thing, but I'm not fragile."

"I don't want to hurt you," he admitted.

She lifted up from the mattress long enough to give him a quick, hard kiss. "You won't. I can take whatever you have to give and then some."

There was only one way to respond. "My pleasure."

His tongue flicked out to tease a ripe pink nipple, and he was smugly satisfied to feel a shudder ripple through her long, lithe form. He kept at it, wetting both tips, suckling them into stiff, rigid peaks.

When he had her shivering in his arms, grasping at his hair and whispering his name, he began to scoot her back, sliding her naked, pliant body across the silky coverlet. Then he grasped her hips and rolled, bringing her over him while he lay flat on his back.

"They say a woman is responsible for her own pleasure. Show me what you want."

Alandra stared down at him, her heart fluttering as she went from being startled by the sudden change of position to feeling empowered by his sensual declaration. His low voice rumbled through her, bringing goose bumps out along her flesh, and he held her hips when she straddled him.

A dozen sultry images of being in the lead and having Nicolas at her mercy played through her mind, and she loved every one.

Spreading her fingers, she pressed her palms on his chest and leaned forward. Her hair fell around her shoulders, the ends tickling his skin. She saw his impressive pectoral muscles jerk, and felt him swell inside of her.

Biting back a grin, she brushed her lips across the line of his jaw. "This is nice," she murmured, kissing her way to his ear. "Having you beneath me, defenseless."

His fingers flexed where he gripped her. "I only hope I have the strength to withstand your torture."

"So do I."

Taking the soft lobe of his ear between her teeth, she tugged gently. At the same time, she rose up on her knees, just an inch, then slowly lowered herself back down. Nicolas groaned deep in his throat, and heat burst in her center.

"Do you know what I really want?" she asked, watching her breath flutter the strands of his brown hair.

"What?" The word came out harsh and strangled as he tried to hold back his base desires.

"I want you to touch me. Everywhere. I love the feel of your hands on my body."

Immediately, he began to explore. His palms drifted to her buttocks, where he gave a little squeeze before sweeping back up the length of her torso to her breasts. Again his thumbs wreaked havoc with her nipples, and with a moan of her own, she kissed him.

Sensations swamped her, raising her blood pressure and making her insides vibrate like the strings of a well-played violin. As good as she'd always thought sex might be, she'd never expected it could be *this* good. That a man—any man—could make her feel both hot and cold at the same time. Make her pant and purr, shiver and shake.

Instinct kicked in and she began to move, her body seeming to have a mind of its own. Her hips canted back and forth, and she rose and fell on his rigid length.

He filled her completely, pressing deep and rubbing with a glorious friction along her hidden folds. Pleasure wound inside her like a spring, from her lips all the way to the apex of her thighs, growing tighter and tighter as the two of them picked up speed.

Feeling as though she were about to explode, she sat up, gasping for air. Her eyes drifted shut and she dragged her nails across his chest.

Beneath her, Nicolas seemed possessed of the same frantic need to plunge and writhe and buck to completion. He met her thrust for thrust, pound-

ing into her on every downward slide. And when
that coil of delicious tension building up inside her
finally sprang loose, he was right there with her,
gripping her even harder and giving a guttural
shout of completion.

Alandra's own body shook with climax, rocking her to her very soul before melting into a pile
of boneless limbs and damp, exhausted flesh on
top of him. His arms slipped around her waist, and
where her head rested on his chest, she could hear
his heart thudding beneath her ear.

Her last thought before slipping into sleep was
that she was glad she'd waited all these years to be
with a man. And that when she'd finally taken the
plunge, she was glad that man had been Nicolas.

"Now tell me how it is that you got to the age
of twenty-nine with your virginity intact," Nicolas demanded.

It was late, the sky darker than before. They
were lying in bed, half-asleep after another bout
of strenuous, passionate lovemaking.

He'd protested that twice in one night was too
much for her, that she would be sore in the morn-

ing. But she was having none of it, and had proceeded to convince him otherwise.

Now that she knew the pleasures that awaited
her, she had no intention of sleeping the night
away. In fact, she was already anticipating the third
time being especially charming.

At the moment, however, she was content to lie
in his arms, blissfully sated and tucked between
cool satin sheets.

"Don't you think my high moral fiber is reason
enough?" she replied sleepily.

"It might be, if you weren't more beautiful than a
supermodel, and hadn't recently been accused quite
publicly of having an affair with a married man."

With a sigh, she pushed herself up on one arm,
using her other hand to press the sheet to her breasts.
If he wasn't going to let the topic go, she might as
well tell him everything and get it over with.

"For the record, it wasn't an affair. Except perhaps in Blake's mind. Blake Winters," she clari-
fied. "That was his name. I met him almost two
years ago at a fund-raising event. He's charming
and good-looking, and I admit I was attracted to
him. He started calling, sending flowers and gifts.

We went out a few times, and he was nice enough, but I didn't think we hit it off quite as well as he apparently did. And I *didn't* know he was married and had a family," she stressed, finally finding the courage to meet Nicolas's gaze.

"Even after I decided not to see him anymore, he wouldn't leave me alone. He kept calling, kept sending presents. He attended my functions and did his best to get me alone. Just about the time his attention started to border on frightening, he stopped trying to contact me."

She shifted uncomfortably, readjusting the sheet around her torso as she went back to looking anywhere but into Nicolas's eyes. "I thought that was the end of it, and then suddenly photographs of the two of us showed up in the press. They were probably taken at the charity events, but they were just suggestive enough to get tongues wagging—especially when a so-called 'source' leaked the information that we *had* been intimately involved. I think it was Blake himself. I think he *wanted* people to believe we were having an affair, maybe even thought, in some sick way, that it would make me go back to him."

She shook her head and took a deep breath, shrugging off the bad memories and any lingering remnants of the shame she'd felt when the story—however incorrect—had broken.

The hair on her nape rose when Nicolas reached out to run the back of his hand over her bare arm. His knuckles rasped along her skin, drawing gooseflesh everywhere he touched.

"Poor Alandra, working so hard to take care of everyone else, but having no one stand up for you when you most needed it."

His words, as well as his tone, surprised her, and for a moment she let herself believe them. A second later, though, self-pity transformed into her usual streak of independence, and she gave an unladylike snort.

"I had plenty of people to defend me," she told him. "Unfortunately, my family is no match for all of Texas high society. In situations like that, the only thing you can do is lie low and try not to do anything even more newsworthy until it all blows over."

His hand moved from her arm to her back. The light stroking lulled her and made her want to curl up beside him once again.

"Is that what you're doing here, in Glendovia?" Nicolas asked softly. "Lying low?"

She snuggled down again, draping herself cozily along his hard length. Resting her head on the curve of his shoulder, she asked, "Is this low enough for you?"

He gave a chuckle, then shifted slightly and pulled her tighter against him, readjusting the cool sheets so that they were both covered from the waist down.

Silence surrounded them, heavy but comfortable. It gave her the chance to listen to Nicolas's breathing and the sound of his heart pumping rhythmically beneath her ear.

"That explains the scandal that surrounds you back in the States," he said at last, his fingers drawing random circles on her upper body. "It doesn't, however, tell me how you managed to remain untouched for so long."

Her mouth twisted wryly, even though she knew he couldn't see her expression. "I'm a good girl. What do you think?"

"I think you're a very good girl," he murmured, his words edged with innuendo. "But no one who looks at you would ever believe you were a virgin."

She cocked her head back to glower at him. "Why? Because I forgot to wear my sweater with the big red *V* on the front?"

"No," he responded calmly. "Because you're one of the most beautiful women I've ever met, and sexuality trickles from your every pore. No heterosexual man could be in the same room with you without wanting you, and I find it hard to believe that one hadn't convinced you to sleep with him before now."

Sighing, she relaxed and settled back against Nicolas. "I don't know how to explain it, except to say that no man has truly enticed me enough. I've dated a lot of men, yes. Wealthy, attractive men. And there were a few times I came close, a few I thought I might be falling in love with. But something always stopped me."

"Until now."

Beneath her ear, his heart seemed to jump against his rib cage and double its beat. Her eyelids, already half-closed, drifted all the way shut, his pulse acting like a lullaby.

"Until now," she agreed, her voice growing faint as sleep began to tug at her. "I guess you could say that your invitation came at a very beneficial time. For a number of reasons."

"One of those reasons being that it gave me a chance to finally get you exactly where I wanted you." With one sinewy arm around her waist, he dragged her up so he could see her face, jarring her into full wakefulness.

Alandra wanted to argue the point or chastise herself for falling so effortlessly into his trap. But right now, in the darkest part of the night, with him lying warm and solid beneath her, she couldn't find it in her to be angry.

Later, maybe, but not now.

Ten

Rays of warm sunlight slanted through the French doors, crossing the carpeted floor and part of the bed, and pulling Alandra slowly awake.

She stretched and yawned and reached out an arm, expecting to find Nicolas asleep beside her. When her hand met nothing but cool, bare sheets, she opened her eyes and blinked until her vision focused.

She was naked and alone in a tangle of pale, wrinkled bedclothes.

Sitting up, she glanced around the room, but didn't find him there.

A sliver of disappointment snaked through her belly. Maybe it had been too much to hope that she'd be able to wake up in his arms. It wouldn't do, after all, for him to be caught sleeping with the hired help.

With a sigh, she rolled out of bed and reached for her robe. Knotting the belt at her waist, she glanced at the clock, her heart pitching when she saw that it was well past 10:00 a.m.

Good Lord, how could she have slept so late?

Not looking forward to the greeting she would receive when she finally made her way downstairs, Alandra showered and brushed her teeth, then started to dress. She wore a simple white sheath with a silver-bangle belt, and white platform sandals. Nothing too provocative, but nothing too dowdy, either.

She wanted to appear cool and confident when she next ran into Nicolas.

Sleeping with Nicolas—a prince, her employer and the man who had propositioned her at their first meeting—wasn't the smartest move she'd ever made. She should have been stronger, more resilient.

Because there was no way she was about to become his mistress for the rest of her time in Glendovia.

Resolve firmly in place, she strolled along the palace corridors and down the wide, curved, marble staircase. There was no one around, not even a servant, making her feel even more awkward about sleeping in so late.

She made her way to the dining room, where she'd spent the majority of her time with the royal family thus far, but the room was empty, long ago cleared of any traces of breakfast. From there, she drifted back across the foyer and down the opposite hallway toward Nicolas's office. She wasn't in a particular hurry to run into him, but he was her primary employer and she was already late getting to work.

The door was closed and she rapped softly, half hoping he wouldn't be there. But he called for her to enter after the first knock.

She schooled her breathing and stepped inside, closing the door at her back. He was seated behind his desk, working, but raised his head to greet her.

Scorching familiarity flashed in his eyes. The look made her heart hitch in her chest.

"Good morning," he murmured, setting down his pen and rising to his feet. "I trust you slept well."

His tone was formal, more formal than she would have expected from the man who'd shared her bed only hours before, with no hint of teasing or double entendre. Yet his gaze consumed her, sliding over her like warm honey, and making her want to do nothing more than relax into it, surrendering her body and her will to him once again.

"Very well, thank you." If he could be this decorous, then so could she. "I'm sorry to be running late this morning. Just because the children's Christmas event was a success doesn't mean I should be allowed to dawdle on the other causes you brought me here to deal with."

She purposely avoided any mention of how they'd spent their time after the Santa gift giveaway, sticking to a professional mode. It was better that way and would help her remain on an even keel.

One side of his mouth lifted, as though he knew exactly what she was trying to do. "I don't think sleeping in a few hours can be considered shirking your duties. However, if you have ideas for other fund-raising events, I'd love to hear them."

He waved a hand at one of the chairs in front of his desk, motioning for her to sit down. As soon as she did, he returned to his seat.

"Actually, I do have another idea," she said, feeling some of the tension seep from her body. Talking business was much better than discussing last night. "Not for a fund-raiser per se, but for the development of an organization."

"Really?" His brows rose and he leaned back in his chair, propping his fingertips together as he listened intently.

"Yes. Back in the States, we have a nationwide organization that works to fulfill the wishes of terminally ill children. I've noticed that you don't have anything like that set up here in Glendovia, and I think it would be a wonderful project for the royal family to undertake. It would bring you some outstanding press, and also fill a very real need for kids who are sick in the hospital or even at home, with no hope of recovery. I thought we could call it Dream a Little Dream."

After considering her proposal for several long

seconds, he asked, "And what kind of dreams would we be fulfilling for these children?"

"Whatever they wanted. Their dearest wish, if it's at all feasible. At home, the organization arranges for children to meet their favorite celebrities, spend an entire day at an amusement park that's been rented out just for them and their friends, go for a hot-air-balloon ride or learn to fly a plane. Things that the kids have always wanted to do, but otherwise wouldn't get the chance to because of their condition."

Nicolas returned her grin. "I suppose that could be arranged."

"So it's something you'd consider?" She leaned forward eagerly. "There would be much more involved than simply planning a fund-raising event. We're talking about renting office space, hiring employees, enormous national and possibly international publicity, probably even a press conference or two. And the organization would need continued support long after I return to America."

She thought she saw a flicker of unease cross his face at the mention of her leaving, but it was gone in an instant.

"It's a noble endeavor," he said, shifting so that his elbows once again rested on the desktop. "A good cause, and something that would bolster Glendovia's reputation and its citizens' esteem. I'll have to discuss it with the rest of the family, of course, but I would certainly be in favor of getting the ball rolling."

"Excellent." She grinned broadly, pleased that he was in favor of a project she'd begun to feel very passionate about.

"You have only a little over a week left of your stay," he pointed out.

His mouth was a flat line and his words were curt, as though he found that fact distasteful. The ripple of unease low in her belly told her that she wasn't entirely comfortable with it, either.

When she'd first arrived and discovered exactly who Prince Nicolas Braedon was, she'd threatened to turn around and fly back to Texas, even if it meant breaking her employment contract with the royal family. But now that she'd been here for a while and had really begun to dig into the work, she was enjoying her visit. Enjoying the palace and the country and its people.

She missed her family and was eager to return

to Texas to be with them again, but she was no longer looking forward to leaving, as she had been only a couple of weeks before.

"Do you think that's enough time to establish this organization and get it to the point where it can be turned over to others and still run smoothly?" Nicolas asked.

"I do."

"Even with Christmas coming up?"

"I'll work through the holiday. I was planning to do that, anyway."

Without her family to share in the festivities, and with a multitude of servants who had already decorated the palace from top to bottom, she suspected Christmas this year would end up passing much like any other day.

She'd been prepared all along to spend that time alone in her room rather than intruding upon the royal family's celebrations. At least this way she would have a nice, meaty project to work on and keep herself occupied.

She thought she heard him mutter, "We'll see about that" beneath his breath. But then he pushed himself away from his desk and stood, and in a firmer voice said, "All right. I'll bring it up with the family and see how they feel about it, then get back to you with a decision."

Nodding, she rose to her feet as he crossed the office to hold the door for her. She took a couple of steps in his direction, then stopped.

"Is there anything else?" he asked, noticing her hesitation.

She curled her fingers into fists at her sides, then released them, fidgeting anxiously while she tried to decide whether or not to voice the concerns circling through her brain.

"Alandra," he murmured softly, and started in her direction.

Straightening her shoulders, she met his eyes, stopping him in his tracks. "About last night..." she began, steeling her nerves for a conversation that filled her with dread.

"Yes?" he asked without inflection of any kind.

Obviously, he was in no mood to make this easier on her.

"It can't happen again," she told him quickly and succinctly, as if pulling off a bandage before the pain or aftereffects sank in.

"Oh?" Again his voice lacked inflection, but this time he raised an eyebrow, the only hint that he had any interest in what she was saying.

"No. I realize it's exactly what you wanted, your whole reason for inviting me here to begin with, but it was a mistake and it's not going to happen again."

For a long minute, Nicolas studied Alandra, taking in her rigid stance and stern countenance. He wondered how annoyed she would be if he told her how attractive she looked when she tried to be authoritative.

Deciding not to risk her wrath over that, when he was about to commit a much worse offense to her sensibilities, he pushed the door shut with a quiet click and slowly closed the short distance between them.

"I'm afraid that's unacceptable to me," he replied, raising a hand to touch her hair, which hung straight and silky around her shoulders.

He watched her head tip just a bit away from his hand, as though trying to move away from his touch. And then the tendons of her throat tightened and released as she swallowed, her gaze not quite meeting his.

"It doesn't matter whether you agree or not," she said. "I'm simply telling you the way things are going to be. What happened last night isn't going to happen again."

She sounded resolute. So much so that he couldn't help smiling.

Not that he could hold her response against her. She hadn't known him long enough to realize that he was a man who got what he wanted. He had no intention of giving up so easily or letting her go purely because she claimed their lovemaking last night was a mistake.

He disagreed. Strongly.

Still grinning, he let his hand graze her soft cheek and tuck a strand of hair behind one ear. "I beg to differ. Last night was magnificent."

Her gaze flitted away and a pale pink blush started to creep across her face.

"You have less than two weeks left in Glendovia, and I fully intend to enjoy them. To enjoy you. I know that you'll need to spend your days working, especially if you undertake this new project you've proposed. But your evenings will be free, and I want you to spend them with me, in my bed."

"Absolutely not." She shook her head and took a step back, breaking away from his touch.

As much as he wanted to close the distance between them and grab her up, kissing the quarrel from her luscious, red-tinged lips, he remained where he was, allowing her to believe a few inches of space would keep her safe from him.

A wry smile lifted the corner of his mouth. "You think that I lured you here, created a position for you within my country, to sleep with you for only one night? Alandra," he breathed softly, almost teasingly, "even if you didn't know me well enough by now, you have to realize that no prince would go to such lengths for a single night of sex, no matter how spectacular that sex might be."

Determination straightened his spine and pushed his shoulders back. "I am a bit more dedicated than that," he added, slowly stepping forward. He was encouraged to note that her wide eyes remained locked with his, and she barely seemed to register his approach.

"And now that I've had you, I have no intention of letting you slip away. I wanted to make love to you, and I've done that, but I'm far from sated."

Even as his voice fell, becoming low and rich and seductive, his finger lifted to gently brush against her body. First the curve of her waist and the underside of her breast, then the tender flesh of her upper arm. He kept the contact brief and featherlight, just the tips of his fingers grazing the material of her dress and her bare skin.

And even though he was scarcely touching her, he still felt the shiver of awareness that rippled through her. It sent a jolt of white-hot sensation through his system, gathering and pooling in his groin. He went hard and heavy in an instant, nearly desperate enough to throw her to the floor and make love to her right then and there.

He wouldn't, of course, though it wasn't his royal blood keeping him from doing anything so crass. When it came to being alone in a room with Alandra Sanchez, his royal blood be damned.

No, it was Alandra herself who kept his more base instincts in check. She was already nervous and shy and regretful about what had passed between them last night, and jumping at her now would only cause her to crawl deeper into her shell, to move further away from him.

Instead, he knew he would have to go slowly again, returning to his original plan of smooth, flawless seduction.

Oh, he would have her in his bed again—tonight, if he had anything to say about it. But it would require a bit of persuasion to get her there.

Alandra's chest rose as she inhaled, and her bright, expressive brown eyes drifted closed for a moment, her head tipping down in defeat.

"Please don't do this," she breathed raggedly. "Don't make me do something that I'll hate myself for later."

Her eyes fluttered open and she raised her head to meet his gaze. Her expression was resolute, if somewhat sad.

"I don't want to be Prince Nicolas's secret mistress. A temporary entertainment to be enjoyed while I'm here, then sent away when you're finished with me, never to be thought of again."

Something about her words twisted his heart painfully, and for a second he reconsidered his single-minded determination to have her, regardless of the consequences.

He didn't want to hurt her, didn't want to bring that look of misery to her face.

He wanted to hold her, kiss her, savor her like a glass of expensive brandy.

Why should it be more complicated than that? They were both mature adults, able to make their own decisions and spend time with whomever they chose.

Leaning in slightly, he let his warm breath fan her cheeks as he hovered a scant inch from her lush, kissable lips.

"I don't want you to hate yourself," he murmured quietly. "I just want to be with you. And though I can't change who I am or the prudence my role in this family requires, I don't think it needs to have any impact on our time together. What we do when we're alone, away from the public eye, is no one's business but ours."

He threaded his fingers through her hair, holding her tight and tipping her head back so he could better reach her mouth. He brushed his lips across hers, tasting her, feeling her, absorbing her energy and spirit into himself.

"I only want to be with you," he said without

breaking contact. "And after last night, I believe you want the same thing. You'll have to work very hard to convince me that isn't true."

She didn't answer, didn't pull way. He wasn't even sure she was still breathing. Pressing his advantage, he kissed her again, deeper this time, until her spine bowed against his body and her nails dug into the material of his jacket.

When he finally raised his head, they were both breathing heavily. A shaft of satisfaction rolled through him at the cloudy, unfocused look in her eyes.

"Very hard," he whispered.

Eleven

It was beyond difficult to convince Nicolas that she didn't want him. So impossible, in fact, that she'd given up trying.

How could she claim she wanted nothing to do with him when one touch of his hands or mouth melted her insides like a pot of chocolate fondue?

He'd discussed the idea for the Dream a Little Dream Foundation with his family, even asking Alandra to draw up an official proposal he could take to them. He'd also done a bit of research on his own into its American counterpart, so he could show them what the end product of such an endeavor might be like.

Reaction so far had been positive, and she and Nicolas had been working together on a daily basis to plan things in more detail, crossing all the t's and dotting all the i's. Once the king and queen approved, as well as the board of Glendovian officials who oversaw this type of thing, she would be given the freedom to get the ball rolling on establishing the foundation.

Daylight hours were not her problem. She had plenty to do to keep her busy, and managed to make sure she wasn't alone with Nicolas any more than necessary.

The door of his office stayed open while they were working, and if for some reason it was closed, she found a way to get it open again. If they were alone and things began to feel too tense, too dangerous, she'd make an excuse to get someone else into the room with them.

It was nighttime that caused her the most anxiety. After dinner, when Nicolas would walk her back to her rooms…holding her hand, standing too close, leaning into her at the door.

He kissed her cheek or sometimes her lips. Stroked her hand or shoulder. And always, *always* his eyes blazed with the clear desire to sweep her up in his arms and cart her off to bed.

She prayed he'd never figure out how very often she wished he would do just that.

Obviously, she wasn't safe around him, and she didn't know how she was going to make it another ten days without either giving in or going crazy.

Ten more long, arduous days and she could fly home, fly away to safety.

For some reason, though, that knowledge didn't comfort her as much as she would have hoped. In fact, it almost saddened her.

But that was an emotion she refused to examine. Her entire existence had been turned upside down, and as soon as she arrived home, life would begin to right itself and return to normal.

She hoped.

For now, though, it was late, and she'd thankfully managed to survive another day, another dinner, another long, excruciating walk back to her suite.

She'd changed into a pair of comfortable black satin pajamas and was ready to climb into bed when a soft knock sounded on the sitting room door.

A petite young woman in the uniform of the palace's household staff stood on the other side.

"Miss," she said, bobbing a slight curtsy. "Prince Nicolas sends this message and requests an immediate response." She held out a square envelope.

It was Nicolas's official stationery, Alandra saw, with her name scrawled in his expansive script across the front, and a dab of wax sealant pressed to the back.

Whatever was inside, she suspected, was either very important or very private.

Running a finger under the flap of the envelope, she broke the seal and removed the folded sheet of paper.

Alandra—
Your presence is required at a very important meeting concerning Dream a Little Dream. We fly to the other side of the island tomorrow morning. Pack for at least one night. Be ready to leave at 7:00 a.m.
Nicolas

She wasn't sure exactly what response he was awaiting, since he didn't seem to be giving her much choice in the matter. He hadn't asked if she wanted to go or would be willing to go, or was even able to go…he'd simply told her to be ready.

Refolding the note, she stuffed it back in the envelope before returning her attention to the servant. "Tell the prince I'll be in the main foyer by seven o'clock. Thank you."

The woman nodded and hurried off, ostensibly to deliver the message. More like announce Alandra's compliance, she thought crossly as she shut the door and headed back to the bedroom.

Though she wasn't particularly happy about this new development, she dragged an overnight bag from one of the closets and began to pack.

By the time she'd finished, she was truly exhausted. Climbing into bed, she hoped for a good night's sleep.

She would need all the rest she could get if she was going to be alone with Nicolas—away from the palace. Overnight.

She met Nicolas outside the palace at exactly 7:00 a.m. The entire place, inside and out, was decorated to the nines in anticipation of the Christmas Eve party the royal family was hosting in only two days' time.

"Good morning," he said.

"Good morning."

"I'm glad you were able to accompany me to this meeting," he told her once they were inside the car and heading down the driveway.

"I didn't have much choice in the matter, did I?" she replied, avoiding his gaze by staring out the window.

"You always have a choice."

She turned her head, meeting his blue eyes. "Well, your note didn't seem to *ask* if I'd like to go with you."

"I was afraid that if I did ask, you would have said no," he confessed.

"Of course I wouldn't have said no. As long as this meeting actually does concern the Dream a Little Dream Foundation. Or did you just say that to get me alone and away from the palace for a few days?" she asked quietly.

A moment passed before he responded. "This trip *is* about the foundation, and though I could probably handle things well enough on my own, I think it's important that you're there. I think you'll be glad you came."

He paused again, letting the silence fill with tension as his sharp gaze bored into hers. "But I'm also quite happy to get you away from the palace and to myself. I think you'll be glad for that, too—eventually."

His voice lowered to a warm, honeyed tone, and it took all of Alandra's willpower not to suck in a deep breath of air to replace what had gotten stuck in her throat.

She should be angry. He was manipulating her again, moving her how and where he wanted her in an effort to change her mind about sleeping with him.

One thing could be said for Nicolas Braedon—he knew what he wanted and didn't take no for an answer.

She didn't want to admit it, not even to herself, but the truth was his single-minded determination to seduce her made her feel…special.

It wasn't her intention to play with him, to turn this…whatever it was between them…into a game, but she suddenly realized she was enjoying herself. She enjoyed knowing that he wanted her.

Instead of arguing or giving in too soon, she merely shrugged and said, "I guess we'll have to wait and see."

The flight to the other side of the island was a short one, and they went straight from the small private airstrip to the office where the meeting was scheduled.

Alandra was stunned to learn that they weren't simply meeting with a few people *about* establishing the new foundation, but were meeting with many people to actually get the organization up and running.

As the morning meetings progressed, she realized Nicolas had been right. She was glad she'd come along.

She was also thrilled with the amount of progress they were making in such a short time. Over a working lunch she met wonderfully enthusiastic people raring to get started. She had no doubt they would do an excellent job of running the organization, whether she was there or not.

She and the prince said goodbye to the future Dream a Little Dream staff at five, and Nicolas instructed his driver to take them to a hotel where the royal family kept a suite of rooms.

Alandra wasn't taken aback, and she wasn't upset. In fact, she belatedly realized she'd expected as much. After her little revelation in the car on the way to the airport that morning, she even found herself looking forward to what the evening might bring.

The royal suite was gorgeous. Nicer, even, than her rooms at the palace.

The walls, carpeting and drapes were all done in varying shades of blue, with touches of white and tan. A set of dark mahogany French doors opened onto a small lanai overlooking the city and the coastline beyond. One of the doors was open, allowing a cool breeze to ruffle the long, diaphanous curtains, bringing in the salty scent of the sea.

"Are you hungry?" Nicolas asked, stepping to a desk that held a thick, black binder of hotel amenities.

She nodded, moving slowly in his direction as she continued to take in her surroundings. She wondered if she should bother unpacking, or simply live out of her overnight bag.

"I'll have something brought up," he said, flipping through the room service menu and then calling down to order what sounded like a veritable buffet of appetizers and entrées. Before hanging up, he asked for a bottle of their best wine, and strawberries with fresh whipped cream for dessert.

"We have about thirty minutes before the food arrives." Loosening his tie and shrugging out of his suit jacket, he draped both over the back of a chair as he crossed the room. "Would you care to change into something a bit more comfortable before it gets here?"

His gaze raked her from head to toe, raising gooseflesh every inch of the way.

She knew when to admit defeat—and when to enjoy a very handsome man who was more than willing to pleasure and worship her, if only for a short while.

"Do you have any special requests?" she asked, slowly removing her watch, and then her earrings.

Next she raised a hand to the top button of her blouse, slipping it through its hole.

His eyes followed her actions intently, glittering with longing and sending sparks of awareness through her.

"Naked works for me," he murmured, his voice gravelly with desire.

She chuckled, feeling a thrill of empowerment swelling in her veins. "Not just yet, I don't think," she said, turning on her heel and heading for the bedroom. "I wouldn't want to shock the waiter when he arrives."

"If he sees you naked, I could have him killed."

She laughed again, facing him with her hands on the knobs of the double bedroom doors.

"Let's not turn this trip into a crime spree just yet. Not if we can help it," she told him as she swung the doors closed. "I'll see what I can come up with on my own."

She stayed in the bedroom until she'd heard the room service waiter deliver dinner and leave again.

Opening one door a crack, she saw Nicolas standing before the round table on one side of the sitting area. It had been set with an array of dishes and stemware.

Stepping the rest of the way into the room, she paused and waited for him to notice her. When he did, his hand froze on the silver serving lid he'd been about to raise, and his gaze zeroed in on her like a heat-seeking missile.

She'd changed into a long black nightgown with spaghetti straps and lace-lined slits running from ankle to midthigh on each side. Her feet were bare, her red-tipped toes peeking out from beneath the hem of the nightie, and she'd combed her hair out to fall in a straight, silky curtain around her shoulders. The look on Nicolas's face told her how completely he appreciated her efforts.

"It's not naked, but I hope you approve."

He swallowed hard. "Very much so. I didn't think it was possible, but that gown may just be better than full nudity."

An amused smile tugged at her lips. "I'm glad you said something. Now I know not to take it off, no matter how much you beg."

"Princes don't beg," he informed her, stalking slowly toward her.

"No?" she asked, her mouth going suddenly dry.

"No."

He was standing in front of her now, close enough to touch, but keeping his arms at his sides. Her heart was pounding in her chest and she had to fight the urge to wiggle nervously.

"What do princes do, then?" she asked, her voice husky with growing pleasure.

Reaching out, he stroked the back of his fingers across her cheek. "It would be better if I showed you."

"Won't dinner get cold?"

"Do you care?"

Twelve

Late that night, Alandra lay in bed, wrapped snugly in Nicolas's arms. She couldn't have been more physically comfortable and sated…but her emotions were in an uproar.

She had done the very thing she'd sworn not to—she'd become Nicolas's lover.

As disturbing as that was, as much as it made her question her own character, it wasn't what had her teetering on the edge.

She'd realized not an hour before—while

Nicolas was kissing her, stroking her and making her sigh—that she was falling in love with him.

She swallowed hard, blinking to keep the moisture collecting at the corners of her eyes from spilling over. Beneath her cheek, Nicolas's chest rose and fell with his easy breathing.

This was bad. So bad. An affair was one thing. But how was she supposed to leave for home with a smile on her face if her heart was left behind, broken and bleeding?

How was she supposed to pretend that what had passed between them was just a holiday fling, when it had become so much more than that to her?

Nicolas shifted slightly in his sleep, causing her breath to catch. When he didn't wake up, she relaxed, feeling a bit steadier.

Since she knew she was merely a temporary distraction for him, and that he didn't share her newfound sentiments in the least, she would simply have to deal with the situation as best she could. Hide her feelings. And then, when the time came, she would walk away.

Closing her eyes, she began to drift off, telling

herself to get used to the pain squeezing her heart. It was going to be with her for a long time to come.

They returned to the other side of the island the following morning, Christmas Eve, with many hours to spare before the family's annual holiday party. Nicolas had made certain Alandra knew she was to attend, though she wasn't entirely looking forward to it.

Stepping off the plane, they were accosted by a large group of reporters, all snapping pictures and screaming out questions. She had trouble making out the exact words, and Nicolas bustled her into the back of the waiting limousine before she could decipher them.

"What was that about?" she asked breathlessly as the car shifted into gear and headed toward the palace.

He shook his head. "The press probably caught wind of our travels and are trying to see if it's worthy of front page news."

The media attention still seemed odd to her, since the trip had been business-related and the palace likely would have already delivered a press release outlining the prince's plans. But she pushed aside her misgivings and relaxed in the comfortable, stuffed leather seat.

When they arrived at the palace, the queen was waiting for them in the main foyer. Her face was pinched, her mouth set in a flat, angry line. Though she didn't raise her voice, the disapproval in her tone was clear as glass.

"In the library," she snapped. "Now."

Nicolas and Alandra exchanged a questioning glance, then slowly followed in the queen's rapid-fire footsteps.

As soon as they stepped into the library and closed the door behind them, Eleanor spun back around, holding a newspaper in her shaking hands. *"What,"* she demanded through clenched teeth, "is the meaning of this?"

Alandra stood perfectly still, stunned by the queen's obvious displeasure, but unsure of the cause. As hard as she tried, she couldn't make out the headline of the article being waved between them.

Seemingly unfazed by his mother's mood, Nicolas reached for the paper. There, taking up nearly all of the top half of the front page was a close-up photo of Nicolas and Alandra. They were standing on the balcony of the hotel suite, caught in an un-mistakable embrace.

The photo had to have been taken after they had made love, then gone out on the balcony for a breath of fresh air…only to end up kissing for long, stolen moments before drifting back inside to make love again.

Alandra's cheeks flamed at both the memory and the knowledge that someone had been out there, snapping pictures of a very private moment.

Above the photo, sending a wave of nausea through her stomach, was a bold, glaring headline that declared her Prince Nicolas's American Tart.

Nicolas muttered a dark curse beneath his breath and lowered the newspaper.

Still vibrating with anger, the queen said, "You and your little…*American* are on the front page of every newspaper in Glendovia. I told you, Nico-las. I *told* you not to get involved with her, that she would only bring shame and embarrassment to our family."

The sick sensation clawing at Alandra's insides grew worse. She'd come to Glendovia to get away from one scandal, only to find herself smack in the middle of another.

And this one was even worse, because now it was true. She hadn't had an affair with Blake Winters, as the American press had claimed, but she *had* been sleeping with Nicolas.

"Mother," Nicolas growled.

His jaw was clenched, and the single word was clearly a warning. One the queen chose to ignore.

"Princess Lisette arrived less than an hour ago—in tears. She's crushed, and her parents are furious. Do you have any idea how this indignity will affect your upcoming nuptials? If she backs out of the engagement, our family's ties with hers will be fractured. The political future of Glendovia could be in peril."

"I think you're overreacting," Nicolas remarked, but it was obvious from his expression that the entire situation had him concerned.

Alandra's brain had gotten stuck on two words that made her heart feel as though it were being squeezed in a vise.

She turned her head toward Nicolas. "You're engaged?" she asked.

"It's not what you think," he said shortly. "I can explain."

But she didn't want to hear explanations, excuses, lies or more of the persuasive and creative arguments he seemed only too talented at spinning.

It was her turn to shake her head as she backed away.

"I'm sorry," she murmured shakily, directing her apology to the queen, not Nicolas. She had nothing to apologize to him for.

"I'm sorry," she said again, "I didn't know he was betrothed. I certainly didn't come here with the intention of getting involved with Nicolas. I would never have knowingly brought any embarrassment or undue attention to your family. I hope you can believe that."

The queen's pinched expression did not change as she turned to look at her son. "I'll expect the two of you to keep your distance from now on. You will conduct yourselves with the utmost decorum and stay as far from each other as possible while we rectify this situation. Is that understood?"

Nicolas looked as though he wanted to argue, but Alandra was already nodding. She blinked to hold back tears of humiliation, even as she licked her dry, parched lips.

"You may go," Eleanor told her, clearly dismissing her. "And you," she said to Nicolas, "will speak with Lisette immediately, and do your best to repair whatever damage has been done. Is that understood?"

Alandra slipped out of the office, closing the doors behind her without waiting to hear Nicolas's reply, and hurried across the parquet floor for the stairs. All she wanted was to get away, get back to her rooms, where she could be alone. What a fool she'd been. Again.

Standing in the doorway of her suite, Alandra took one last look around to be sure she hadn't left anything behind. All had been erased.

Closing the door quietly behind her, she walked down the hall, pulling her wheeled carry-on behind her. Instead of heading for the front of the palace, where guests would be arriving for the Christmas Eve party, she slipped toward the back, where a car was waiting to take her to the airport.

Leaving now meant giving up the hefty bonus

Nicolas had promised for the charity of her choice, but she simply couldn't stay. She wanted to go home, where she would be surrounded by family. Where she could hopefully hide and start to heal.

At the moment, the pain in her heart didn't feel as though it would ever go away, but she was hopeful. Hopeful that the sooner she left Glendovia, the sooner she could put this entire incident behind her. That the farther she could get from Nicolas, the faster she would begin to forget that she'd let herself fall in love with him—and that he'd been lying to her the entire time.

"Thank you for all of your help," she said to the woman who had helped her arrange for the car and a flight back to the United States.

Alandra handed her a stack of thick files and paperwork, with a separate sheet of stationery clipped to the outside. Despite her eagerness to leave, she had taken the time this afternoon to make certain the foundation wouldn't be left in the lurch.

"Please see that Prince Nicolas gets this. It should be everything he needs to continue with the Dream a Little Dream project."

The woman nodded and offered a small curtsy. "Yes, miss. It was a pleasure to meet you."

"Thank you," Alandra said, swallowing back tears. In only a few short weeks she had grown unaccountably close to the palace staff and was sincerely going to miss them.

With her throat too clogged to speak another word, she walked to the waiting vehicle and climbed in the back. It was dark outside, and too dark to see much of anything through the tinted rear windows. But even so, as the car rolled slowly away from the palace, Alandra kept her gaze focused straight ahead, not wanting to catch even one final glimpse of the site where she'd experienced both an incredible amount of happiness and an incredible amount of heartache.

Nicolas kept his expression impassive throughout the night, giving no hint of his dark, foul mood. He was only too relieved when the Christmas party drew to an end and he was able to slip away from his family and their guests.

He muttered a curse through gritted teeth as he made his way down the long hallway to Alandra's rooms. This was *not* the way he'd hoped things would turn out between them, or how he'd intended her visit to Glendovia to draw to a close.

When he reached her suite, he knocked lightly, then opened the door and entered without waiting for her response.

The lights were on and he heard noises coming from the bedroom, but something seemed oddly out of place.

"Alandra?" he called, striding in that direction.

He pushed open the door, immediately taking in the stripped bed and the lack of Alandra's personal items, which had been scattered about the first night he'd spent with her. A second later, a maid appeared in the bathroom doorway and gave a little squeak of surprise.

"Your Highness," she said, bowing her head.

"Where is Miss Sanchez?" he asked, frowning in consternation.

"I'm sorry, sir, but she's gone. Left just before the party began."

"She's gone?" he repeated, feeling as though his feet had been swept out from under him.

"Yes, sir. I believe she left something for you, though, with Delores. Shall I get her for you?"

"Yes, thank you. Have her bring it to my office, if you would, please."

"Yes, Your Highness."

The maid rushed around him and out of the room. Nicolas trailed behind at a much slower pace, taking a back stairwell to the first floor and heading for his private office. Ten minutes later, Delores arrived. She had a stack of folders in her arms.

"Miss Sanchez left these for you, sir," she said, handing them across the desk to him.

He thanked her, waiting until the servant had gone before opening the note on top of the pile. Alandra's letter was oddly lacking in emotion, simply explaining that she couldn't stay any longer, regardless of the requirements of her contract, now that she knew he was engaged to be married and those pictures had become public. The files, he discovered, held pages upon pages about the Dream a Little Dream Foundation.

He should have expected that she wouldn't want to leave unless she was sure all of the project details were in his hands, and that the establishment of the organization would move forward as planned.

The problem was, he hadn't expected her to leave at all. Not without talking with him, letting him explain.

He should have told her about Lisette in the beginning. Should have let her know that it was an arrangement made by his parents and not necessarily his choice. That even though he was betrothed to the princess, they had never been physically involved.

Lisette and his mother would be delighted to learn of Alandra's departure. Without her presence in Glendovia, the scandal of their affair would die a quick death, and life as they knew it could move on, including plans for his upcoming wedding.

He only wished he felt the same. Instead, he found himself wanting to charge down the hall and be driven to the airport, follow Alandra all the way back to Texas.

If only she'd given him a chance to explain.

With a sigh of regret, he crumpled her note.

It was better this way, he told himself as he left his office and strolled slowly to his rooms on the second floor. Now that Alandra was gone, things could return to normal. He could get back to the matters at hand without being preoccupied with thoughts of making love to her just one more time.

Yes, it was better this way. Better for everyone.

Thirteen

The noise from the back of the room buzzed in Alandra's ears. She really didn't want to do this.

After arriving home from Glendovia in the middle of the night—Christmas night, no less—she'd done her best to get her life back on track. News of her affair with Nicolas had yet to trickle back to the States. But if anyone in her immediate circle had heard about the affair they'd wisely chosen to ignore the gossip.

Everyone except her sister. Elena had waited

until they'd gotten home from the airport to say anything, but she'd known instinctively that something had sent Alandra running back to Texas.

The minute they were alone, Alandra had broken down and told her sister everything, pouring her heart out about the situation and how she'd unwisely fallen in love with a man she could never have. And as always, her sister had understood. She'd listened and offered appropriate responses at appropriate times, but never acted as though she thought Alandra had been a fool to get involved with Nicolas in the first place.

Elena was also the one who'd encouraged her most strongly to throw herself back into her work, when Alandra had wanted nothing more than to curl up in a ball and hide under the covers for the next month or two.

Which was how she'd ended up backstage at the Gabriel's Crossing Country Club. Long before she'd left for Glendovia, she had not only helped finalize the evening's New Year's Eve bachelorette auction, but she'd somehow allowed herself to be roped into being one of the bachelorettes, as well, and now they were holding her to her promise.

The event was in full swing. Six other women had already pranced down the runway to a smattering of applause and generous, good-hearted bidding by the interested bachelors in the audience. Two more ladies were set to take their walks, and then she would be next.

She swallowed hard, taking deep breaths to keep from drowning in panic. This wasn't her idea of a good time. She far preferred to remain behind the scenes at these events. Being the center of attention—especially with all of the publicity that had surrounded her lately—made her knees shake and her teeth rattle.

One bachelorette down, one to go.

"Alandra," a woman who was helping out backstage called in a loud whisper. "Get ready, you're next."

Oh, God, oh, God, oh, God.

For a brief second, she wondered how far she would be able to run in four-inch heels. She probably wouldn't get far, but it was still worth a try.

Inhaling deeply and praying she wouldn't trip over the hem of her gown, she started slowly down the makeshift runway to the sound of scattered clapping and the voice of the master of ceremonies, who extolled her many feminine virtues and outlined the details of the date she'd agreed upon beforehand.

She felt like an animal at a zoo, on display for the whole world to gawk at and appraise. And as she neared the end of the runway, her stomach plunged when she realized that not a single bid had been called out yet.

Oh, Lord, please let the floor open up and swallow me whole, she thought.

At the end of the runway, she stopped and posed, more from embarrassment than any wish to act like a supermodel. Except for the MC asking if there were any bids, any bids at all, the room had fallen into utter silence. The scandals, it seemed, hadn't quite died down, after all.

Alandra blinked, feeling the stares of a hundred people boring into her like laser beams. She was just about to turn in disgrace and walk back to the curtain when a voice rang out from the rear of the room.

"Two hundred and fifty thousand dollars."

Her heart stopped, and she strained to see who had made such an outrageously extreme offer. The rest of the crowd did the same, twisting in their seats for a glimpse of the mystery bidder.

Elated, the MC quickly declared Alandra "sold!" to the gentleman at the rear of the room. At that announcement, the bidder started forward.

As the bachelor walked toward her, he moved into better light, and Alandra's heart stopped again, but for a much different reason this time.

Nicolas, in all his royal finery, stepped through the crowd. A couple of hulking, black-suited bodyguards trailed behind, making his presence stand out all the more.

She opened her mouth to breathe his name, but no sound emerged.

At the end of the raised walkway, Nicolas stopped to gaze up at her. He stretched out a hand, his face showing nothing as he reached toward her.

"May I?" he asked in that rich, deep voice that sent shivers down her spine.

Without conscious thought, she put her hand in his and let him lift her bodily from the runway, then lead her back through the crowded room to the rear of the building. She let him take her away from her own event, away from the gawk-

ing stares and curious onlookers, to the limousine
that waited just outside, on the paved country club
driveway.

Nicolas handed her inside and climbed in behind her, allowing the driver to close the door. A
second later, she heard the driver's door slam shut,
but the partition was up, and she knew that for all
intents and purposes, she and Nicolas were alone.

"What are you doing here?" she asked when she
finally regained her senses and found her voice.

"I bought you," he replied easily, purposely
ignoring the seriousness of her question.

The look in her eyes must have warned him he
was skating on thin ice, because he sighed and
shifted lightly on the leather seat.

"There have been some developments back in
Glendovia since you left. Positive ones, in my es-
timation. For one, plans for the Dream a Little
Dream Foundation are moving forward. We're es-
timating a March first start date for having everything up and running."

"I'm glad," she said softly. She was happy that
things were moving smoothly with the plans she'd
put into effect before leaving. But she doubted

Nicolas had flown all the way to America just to deliver an update.

"For another, I've reconsidered my original desire to have you as my mistress." His eyes met hers then, hard and unyielding. "It was short-sighted of me to believe that having you only temporarily would ever be enough."

Sliding across the seat, he wrapped his arms around her and tugged her against his chest. She went willingly.

"I've missed you, Alandra," he whispered against her hair. "I tried to forget you, tried to put you out of my mind and move on with what I knew I had to do."

His hands stroked her back, her neck, the side of her face. "But I couldn't go through with my engagement to Lisette when only one woman filled my heart. You're the one that I want, Alandra. Not as my lover or mistress, but as my wife."

Tipping her head back, she met his gaze, searching his startling blue eyes for the truthfulness in his words. And still she was afraid it was all a dream, that she would wake up to find herself alone, in her bed, with Nicolas nowhere around.

"I broke my engagement to Princess Lisette. It's caused a few hurt feelings and political problems between our two countries, but nothing that won't heal in time. And I've informed my family—my mother, especially—that I was coming to get you and wouldn't return unless you were at my side."

He slid his fingers through her hair, tugging loose the elaborate knot at the crown of her head and dislodging the tiny diamond clips holding it in place.

"Tell me you love me, Alandra, as much as I love you. Tell me you'll come to Glendovia with me, marry me and be my princess. My wife."

Her lashes fluttered as she struggled to absorb everything that Nicolas was saying. His determination and declaration of love, his willingness to put her before his responsibilities to the royal family and his country.

There were so many questions spinning through her brain, but when she opened her mouth, only one thing came out.

"I love you," she murmured, her own arms lifting to curl around his shoulders and hold him as tightly as he was holding her. "It wouldn't have hurt so much to leave if I didn't."

His mouth curved in a gentle smile. "I'm very glad to hear that. Does this mean you'll be my bride?"

A thrill of happiness squeezed her heart. She wanted nothing more than to say, "Yes, yes, yes!" and cover his face with kisses. But fear had her tugging away, watching his expression to be sure everything really was okay and that she could accept his proposal without making matters in both their lives so much worse.

"What about your mother?" she asked. "I don't need to tell you how much she dislikes me, and she was horribly upset about those photographs showing up in the papers. I can't imagine she'll be very pleased to hear you've asked me to marry you."

"Whatever problems my mother has with you are her own, and she'll have to learn to live with them. *My* feelings for you are what matter, and I can tell you quite unequivocally that I adore you." The corners of his mouth curved up in a grin, and he paused a brief moment to press a kiss to her lips. "And I'll have you know that the rest of my family is equally fond of you. They supported me one hundred percent when I told them of my plans to come here and try to win you back. My father in-cluded, and you can bet that he'll do his best to bring my mother around."

"You're sure about this?" Alandra asked softly. "I don't want to do anything that could hurt you or bring trouble to your family and country."

"I couldn't be more certain," he told her, and the conviction in his tone filled her with relief. "I would give up my title for you, and if you ask it, I will. You're all that I want, and I'll do whatever it takes to have you."

She couldn't decide whether to laugh or cry as pure delight poured through her clear to her soul. "Would you take me to a hotel—one without balco-nies, thank you very much—and make love to me?"

His eyes glittered dangerously, his hold around her waist tightening enough to have her gasping for breath.

"A prince's job is never done," he murmured a split second before his mouth touched hers.

* * * * *

ROSSELLINI'S REVENGE AFFAIR

by
Yvonne Lindsay

Dear Reader,

It's a real thrill to bring you my first European hero in the form of Raffaele Rossellini.

While growing up, I feasted on books about gorgeous Mediterranean heroes, popular in category romances of the time. The conflict of cultures and social behaviours always made for a meaty story between a strong alpha male and his reluctant mate. Even though their romance seemed impossible at times, the final delivery of a promise of unending love never failed to produce that "ahhhh" moment I craved as a romance reader.

I hope you enjoy Raffaele and Lana's story and their journey to admitting they belong to one another despite all their trials along the way. The story was challenging to write, but immensely satisfying to finish. I hope I have delivered on that deeply romantic and soul-sweeping satisfaction for you.

With very best wishes from New Zealand,

Yvonne Lindsay

YVONNE LINDSAY

New Zealand born to Dutch immigrant parents, Yvonne Lindsay became an avid romance reader at the age of thirteen. Now, married to her blind date and with two surprisingly amenable teenagers, she remains a firm believer in the power of romance. Yvonne feels privileged to be able to bring to her readers the stories of her heart. In her spare time, when not writing, she can be found with her nose firmly in a book, reliving the power of love in all walks of life. She can be contacted via her website, www.yvonnelindsay.com.

This one is for Louise,
my special first reader, in deep appreciation
for your honesty and your friendship.

I would also like to express my thanks to
Sarah Glass for her information on the care of a
comatose pregnant mum and her unborn child.
Any mistakes in the story are mine entirely.

One

He despised and loathed her with every breath in his body.
She was there, a woman apart. Alone. Widowed.

Widowed when she should have been divorced.

Tall, elegant, unnaturally composed. Had she even loved her dead husband? He doubted it. If she'd loved him, she would have let him go. Let him go to Maria instead of clinging to a marriage long dead.

Oblivious to the biting wind that drove unrelenting sheets of rain against his skin, Raffaele Rossellini stood some distance from the scattering graveside mourners.

He fed the anger that rose within him as if fuelling a log-filled fire with dry kindling. Would his treasured sister be lying in a hospital bed now, supported only by life-giving machinery, if the cool blonde in black had given in to her husband's repeated requests to be set free? Set free before the birth of a child who would now never know its father or its mother.

Grief rent him anew, dragging an unwilling groan of loss from deep inside his chest.

He had done his duty and come today out of respect for the man his sister had loved. A man he himself had done business with and considered a friend. Soon Raffeale would be back at his sister's side. Whether she knew he was there or not.

Her life support would be terminated after the birth of the child. A birth doctors hoped to delay as long as possible to give the infant a chance at a stronger start to life. While Raffaele warred with the barbaric reasoning that another life should not be unnecessarily lost, it contradicted every measure of decency and grace his vibrant younger sister had possessed to keep her in suspension until the safe delivery of her child.

He tried to tell himself it was what she would have wanted—she'd loved the baby so very much and looked forward to its birth—but knowing she would have given her life for her child did little to assuage the devastating loss of knowing she was already gone. There but not there. Living, yet not alive.

Raffaele narrowed his eyes against the rain as he focussed on the golden head of the woman he knew only from hearsay. The widow of the man whose lifeless form had been laid to rest in the yawning grave before her. She stood in frozen isolation at the graveside without so much as a tear gracing her smooth pale complexion. Not even now, long after the last of her fellow mourners had gone, did she even have the decency to show any sense of loss.

Bitterness warred with the rage that billowed inside

him. He'd failed in his promise to his dying mother many years ago that he would protect his sister with everything in his power. Now it was too late to mend the irrevocable damage his indulgence in Maria's whims had wreaked.

When he'd discovered her affair with a married man he should have stepped in earlier, even though trying to stop his headstrong sister would have undoubtedly been impossible. Yet he should have done something to see her achieve her dream of marriage to the father of her child. He should have wrangled an introduction to Lana Whittaker and somehow, some way, used his considerable power to coerce her into agreeing to her husband's request for dissolution.

Too late. He was too late.

The vivid image of his sister's body, inert in her hospital bed yet swollen with the advent of new life, burned like a brand in his mind. Yes, he'd failed to protect Maria but he would *not* fail her unborn child.

Raffaele Rossellini never made the same mistake twice.

The child would grow up as his own; that was now his promise to Maria. Her son or daughter would be totally loved and, in time, would know all about his or her mother so she would not fade away as a distant memory.

His eyes burned with unshed tears as he stared at the back of the woman at the graveside.

He would not fail again.

He swallowed against the grief that fought to escape from deep within him. One way or the other, he vowed silently, Lana Whittaker would know the power of the Rossellini wrath. He would make her pay. Make her pay for Maria's suffering—the anguished phone calls he'd received at home, in Italy, when her pregnancy had been confirmed and she'd realised that Kyle would not be able to marry her before their child's birth.

Lana Whittaker would know regret as he knew it.

She would know loss.

Lana shivered beneath her sodden black wool coat acutely aware of the tall dark stranger who had hovered on the periphery of the crowd during the brief service and who now remained rooted to the spot, his gaze burning a hole in the back of her head.

Who was he?

She daren't look back at him. If he was paparazzi, the last thing she needed right now was her face plastered across the tabloids. The circumstances of her husband's death would filter out soon enough.

How could Kyle have done this to them? To her? How could she not have seen—not have known—he was having an affair? She tried desperately, as she'd done so frequently in the past forty-eight hours, to remember if there had been a sign or a clue he hadn't been happy. But there was nothing. He'd been his demonstrative and loving self even as she'd driven him to the airport for his business trip down to New Zealand's capital city, Wellington. A trip he'd taken for one week each fortnight for the past three years.

A trip he'd been taking to be with his lover!

For a moment Lana almost gave into the welling urge to scream and rant and wail. To pull at her hair, her chest, her clothing. To give in to the wild anger and fear that tore at her equilibrium. It wasn't supposed to be like this. They'd been the perfect couple—devoted—everyone had said so.

Tiny black spots spun wildly in front of her eyes.

Breathe, she commanded, breathe. Don't give in. Don't give up to this. Keep the emptiness away.

Lana dragged moisture-laden air into tightly squeezed lungs, desperate for some measure of purity back in her life. But nothing could assuage the yawning black hole that remained in her heart.

"Mrs Whittaker? We should go now. The caterers have called to say the first of the mourners have arrived at the apartment." The undertaker's carefully modulated voice penetrated the chill that enveloped her mind. What was it about these people that they all talked in the same measured way? Didn't they feel emotion?

"Mrs Whittaker?"

Lana drew in another breath and closed her eyes briefly, the shape and shadow of Kyle's coffin as it lay in the ground embedded against her eyelids.

"Yes, I'm ready." But ready for what? Where was her future now? Her life—her dreams, her deepest love—lay in the ground with her husband's lifeless body.

The short journey home to her inner Auckland city apartment passed in a blur. People would be there, pressing their interminable, yet well-meant, condolences upon her. She had to hold it together for their sakes. Let them think for a little longer that Kyle had been the kind of guy they could mourn and remember with respect, instead of the man he really was.

He'd lied to them all.

The mood in the apartment was sombre, a fitting tribute to the loss of a man who'd been revered by many as a financial genius. A man whose opinion had been sought on all levels.

Within a couple of hours the caterers had cleaned up and

the last of her guests were gone. Lana wondered if she would see any of them again once the truth hit the papers. Whether their condolences would wither into pity or, worse, scorn.

Her lawyer had managed to get an injunction against the release to the media of details surrounding Kyle's death only two short days ago, but it would expire at midnight.

Then the onslaught would begin.

Unbidden, the memory of the stranger at the graveside service plucked at her memory. Who was he? If he wasn't paparazzi perhaps he'd been one of Kyle's clients? She knew she'd never met him before, that much was certain. While she'd only caught a glimpse of his face, she would never have forgotten the gently sloping forehead, the slightly aquiline nose between deep-set dark eyes and the strong determined chin. His wasn't the kind of face a woman forgot. Everything about him, even the cut and length of his coat, had shrieked European elegance.

Lana shook her head in disgust. Here she was, her husband barely dead two days and she was looking at another man. Even though Kyle had been unfaithful it still didn't give her the right to seek another. Not within *her* code of ethics.

She walked slowly across the spacious formal lounge of the apartment, trailing her hand across the back of the expansive white leather couch where she and Kyle had curled up together, and watched the sun disappear across the distant Waitakere Ranges bordering Auckland's western suburbs, before escaping to their room to make love. Sometimes they hadn't even made it that far.

Her fingers curled into a tight fist as the pain of his duplicity carved through the protective mantle of stoicism she'd hidden behind all day. How did women cope with the discovery that their husband had a mistress? How did they shoulder the weight of the lies they'd unknowingly been living and manage to go on?

She felt angry—cheated. How dare he die like that—leaving so many questions unanswered? She didn't even want to think about what she'd discovered on his laptop last night after the police had delivered his belongings from the wrecked vehicle to her. Miraculously it had survived the head-on impact of the crash, but a part of her wondered if she would have been better off not knowing its contents.

Not knowing how he'd abused the trust of so many of his clients by filtering their investment funds to support his mistress in a waterfront home on Oriental Parade in Wellington. Not knowing how he'd used money from their joint savings account for the same purpose.

Not knowing he was probably already under investigation for fraud. She would need to get the computer back to the police. They'd be very interested in its contents.

Pain dragged like a serrated knife through her body, sending her to her knees on the plush cream-carpeted floor. She braced her hands on the carpet in front of her and let her head drop between her shoulders, pulling one shuddering breath into her lungs after the other. It was more than she could bear.

On the coffee table at her side a picture frame caught her eye. She and Kyle had been out on a friend's yacht, laughing at a private joke, their love and intense connection to one another shining from their eyes when the snap had been taken.

A lie.

Her marriage—the envy of all her friends and the union

the society pages had, on their anniversary last year, extolled as the perfect example of a happy marriage—had been over for three years and she hadn't even known it.

With a sudden surge of anger, Lana reached out and hurled the portrait against the far wall. Oblivious to the shattering glass and buoyed by her fury, she lurched to her feet and, like a woman possessed, denuded the apartment of every last photo of the 'perfect couple'.

She ripped each celluloid image from its individually chosen frame, letting the frames jumble in an uneven stack on the table and tearing at the pictures frantically until they lay in a fractured mass of broken promises at her feet.

Lies, all of them, lies.

Only then did she give in to the grief that had plucked at her since the police had delivered the devastating news. Tears coursed down her cheeks and a shattered howl burst from her throat. She dropped onto the couch, oblivious to the sunset, oblivious to the passage of time. Aware only of the gaping empty hole that ached in her chest where her heart should be.

Buzz! The strident sound echoed through the now darkened room and jolted her from her numbed misery. Her heart shuddered in her chest so loud she could almost hear its erratic beat echoing in the silence of the apartment. The security intercom, she finally realised through the fog of despair that enveloped her. Oh, no, she shivered, oh, please no. Not the press already?

The intercom buzzed again. Who was on duty today? She couldn't remember. But she *should* know. It was the kind of detail she always made a point of knowing. Hot tears filled her eyes and she blinked them away furiously. She would not cry. She had to hold it together. It was what she'd been trained to do her entire life as a diplomat's daughter and what she perpetuated in her role as the head of fundraising for the underprivileged children's charity she worked with.

Suddenly the night security guard's name sprang into her mind. With a shaking hand Lana pressed the talk button. "Yes, James."

"Sorry to disturb you, Mrs Whittaker, but there's a gentleman here to see you. I know it's late, but he's most insistent."

"I'm not seeing any reporters, James."

"He's not a reporter, madam. He says this is a personal matter. His name is Raffaele Rossellini."

"I don't know a Mr Rossellini. Please ask him to leave."

"Mrs Whittaker?" A deep, accented voice penetrated the air. Even through the speaker, it vibrated with strength and raw masculinity. "We haven't met before, but I must see you. I was a friend of your husband's."

"I knew all of Kyle's friends, Mr Rossellini. I don't know you."

"*All* of them, Mrs Whittaker?"

The reality of his question hit her like a hard-fisted punch to the stomach. She hadn't known about Kyle's lover.

"Come up." She ground out through clenched teeth. "I can see you for ten minutes only."

"What I have to say will not take long."

Silence.

He was already on his way.

Lana quickly flicked on several lights, bathing the room in a warm glow that was in contrast to the cold ball of lead settled in the pit of her stomach.

A sharp rap at her door saw her automatically smooth her dress over her hips and drag her fingers quickly through her hair. Too late to do any more than that. Whatever this guy wanted, it certainly wouldn't make any difference how she looked.

Raffaele stiffened as his nemesis opened the door before him. *Dio!* But she was beautiful. Surely this wasn't the same woman whose composure had stung him so viciously at the funeral.

Spiky dark lashes flanked her soft blue-green eyes, as if she'd recently wept. Her face was flushed and her hair tumbled. She looked soft, wounded, desperate for comfort—the kind of woman a man like him sheltered from the harsh realities of life. The kind of woman a man like him made love to long into the night, revelling in the length of her body, drowning in the glory of her hair and cherishing with every instinct known to him.

Then, before his eyes, she metamorphosed into the cold-eyed and coolly dignified widow who'd stood at the grave-side. He must have been mistaken. The glimpse of someone—something—totally different, an aberration only. The transformation was a stark reminder of his reason for being there.

"Mrs Whittaker, Raffaele Rossellini. May I come in?"

She looked surprised at the sight of him, as if she recognised him from somewhere. But that was impossible. He'd stayed well to the rear of the crowd at the cemetery, and their paths had never crossed before that. But there was something that intrigued him about her, about how swiftly she'd masked her features. As if she hid behind a thick, yet transparent, wall.

Of course she did, he chided himself. This was the real Lana Whittaker. The ice queen incarnate. The woman who'd insisted on holding on to a semblance of marriage, and therefore her pride, rather than let go of a man who no longer loved her.

"Please, come in." Leaving the front door open, she led the way down the short hall and through to the spacious, expensively decorated formal lounge. No wonder Kyle had needed money from him. Lana Whittaker was—as the Americans so charmingly put it—high-maintenance.

Following in her wake, his nostrils were tantalised by a suggestion of her fragrance—surprisingly there was nothing harsh or dominating about the scent, instead it was intriguingly gentle and slightly sweet. A total contrast to the woman he knew she was.

Did she do that deliberately, he wondered. Just to set the minds of weaker men astray? To lure and entice, then to coldly spurn any advances, all the while maintaining her formidable control? He silently vowed to see that control shattered before he left here tonight.

Without even asking him to sit down she spun around to face him, squaring her shoulders as she met his gaze.

"Well, Mr Rossellini. You wanted to see me. You have nine minutes left."

Anger rose within him, swift and sharp. She dared to challenge him without even knowing who he was? Raffaele clenched his jaw, bit back the retort that sprang to his lips and drew on the strength that had seen him drive and expand his family's olive oil export business onto the fore-front of the world stage, and successfully keep it there.

"I am sorry for your loss."

"Thank you, although I'm sure you didn't come to pass on your condolences." She held herself erect, her arms resting gracefully at her sides although for all the prickling vibes she gave off they could have been crossed across her willowy frame. "What do you want?" She demanded more insistently.

Raffaele began to see why Kyle had found his curvaceous, bubbly sister attractive. What on earth had possessed the man to remain with this frozen excuse for femininity? And yet, beneath the ice there was something—a fire simmering in the back of those sombre cat's eyes—something that forced a rush of heat over his skin and down deep past his belly.

"Your husband never mentioned me I gather?"

"Should he have?"

The insolence in her tone rankled, making his response clipped. "We were friends as well as business partners."

"Kyle never had a business partner."

"I stand here before you. It is true." Raffaele pushed his hands deep into his trouser pockets, nailing her with a hard stare, trying to see whether he could find some edge, some advantage. A way to rattle that unnerving calm she'd cloaked about her. "Your husband owed me money, Mrs Whittaker. A rather large sum of money." He watched her already pale features blanch even more as he mentioned the total sum. The darkened smudges under her eyes looked like bruises on her delicate skin.

"That's impossible!" she denied vehemently, her fingers suddenly curling into fists at her side. Ah, he thought with bitter satisfaction. Money *was* her trigger. Understandable given the polish on her looks—the perfectly manicured nails, the even tan on her skin, the expertly cut swathe of golden hair. High-maintenance indeed. It was time to go for the jugular.

"Kyle's death has put our business plan into an unfor-

tunate position. My Italian investors have already indicated their intention to pull out. Without your husband to
see to the balance of New Zealand investors, I have to
recall the loan." She didn't need to know that his own
company was the Italian investor he referred to, or that the
scheme—to expand a large scale organically grown olive
oil distribution network—was merely in its infancy. But the
loan itself had been real.

"Recall the loan? Just like that?" Her eyes widened, fear
making them appear huge in her ashen face.

For an infinitesimal moment, Raffaele felt a twinge of
pity but then reason, sanity, prevailed. A child would grow
up without either of its natural parents because of this
woman. There was no room for pity in his dealings with
her. One way or another, she was going to pay dearly for
what she had done to his family.

"*Si*. Just like that. I assume you'd prefer that I deal
directly with your lawyer?"

She didn't respond. If anything, she looked as though
she'd withdrawn into a part of her mind where no one and
nothing could touch her. Had he pushed her too far? It was
possible. After all, she'd only buried her husband this afternoon. Perhaps he should have waited another day.

Did Maria have another day? The question flung harshly
from the depths of his mind. No, she did not. He reached
a hand towards the silent woman standing opposite him and
touched her briefly on her arm.

"Mrs Whittaker?"

She recoiled instantly from his touch as though he'd
burned her with a red-hot poker instead of grazed the
merest contact of his fingers on her bare forearm.

"I…I'll get you his card."

Again she made that miraculous recovery, as if drawing from deep, deep down inside of her and pulling up every vestige of serenity to paint a totally poised exterior.

She walked with quiet elegance to what he assumed was the master bedroom. While she was gone, he looked about the room mentally pricing every item within it. He didn't care much for the pristine perfection of the furnishings, nor the modern art on the walls. He much preferred warmth and comfort in his home—and in his women.

His eyes suddenly lit on the scatter of torn photographs on the floor at the end of the couch. Raffaele walked closer and bent to lift one mangled image from the floor. So, she couldn't wait to get rid of every last reminder of her husband. He clamped his teeth together hard and let the shred of another man's memory float back down. He had made the right decision. Lana Whittaker deserved no sympathy.

When she returned with a white business card, some perverse imp of mischief made him hesitate before taking it, forcing her to wait. When he finally reached for the card, he trained his eyes on her face and deliberately allowed his fingers to brush against hers.

Her pupils, pools of black on a stormy background, dilated at his touch. Interesting, he thought. She was not immune to his touch. Very interesting indeed.

Her voice was cool when she finally spoke, belying the sudden flush that stained her cheeks. "Your ten minutes is over. Please deal directly with Mr Munroe in future."

"Of course. Good night, Mrs Whittaker."

"*Good bye*, Mr Rossellini."

His lips twitched into a smile at her emphasis. A smile

she couldn't help but notice as he turned and left her standing in the lounge. He let her have the final word— this time. She would be in for a surprise if she thought she'd seen the last of him.

Two

The tremors started the moment Lana heard the front door click closed. Kyle owed this man money, too? What else had he hidden from her?

When they'd learned three years into their marriage they'd never have a family of their own, she had thrown herself into her charity work, bit by bit letting Kyle assume full financial responsibility for their affairs. A responsibility he'd said he didn't mind—after all, he was supposed to have been the financial genius.

How long would it have taken her to find out, she wondered, if he hadn't died in the accident? How long would she have continued to live in a bubble of false security?

Weariness dragged at every pore of her skin and every muscle in her body, making her feel as if she'd aged forty-eight years in the past forty-eight hours. She could do no more tonight. Tomorrow she would see Tom Munroe, her lawyer, and go over the information in Kyle's laptop. Information which hadn't shed any light on Raffaele Rossellini, unless it was hidden elsewhere in his files.

Without bothering to turn off any lights, Lana trudged to the bedroom, but one look at the wide custom-made bed dominating the room sent nausea coasting through her like a tidal wave. The intimacies they'd shared under the cloak of night, the whispered dreams and promises, the shared grief when they finally accepted they'd never have the children they'd so desperately wanted, all swirled around her. Painful, tangible pieces of her past.

She could never sleep in that bed again, never!

Lana dragged a blanket and spare pillow from the elaborately carved chest at the end of the bed and went back into the lounge, collapsing on the vast leather suite. Then, finally, she let sleep claim her from a world that had become unbearable.

The winter sun had barely begun its subtle caress of the new day when the burr of the telephone jarred Lana from her slumber. Disoriented, she took a moment to catch her bearings before padding over to the nearest phone.

"Hello?" she croaked, her voice rusty with sleep.

"Is it true that Kyle Whittaker was with another woman when he died?" The intrusive male voice jerked Lana into full awareness.

So, the news was out and the wolves were already baying for blood. Slowly and quite deliberately, she replaced the receiver and flicked the switch on the handset to mute the ringer. Before she could cross the apartment and do the same to the phones in the office and the master bedroom, the line was ringing again. Without answering, Lana yanked the cords from their wall sockets and retreated to the en suite bathroom.

Kyle was everywhere. His toiletries still scattered on the black marble vanity, his robe behind the door. The vast double shower stall stood jeeringly empty.

She grabbed the wastebasket and swept his things off the vanity to jumble in an untidy mess of cologne, lotion, toothbrush and deodorant.

It was only when she looked in the mirror that she realised that once again her face was wet with tears. She slid out of the severe black dress she'd worn to the funeral the day before and peeled away her underwear, kicking it sharply across the floor instead of placing it in the hamper for their housekeeper—her housekeeper, she corrected herself—to take care of. If she had a fireplace she would burn the lot.

She snapped on the water for the shower and stepped beneath the stinging hot spray, seeking solace in the rhythmic pulse of the jets. Yet nothing penetrated the cold that encapsulated her heart.

Later, with her hair turbaned in a towel and wrapped in a voluminous robe she surveyed her clothes trying to decide what to wear for her appointment today with Tom Munroe to ascertain just what Kyle had left her with. She'd need to show him the contents of the laptop too—the thought made her sick to her stomach all over again. Finally she made her selection—a simple fine wool trouser suit in a vibrant teal, offset with a multicoloured scarf in softer sea and coral tones. That decision made, she needed coffee. Strong, hot, black coffee. She would survive this—somehow.

Leaving the apartment building's basement car park proved to be a nightmare. Security had already warned Lana not to depart via her first and preferred option—a taxi at the front door. Forced to use her own vehicle, Lana reluctantly nosed the late model Mercedes soft-top convertible up the ramp that lead to the street. Already she could see a wave of faces, cameras and boom mikes. Maybe it would be better to ask Tom to visit her here, at the apartment. But she knew if she stayed in there one moment longer, surrounded by the contradiction of so many happier memories, she would go completely mad.

Lana took a deep breath and pushed down on the accelerator. The security grill began to lift, slowly. Too slowly. Instantly, reporters, eager for the latest scoop, beset her car. To avoid hitting one of them she was forced to slow down. Thankfully, security at the apartment complex was thick on the ground. Uniformed guards cleared a path and urgently waved her on.

With her stomach clenched as tight as knotted ribbon, Lana drove forward, temporarily blinded by the recurring flash bulbs bursting like supernovas and bouncing light off her windscreen. Finally she was clear and accelerated away before the maddening crowd could follow.

At her lawyer's office she was ushered swiftly into a private waiting area. Clearly, bad news travelled fast. Lana sank into the plush chair. A subtle fragrance lingered in the air. Masculine, slightly musky. She'd smelled it somewhere before but couldn't put her finger on where. It was nothing like what Kyle had worn—he'd always preferred crisper citrus colognes. From her lawyer's inner sanctum she heard the rumble of male voices and the hairs on the back of her neck stood up as though someone had stepped over her grave, or Kyle's grave to be more precise.

Raffaele Rossellini.

He was here already? Bile rose swiftly in her throat and she swallowed hard against the acrid burning sensation. He couldn't even wait a day. Through the panelled walls she heard Tom's outer office door open and close before the inner door to the private waiting room opened.

"My dear—" Tom stood on the threshold, his hands reaching for hers. His wife had been a close friend of her mother's from their university days and Tom Munroe had been a part of Lana's life for as long as she could remember. She'd missed his solid presence during the funeral service, but a prior court matter had kept him from her side.

The sympathy in his eyes was almost her undoing. She put her hands in his and allowed him to pull her to her feet and into the relative comfort of his arms. A sob struggled for life from deep within her chest, but she pushed it down, determined not to give in to the fear and loss that had rent every last vestige of security from her life.

He ushered her into his office and settled her on a leather visitor's chair. Through the soft wool of her trousers she imagined could still feel the warmth of its last occupant caressing the backs of her legs. Sheer foolishness, she knew, but her skin prickled just the same.

There was no easy way about this. "You've had a visit from Raffaele Rossellini." Her voice trembled slightly. Lana clutched the laptop case more firmly between her fingers as if that would lend her strength.

"Yes, charming gentleman. Although somewhat concerned about some money he'd loaned Kyle. Did you know anything about that?" Tom leaned back in his chair and peered at her over steepled fingers.

"Nothing." Lana unzipped the computer case. "And that's not the worst of it."

By the time she'd finished cataloguing her financial

position as she'd discovered it, Tom had fallen completely silent. A worried frown puckered his brow.

"This puts an entirely different complexion on things, as I'm sure you know."

Lana's stomach did that awful twist thing again at the tone in his voice. "I've looked for our life insurance policies too, and I can't find them. You don't think he cashed them in do you?"

"No, more likely he assigned them to the bank as security for an additional loan. He didn't do it through me but as the appointed executor and administrator of his Will I can start making enquiries for you."

"But that will take days, weeks even. I need to know now. I can't sit around waiting for the next loan shark to come darting out the woodwork."

"No, I agree. Don't worry. I'll get my team onto it now. Are you going back to the apartment?"

The very thought of going back there made Lana's head whirl and the pain in her stomach increased.

"No. I can't. The press are all over the building. If I go back today none of the other tenants will get any peace at all."

"Why don't I give Helen a call, I'm sure she'll be thrilled if you come and stay with us until this settles down."

"No, I couldn't, but thank you. The press are insufferable already. When they find out Kyle was being investigated it'll only get worse. Don't worry about me. I'll check into a hotel."

"Sounds like a good idea. Make sure reception screens your calls." Tom stroked his chin thoughtfully. "Are you okay for money?"

"Of course."

"Well, if you're certain."

"Truly. I'll be fine." Lana stood and put the laptop back in its case. "The police will need this. You'll let them know?"

"Certainly, my dear." He took the case from her and laid it on his desk. "Remember, call me if you need help. Any time of the day or night, understand?"

"I will. Thank you."

"Thank me when this is all over and you still have a roof over your head."

"Do you think it could get that bad?" Lana clutched the chain-linked strap of her shoulder bag so tight she could feel each individual link impressed upon her skin.

"I'm afraid it might."

"Well, do what you have to." Lana reached up and planted a swift kiss on his cheek. "I'll call you and let you know where I'm staying."

"Make sure you do, and Lana…"

"Yes?"

"Stay away from Raffaele Rossellini. As charming as he appears, something about him troubles me."

"You think he's dangerous?"

"Not in a physical sense, but I suspect there's more to that young man than he's letting on. I'll get someone onto that too."

Staying away from Raffaele Rossellini wouldn't be a problem, Lana decided as she guided her car into the flow of traffic and headed for one of Auckland's premiere hotels in the central city. She had no plans to ever see him again.

The warmth in the foyer enveloped Lana like a much needed embrace. The hotel was busy, as usual, yet the elegant furnishings lent an air of solid permanence and longevity that both comforted and revived her. Even the scents in the air of cut flowers and the blend of expensive fine fragrances, both male and female, all combined to remind her of her childhood. Of security.

At the front desk Lana completed her registration details and handed them back to the smiling clerk together with her credit card.

"I'm not sure how long I'll need the room, but I imagine it will be at least a week." Surely after a week the press would be after their next nine-day wonder and be off hounding some other poor person.

"Certainly, madam."

Lana tapped her foot restlessly. The first thing she'd do when she reached her room was run a hot bath to soothe the tension that held her in its vice.

"Excuse me, madam. There seems to be some problem with your card. Do you have another you can use?"

"Yes, of course." Lana dug in her bag and tried to ignore the sickening wave of dread that undulated through her body. "Here, try this one."

The clerk swiped the card. A frown puckered his forehead and he shifted uncomfortably. "I'm sorry, madam. But this one has been denied also."

"But I don't understand. That's ridiculous." Lana took back the platinum card and slid it into her cardholder. "Can I use your phone to call my bank?"

"That won't be necessary." A velvet smooth male voice interrupted. "Perhaps I can help."

Lana whirled, her heart hammering against her ribs like a frightened bird in a cage. "You?" Of all the people she least needed right now, Raffaele Rossellini topped the list.

"Why not?"

"A telephone, please." Lana turned her back on him and baled the clerk with her most imperious stare.

He gestured to the bank of call phones against one wall in the lobby.

"Thank you." Her voice was clipped. She spun on her heels and stalked back across the foyer, determined to increase the distance between herself and Raffaele Rossellini as swiftly as possible. But he wasn't easily deterred.

"Mrs Whittaker. A moment, please."

"I'm very busy, Mr Rossellini. Can't this wait?"

"I was only thinking of your privacy. Perhaps you would prefer to use the telephone in my suite?"

Cristo! What was he thinking? It didn't matter to him whether the whole world witnessed her vulnerability when she received the news he'd paid his sources dearly to find out. When she discovered she was destitute.

He watched, dispassionately, as indecision chased across her features, as understanding dawned in her haunted eyes. She inclined her slender neck in assent.

"Thank you, yes. That would probably be best. I won't take too much of your time."

"Please, take all the time you need."

He gestured towards the bank of elevators across the lobby and followed close behind as she made towards them, trying to ignore her fragrance and the way it tantalised and teased his olfactory nerves. Did she wear her fragrance only behind her ears, or on pulse points all over her delectable body? It would be intriguing to find out. To discover first hand whether she was indeed as chillingly cold as her looks and demeanour suggested.

In fact, it would even serve his purpose—in more ways than one—to determine how best to undermine that inscrutable façade she wore, to destroy what little remained of her world of privilege.

He would be charm incarnate until her defences were breached. Then he would act with as much swift precision as a surgeon's laser, to excise her from the cataclysm her selfishness had wrought upon his family.

As the elevator doors slid shut Lana remembered too late her solicitor's words of warning to stay well away from Raffaele Rossellini. In the mirrored enclosure she found it impossible to keep her gaze from straying to his austere Romanesque features—the deep-set hooded eyes, the strong straight blade of his nose, the sensual fullness of his lower lip. She flinched slightly as he reached past her to press the button for the penthouse floor, refusing to acknowledge the rueful smile that chased fleetingly across his mobile mouth.

The penthouse. Of course. A man that exuded his wealth and control wouldn't stay anywhere else. She'd met many men like him, internationally acknowledged for their skill at making money and keeping economies afloat. Before her marriage to Kyle she'd hostessed for many of her father's diplomatic functions and had spent countless evenings shielding her boredom from men such as Raffaele Rossellini. But, a small insidious internal voice reminded her, there was nothing boring about him.

When the doors opened, with a barely audible swoosh, Lana stepped forward onto the thickly carpeted foyer and waited for him to swipe his key card to open the massive rimu double doors that guarded his suite.

"You'll find the telephone over there," he gestured with a sweep of his arm. "Unless you'd prefer the privacy of the bedroom."

Was it her imagination or had his eyes ignited with that last remark—their coal-dark depths glowing with a heat that caught her by surprise. Unbidden, a flush of corresponding warmth suffused her body, flowing in a rush from her extremities before pooling low in her belly.

"Here would be fine, thank you." Lana congratulated herself on injecting exactly the right amount of frost in her tone as the slumberous invitation in his gaze sharpened and cooled.

"As you wish. *Mi scusi*, I must change for another appointment. Please, help yourself to a drink from the bar." Long fingers unknotted the splash of patterned silk at his neck and undid the top two buttons of his shirt, revealing the golden hollow at the base of his throat.

Lana swallowed. All the water in the Clyde Dam couldn't dislodge the lump that had suddenly lodged in her throat. "No, thank you. I'll only take a minute. I can let myself out when I'm finished."

But she was talking to a closed door. A closed bedroom door. Hurriedly, she pushed the image of him undressing behind that door from the forefront of her mind. The bank. She needed to call the bank.

She quickly punched in the free calling number and selected the option to speak with customer services. By the time she laid the handset back in the cradle her hands were trembling. Her accounts were all frozen pending further investigation. No one could help her any further than to say that she currently had no funds available. No funds? But that couldn't be right. Her own salary should have been on the account as of last night. How was she going to survive without any money? What had Kyle done?

She stood, quickly gathered up her bag and lurched

towards the door. She had to get to the bank in person. Surely the manager could sort this out. A roaring sound in her ears drowned out the noise of the bedroom door opening. Black spots swam before her eyes and the sumptuous decor of the suite shifted sharply to one side.

A steadying arm hooked around her waist. As much as Lana craved the opportunity to lean on someone else's strength she knew she had to break free.

"Let me go. I'm all right." Damn, but her voice was weak. She was still fighting him as her legs buckled and the black spots converged into one overwhelming blanket of darkness. Vaguely she was aware of a muffled curse before she was swept into the strength of powerful arms.

Raffaele strode through his suite barely noticing the slight weight of the unconscious woman in his arms but painfully aware of the tempting bow of her parted lips and the shallow breaths that caused the faint rise and fall of her chest.

Eschewing the long sofa in the suite's sitting room he made for the open bedroom door and laid her inert form on the plush comforter of the bed. A shank of honey-blonde hair had escaped the confines of her hairdo and swept across her pale cheek. His fingers itched to brush it aside but instead he reached for the carafe of mineral water on the bedside cabinet and splashed a liberal measure into a glass.

She wasn't unconscious long. Her blue tinged eyelids flickered—once, twice—then snapped open, dawning realisation of her surroundings painting fear on her face.

"Here, drink this." Raffaele slid one arm behind her to help her up and held the glass to her lips.

"I can manage, thank you." She pulled her body away from the support of his arm, her voice stilted.

No wonder she'd driven her husband away. A man could

only stand so much independence before he felt unneces-
sary—unwanted. Here she was observing formalities when
only a moment ago she'd been lying in his arms. Vulnerable to his intent. A shaft of heat flared deep inside him
as she lowered the glass from her lips and swept their soft
fullness with the tip of her tongue.

"Better now?" The words scraped like gravel from his
throat.

"Much. I don't know what came over me. Thank you."
The fabric of her trousers twisted and clung at her hips and
thighs as she swivelled her legs around so she could set her
feet back to the floor and sit up fully.

She was still far too pale. Would she flush with colour
when in the throes of passion, he wondered, or would she
lie still as a marble statue and just as colourless?

"Let me help you." He took one of her slender hands in
his, giving her the necessary leverage to stand up. He tried
not to dwell on how fragile her fingers felt, or how easily
he could crush them inside his own.

"I must go."

"Go? Go where? To your apartment? Let me arrange a
car for you."

"No!" Panic streaked across her features.

"Then where?" He asked as patiently as he could.

"Look, thanks for your help. I'll be fine from here. Really."

"You think so?" He swivelled her around to face the full-
length mirror that adorned the wall opposite the bed. "You
are as pale as a ghost, you tremble like the last leaf on a
vine in an autumn breeze and you tell me you are fine?
How long has it been since you ate?"

"That doesn't matter. I have business I must attend to.
Please, let me past."

"No. What kind of host would I be if I let you go in this state? Kyle would have expected better manners of me than that. Before you go you must eat something. Then I will arrange for a car for you." His eyes narrowed as he saw twin spots of colour burn in her cheeks in response to the name of her dead husband.

"Please don't speak of my husband to me." Amazingly, she withdrew physically from him even more.

"If I promise not to mention him, will you agree to stay and dine with me?"

"You're trying to bargain with me so I'll have a meal with you? Don't be absurd."

"No, *Signora*, I do not bargain. Common sense dictates you must eat. Why not with me?"

"I thought you had an appointment."

"Easily changed. How long since you last had something to eat?"

Lara thought back. The last thing she'd had was lunch on the day that Kyle had been due home. They always dined out on his first night home. A homecoming date, he'd always called it. That was three days ago. Aside from the gallons of coffee she'd consumed, Lana had taken nothing else. But food was the last thing on her list of priorities. More pressing was her financial situation, and this man was one of her creditors. One of her major creditors if the sum of money he'd mentioned last night was anything to go by. Her throat clenched shut. She couldn't have eaten now, and especially in his company, even if she'd wanted to.

"Thank you for your concern," she managed. "I don't need anything right now."

"Anything right now? Or anything from me?"

Lana felt the flush of heated anger rise up her neck. Was

she that obvious? "I'm sorry if I offended you," she managed stiltedly.

He raised a finger to stroke a gentle line down her cheek. "Offend me? No. You don't offend me."

Icy cold flooded her veins, chasing any vestige of warmth from her skin. She clenched her hands tight at her side. Did she mistake his suggestion? Did he perhaps expect to negotiate their debt by an alternative form of currency?

Lana took a swift step backwards. "Well, that's that then. Thank you for letting me use your phone. I'm sorry about—"

He swept a hand expressively in front of them. "Do not apologise. You are under undoubted stress." He reached into the breast pocket of his suit and withdrew a gold edged black enamelled cardholder. Long tanned fingers extracted his business card. "Here, call my mobile if you need anything. Anything at all."

"Really, I'm sure I won't—"

"Take it. You never know when you might need a friend."

Silently Lana took the card and slipped it into her handbag. A friend? She doubted it. Instinct told her she'd be more likely to make friends with a tank full of sharks than count Raffaele Rossellini amongst her friends.

Three

Retrieving her car from the parking valet forced Lana to reevaluate her position rather more carefully. With her accounts frozen—and the remaining funds in her purse being small bills only—she found herself forced, for the first time in her life, to worry about the size of a tip.

The drive to her bank was thankfully uneventful—she only wished she could've said the same for the frosty reception she received upon her arrival in the bank manager's office.

"Mrs Whittaker, I am very sorry for your loss, but my hands are completely tied with respect to your funds. Your husband has defaulted on several payments. We've been corresponding with him for several months on this issue and were led to believe he was refinancing offshore."

"But our term investments…?" Fear plucked at Lana's mind. Where had all the money gone? What had Kyle done?

"I'm sorry, Mrs Whittaker, but there are no investments. You and your husband broke those funds some time ago. We have your signature on the documents." He swivelled his computer screen around for her to view the scanned forms. There, sure enough, was her signature. Although she had no recollection of doing so there was no doubt that was her own scrawl on the page. A sickening wave of nausea gripped her. How many times had she authorised financial transactions without realising what she'd signed, trusting implicitly in Kyle's direction without so much as a quibble.

God, she'd been such a fool. A stupid, gullible fool. How long had he been fleecing money from their joint accounts to line the love nest he'd provided for his mistress?

Summoning the last scrap of dignity she could dredge from the shattered remains of her life Lana rose from her seat and extended her hand to the bank manager. Even her last paycheque was frozen. The pity on his face was almost her undoing but somehow, from somewhere deep inside, she summoned the courage to smile.

"I wish there was more I could do Mrs Whittaker, but as I'm sure you're aware my hands are tied with the investigation into Mr Whittaker's affairs."

Lana nodded, the action a strain on the tension that locked her neck and spine in a straight line. "I understand. Please, don't worry." Understand? She didn't understand at all. Everything that was constant about her world—the very fabric of her life—had been decimated.

In a daze Lana walked out to the car park, reaching inside her handbag automatically for her car keys. A movement across the pavement caught her eye.

"No." she moaned at the sight that met her frantic gaze. "No! Stop that. What are you doing with my car?"

The burly tow truck driver continued winching her car onto the flatbed of his rig—the silver Mercedes coupe incongruous against the garish red and yellow paint of the truck. Lana closed the distance between them, twisting her ankle on the uneven surface of the asphalt.

"Unhook my car right now," she demanded.

"Sorry, missus. I got my orders from the car owners."

"Owners? You must be joking. *I am the car owner!*" Everything today had turned into some awful joke, except she didn't feel like laughing and realised with awful clarity that it would be a long, long time before she ever would again.

"Here." The driver thrust a clipboard in front of her. The words swam before her eyes—repossession order, defaulted payments. In impotent silence Lana watched as the driver finished attaching the hooks that secured her car to the flatbed and climbed up into the cab.

How long she stood there after he'd gone Lana didn't know, but a fine filtering drizzle eventually stirred her into action. As the drizzle thickened into rain, Lana picked her way carefully along the footpath until she found a sheltered area where she could use her cell phone. By the time she slid the phone back in her bag an hour later, she'd worked through her personal address book. Those who hadn't simply hung up on her had taken approximately thirty seconds to voice their thoughts on Kyle and, by association, Lana. For the first time in her life she was truly alone.

Chewing on her lip, Lana considered placing a collect call to her father at the embassy in Berlin. But what would that do aside from draw his attention to her capacity to disappoint him yet again. No, somehow she had to get through this without crawling back to Daddy. His displeasure, when the news filtered through to him, would be bad enough. She could already hear him saying "I told you so." And she couldn't bring this burden onto Tom Munroe and his wife. Always a frail woman, Helen had only recently had by-pass surgery. Somehow, she had to get through this on her own.

Lana looked around. When had it grown so late? The dim afternoon light had darkened to early dusk and the rain had set in. She thought longingly of the tip she'd given to the parking valet at the hotel. She sure could've done with that right now, although using a taxi was an extravagance she would have to learn to do without. She had no other choice than to hoof it back to her apartment. Thankfully it wasn't too far. She should make it in about an hour.

Exhaustion dragged at every muscle in her body and her twisted ankle was throbbing by the time she reached the front door to the apartment building. No media lurked in the shadows of the portico, thank God. Just a lone security guard remained on duty in the foyer. She recognised him as the same guard who'd been on duty last night. A look of surprise swiftly followed by an expression Lana was learning to recognise with sickening frequency chased across his face.

She drew her shoulders straight and pushed through the door. "Good evening, James. Rotten night, isn't it?"

"Mrs Whittaker, we weren't expecting you back."

"Not expecting me back? What do you mean?"

"Well, not after the bailiffs—"

"What bailiffs?"

James didn't answer.

Lana slowly asked again. "James, *what bailiffs?*"

"I'm sorry, Mrs Whittaker."

"Take me up to the apartment."

"I've been instructed not to do that."

"Instructed not to..? What? Don't be ridiculous. I'll go and check myself."

But James wasn't listening. He was looking over Lana's shoulder. A frisson of foreboding traced an icy finger down her spine as she turned to see what had caught his attention. A black limousine pulled up in the sheltered portico at the front entrance of the building, its paintwork, as shiny as polished obsidian, glistened with the moisture of the unrelenting rain. Without even being able to see through the dark tinted windows Lana knew who was inside.

The back door swung open and Raffaele Rossellini's tall frame unfolded gracefully from the car, his long black coat settling around him like a medieval cape on a shadowed dark knight. She felt it the second his eyes locked on her, and held herself rigid, barely daring to draw breath. What was he doing here?

He was at her side in seconds. "What is the problem here?" His accent was stronger, Lana noticed, as she stole a look at his face.

Dark brows were drawn together in a frown, his jaw set and his lips formed a hard straight line. James wavered under the steely regard.

"Mrs Whittaker wants to go up to her apartment."

"And the reason she can't is?"

"I've been instructed not to let her enter the building."

"By whom," Raffaele demanded.

"The management, sir."

"Take Mrs Whittaker up to her apartment. I will personally vouch for her behaviour."

Lana flinched. "That's not necessary. I just want to—"

"Certainly, sir."

Lana's head swam. What kind of power did this Rossellini fellow have? She didn't hesitate to question it, however as James came around from behind his station and led the way to the open elevator waiting on the ground floor. The journey to the tenth floor had never taken so long. By the time the doors slid open she was operating on automatic. As overwhelming as the memories had been last night at least the apartment had been a familiar place.

At the door, she stepped forward to fit her key to the lock and gave it a twist, the action so automatic she could've done it in her sleep. The key didn't turn.

"There's something wrong with my key. It's not working." She turned to the two men standing behind her. "Why can't I go into my apartment?"

"It's not yours anymore, ma'am. The bailiffs arrived just after you left this morning. They've taken everything and the building manager said you weren't to be given access."

"Show me."

"Mrs Whittaker, I can't."

"Show me right now."

To her chagrin James looked to Raffaele Rossellini for approval. At the other man's nod, James reached for the master keys he kept hanging on the chain at his side. In a moment the door swung wide.

Lana pressed her lips together firmly, fighting to hold back the cry that threatened to escape. On a deep instinctive level she knew that if she let it go she wouldn't be able to stop until there was no breath left in her lungs.

The expansive rooms opened emptily before her. She'd thought the memories were bad enough but this, this was far worse. She moved like a ghost through the vacant rooms. Even the kitchen cupboards were empty. Gone was the Meissen dinner set, gone the Baccarat crystal, her furniture, everything. Even in the bedroom, the walk-in wardrobe door stood open, the shelves and rails jeeringly empty. The realisation that she stood with only the clothes on her back slammed home with the impact of a juggernaut. Not so much as a scrap of paper lay on the floor.

Nothing remained of her life as she knew it. Absolutely nothing.

Somehow she found her voice. "Thank you, James. I think I've seen quite enough."

The guard barely masked his sigh of relief. No doubt he'd expected a more hysterical response. As, for the last time, she walked out of what had been her home, he locked the door behind them.

Downstairs Lana numbly headed for the exit. Where she was headed even she didn't know. All she knew was she had to get out, get away.

"Mrs Whittaker." Raffaele Rossellini hailed her. "One moment."

Lana stopped but didn't turn around.

"Where are you going?"

"That's not your concern." That this man had been there to see her whole life ripped apart was bad enough. She couldn't admit to him that she had nowhere to go.

"Kyle was my friend. I owe it to him to take care of you." He drew her hand through his arm and led her towards the car. "Come, tonight you stay with me at the hotel. Tomorrow we will visit your lawyer again and find out what is happening."

To Raffaele's surprise she didn't so much as murmur a

single objection. He showed her into the back of the limousine and settled himself opposite her. He thought she'd looked brittle last night, but now she looked as though a single breath would see her dissolve into a million tiny particles and float away on the breeze.

He deliberately quelled the protective surge that billowed through him. She was, after all, his sworn enemy. She'd destroyed his sister's happiness. He was only helping her out so he knew exactly where to find her. The more she was indebted to him, the easier it would be when he finally wrought his revenge. And yet, there was a vulnerability about her that tugged at him with a persistence he could not disregard.

At the hotel she didn't speak as he took her up to his suite. He shrugged out of his coat, dropping it across the back of a chair and he called for room service while she sank onto a voluminous sofa, appearing almost childlike on its vast surface. A far cry from the cool and confident woman who'd greeted him in her apartment last night.

Kyle's creditors had acted swiftly once news of his death had hit the papers, and it was all her fault. If his friend hadn't been forced to maintain two homes, two lifestyles—essentially, two wives—Kyle wouldn't be dead today and Maria wouldn't be hanging to a thread of life.

Raffaele fed the anger that smouldered like a burning lump of coal in the pit of his stomach. Lana Whittaker had it all coming to her, and more.

The subtle tone of the doorbell echoed through the room. Room service was at least prompt. Raffaele stood to one side as the two staff wheeled in the trolley, laden with food, and set everything out on the table. From the corner of his eye he saw Lana's head lift up as he opened his wallet and generously tipped the wait staff. Money. She could probably smell it at twenty paces.

"Come, eat." Raffaele pulled out a chair and settled Lana at the table.

"Thank you, but I don't think I could eat a thing." Her voice was little more than a whisper.

"It's been a difficult day, but you must eat." He served a portion of seafood fettuccine onto her plate. "Try this, it's almost as good as my Mamma used to make."

"Your mother cooked for you?"

"Always. Yours?"

"No. We had staff."

Staff. It figured. Not for her the drudgery of shopping at the market and coming home laden with groceries. Not for her the simple pleasure of being covered in flour while making pasta from scratch in a noisy bustling kitchen filled with a happy blend of chaos and delicious aromas. His mother had ensured each of her three children was as capable in the kitchen as she. It had stood them in good stead in the hard years when her husband's business began to fail. It had been a difficult time, leading to his father's premature death, and had been the catalyst that drove Raffaele to excel. One way or another he had been determined to make up to his mother for the hardships she'd endured. And he had—with the exception of his last promise to her to keep Maria safe. In that he'd failed shamefully.

The creamy seafood sauce soured on his tongue and he placed his fork on the plate and reached to pick up his wine.

Lana, he noticed, ate little, but some colour had begun to return to her cheeks. Her skin was like that of a pearl, lightly blushed with the softest pink. No doubt she'd been a wonderful adornment to Kyle's life and been the perfect hostess. But despite her appearance he knew she was cold and grasping to her very core.

Eventually, she too put down her fork.

"Thank you. I feel much better now."

"*Prego*. Is there something else you would like? Some dessert perhaps?"

"No. Nothing, thank you. I'm fine." He watched as she elegantly lifted her napkin to her mouth to stifle a yawn. Ever perfect manners.

What would drive her over the edge, he wondered. What would it take to make her let go of that impenetrable calm, the haughty posture, the mask of perfection that governed her features? Raffaele's fingers tightened around the stem of his glass as the need to push her over that edge swelled within him. Not now, he cautioned himself. Not yet. Her time would come, though. Of that much he was certain.

"Would you mind if I retire now? I am rather tired." Lana's request penetrated his thoughts.

"Forgive me for my rudeness. Of course you're tired. Come. I will show you your bedroom."

On the other side of the suite from his own room he ushered her into a slightly smaller and less opulently appointed bedroom.

"You'll find everything you need in the bathroom through there," he gestured. Lana started forward, but hesitated in the doorway. "Is something not to your liking?"

"No, it's not that." She plucked at her clothing, a look of distaste twisting her lips. "Would it... would it be possible to have my clothes dry cleaned overnight? I have nothing else to wear."

"But of course. My apologies, *Signora*, how careless of

me not to have thought of that. I will take care of it for you straight away."

"Thank you."

As Raffaele went to withdraw from the room and close the door she reached out her hand and stopped him.

"Mr Rossellini, I mean it. *Thank you*."

"Raffaele, and you're welcome. It is a small thing I do."

To his surprise, tears welled up in her eyes. She swung away from him in a vain attempt to mask the raw emotion that painted across her face. He reached out his hand and turned her back to face him.

"*Mi dispiace*. I did not mean to make you weep."

He watched her struggle to regain the composure she'd exhibited most of the day. Struggle, and fail. The shoulders she'd held so straight now shook as gulping sobs escaped her mouth.

He pulled her against his body, offering comfort when his instinct told him to turn his back and leave. Offering strength when his inner voice demanded he cast her off to face her misery alone.

She held her slender frame apart from him, then, with a shuddering breath, her body moulded against the length of his. Her small high breasts pressed against his chest, her hips cradled against his. Every nerve in his body leapt to attention and a deep pulsing heat gathered in his groin. He flattened his hands across her back, determined to pluck her away. Yet almost of their own volition, they swept down the length of her spine, lower to her waist, to her hips, and drew her harder against him.

Raffaele lifted one hand and slid it to her throat, his thumb tilting her chin up. Forcing her to meet his gaze. Her eyes stared back at him, as turbulent as a storm-tossed sea.

Moisture brimmed in their depths, threatening to fall if she so much as blinked.

He pulled her body against his again, more firmly this time. There was no hiding his arousal. She didn't so much as pull away by a millimetre. So, it was to be like that. Two could play at that game. He lowered his head, capturing her lips with his own, feeling the softness of hers yield against the pressure he knew he applied too firmly. She should fight back—reject him—he argued internally. But a tremor raced through him as her lips parted and her tongue swept out to trace his lower lip.

Her arms snaked up and her hands clasped behind his neck. Raffaele walked her backwards until the back of her knees hit the edge of the bed. Still locked in their embrace he tumbled them onto the satin bedcover, one hand cupping the back of her neck, the other tugging her blouse free of the waistband of her trousers. His hand slid beneath the silky fabric, upwards until he reached the gentle mounds of her breasts. His fingers swept over the cup of her bra and higher until they traced over the cool softness of her skin. She trembled beneath the mastery of his touch.

Disgust and anger swept through him. She had been a widow only four days yet now she was his for the taking? He yanked his hand away from her, away from the entice-ment of her body, and pushed himself to his feet.

He drew a deep steadying breath into his lungs and slowly exhaled, his eyes narrowing at the picture she made sprawled on the bedcovers—her clothing in disarray, her lips swollen and glistening like temptation incarnate.

Words failed him. He knew he should say something scathing—cut her down or, even better, cast her out. But as she curled onto her side and away from his gaze he found he could do no such thing.

"My apologies, *Mrs* Whittaker," he said through gritted teeth. "It was not my intention to take advantage of your grief. If you put your things in a laundry bag and leave it outside your door, I'll arrange for housekeeping to attend to it for you."

She nodded, the merest inclination of her head, but not another word passed her lips.

Later, under the pounding jets of his shower, Raffaele tried to wash the feel of Lana Whittaker from his body and out of his mind. But it was useless. The taste of her, the texture of her tongue, her skin, ran through his veins like a drug.

He forced the image of Maria to the front of his mind. For her he would do this. Only for her.

Four

Lana rose from the bed the moment Raffaele left her room and rapidly peeled off her clothing. She grabbed the laundry bag off the hanger in the built-in wardrobe and shoved her things in it. Dressed now only in her bra and panties, she quickly opened the bedroom door and dropped the bag outside before pulling it swiftly closed again.

Automatically, she went through the motions of getting ready for bed—rinsing out her underwear, brushing her teeth, taking refuge in a warm shower—all the while refusing to acknowledge, even to herself, how swiftly she'd fallen into Raffaele Rossellini's arms and under his masculine spell. Wrapped in a dry bath towel and with nothing left to do to occupy her, she finally sat on the edge of the bed and faced the irrefutable truth.

Her husband had been dead less than a week and she'd already thrown herself into another man's arms. What did that make her? Waves of desolate weariness swelled through her. Even if she'd wanted to understand, nothing in her life had ever prepared her for this. Not the private schooling in various cities around the world, not the grooming at a Swiss finishing school, not her duties as her father's hostess or her work with underprivileged children in the city, and certainly not the discovery that her husband—the man she'd sworn to love a lifetime—had been a two-faced lying scoundrel.

When had her marriage started to fall apart? What could she have done differently? Would it even have made any difference?

And what of her behaviour with Raffaele Rossellini? This time last night he'd been the last person she expected, or wanted, to see ever again. Another of Kyle's creditors, and for a huge sum of money. Letting herself be comforted by him was one thing, but to have willingly offered her lips, her body, to him was quite another. And yet, even now her nipples still tightened at the memory of his touch and fire still shot delicious flames through her body. His kiss had been dominating, masterful, and she'd welcomed it with a wantonness that still pulsed through her.

She shouldn't be feeling like this. Guilt should be flaying her with its many tails, not leaving her body awakened and craving more of his touch. She could even still smell him, the musky spice of his cologne, the underlying heat of him.

She wanted him with a force that shocked her to her core. Was it only a knee-jerk reaction to Kyle's infidelity—to the proof that she wasn't woman enough for him, and obviously hadn't been for some time? Thoughts cascaded through her mind, one after the other, like pebbles tumbling in a fast flowing stream.

Lana crawled beneath the sheets on the bed and pulled the covers up to her chin staring unseeingly into the dark. What had her life come to and, more importantly, what came next?

A gentle knock at her door dragged her from sleep the next morning—sleep that had been fractured with dreams of herself entwined in Raffaele Rossellini's arms. She sat up and pushed her hair from her eyes. God, she felt a total mess. The towel she'd wrapped around her last night had twisted and slipped around her body and she grasped at its edges, pulling them up to cover herself as her door swung open.

Raffaele stood in the doorway, a towering dark presence, dressed in what she realised was his trademark black business attire. Cool grey eyes, flicked over her tumbled hair, her bare shoulders and lower to the shadowed valley of her breasts, accentuated by the way she clutched at the towel. Heat bloomed through her body, her skin suddenly ultra sensitive to the texture of the towelling beneath her. She flicked her tongue across suddenly dry lips, her eyes captured by the answering flare of heat in his as he watched the automatic action.

"*Buon giorno*, Mrs Whittaker. I trust you slept well?" There was a steely tone to his voice, almost as if he was angry.

Lana fought to regain her poise. "Please, don't call me that. I don't… I'm not—" she broke off mid-sentence.

It sounded all wrong hearing "Mrs Whittaker" from his lips, it sounded all wrong altogether. She had been Kyle's wife, but it had meant nothing to him. Nothing whatsoever. As she'd lain tangled in the sheets of her bed last night thinking about anything and everything but how she'd wantonly thrown herself at Raffaele Rossellini it had finally dawned on her that she'd been no more than another achievement to him. Something to flaunt before his colleagues. Something to boast about when he'd talked about how far he'd come from the kid who'd dropped out of school at fifteen to panhandle the streets and run odd jobs.

Raffaele's eyebrows drew together in a stark line and his grey eyes grew cool. "You want me to call you Lana."

She shivered slightly as her name rolled off his tongue, his accent lending an entirely new pronunciation to the two simple syllables. "Please, let's not stand on formalities."

"As you wish. Housekeeping has not yet returned your clothing. I took the liberty of ordering some items for you from the hotel boutique. I trust they will be suitable. I've also contacted Tom Munroe's office. They're expecting us at ten-thirty."

"Tom's office?"

"You need to find out what is to happen next, don't you? Where you stand financially."

"Of course. Thank you. You surprised me, that's all. I'll be out in a minute." She'd forgotten for an instant that she owed this man money. A great deal of money. Of course he wanted to know how soon she would repay him.

Raffaele lifted two large shopping bags, embossed with the hotel boutique's insignia on the side, onto her bed. "Let me know if these are not suitable. We can have them changed."

"Thank you. Yes. I will." With each time her words of thanks passed her lips Lana was reminded of how he'd accepted her thanks last night, of how she'd reacted under his touch and how her body flared to life in his presence. It was as if he exuded a drug that intoxicated her senses and drove all thought of her precarious position from her mind.

He was dangerous.

The thought flashed through her mind, identifying the

subtle power he already held over her. She'd do better to focus on each tiny step she would have to take to get through today and each subsequent one after that, in an effort to get through the mess Kyle had left of their lives.

When Raffaele closed the door, Lana carefully tipped the contents of the bags onto her bed. She gasped in surprise at the items that spilled onto the covers, her fingers reaching for the lingerie that slid from its tissue wrapping. The briefs were the sheerest scrap of lace, their colour the shimmering turquoise of a tropical sea, and the matching demi-bra more enticing than anything she'd ever worn before. Something was caught in the tissue and she plucked it from the delicate paper—a suspender belt.

She clutched the items in her suddenly fisted hand and examined the sizes. Perfect. A disquieting thought sprang to mind. Had he chosen these himself, his long fingers caressing the sensuous slide of fabric? A heated flood of desire pooled at her core. Had he imagined her in them when he'd bought them? *No!* She had to stop thinking like this, tormenting herself like this. He'd been thoughtful enough to arrange for a change of clothing. That was all. It was no more than anyone would have done for her under the circumstances, surely.

But there was no-one else, the insidious voice at the back of her head reminded her. Not a single other person for her to turn to. Raffaele Rossellini was it, and who knew how much longer she'd be in a position to rely upon his generosity. No. She was indulging in temporary insanity if she thought there was more to this than met the eye. She had to pull herself together. To remind herself of where she was and what she had to do next.

After a quick shower and brushing her hair, Lana slid into

the exquisite lingerie, forcing herself to ignore the delight of sensation as the fabric caressed and cupped her skin. The deep golden-coloured wool skirt and matching jacket in the bag were tailored to nip in at her waist, accentuating her figure and bolstering her flailing femininity like armour did a marauding knight. Dressed like this, she felt invincible. And to all the world, that was exactly how she'd appear, despite the way her skin reacted to the silk lining of the suit where her stockings left her upper thighs bare.

There was no top to wear under the jacket, so Lana buttoned up to the deep V at the front, noticing in the mirror how the gentle creamy swell of her breasts was exposed. A small frown wrinkled her forehead. A camisole or blouse wouldn't have gone astray right now.

"Are you ready? We have time for some breakfast before we go."

Lana wheeled at the sound of Raffaele Rossellini's voice right behind her. She hadn't heard him open the door, or come into the room.

"*Bella*. The suit looks well on you."

"I'm afraid it's a bit too…" Lana's hand fluttered at chest height and she faltered, lost for words.

"You look wonderful. Come, eat. Then we'll visit Tom Munroe."

Lana had no other option than to do as he suggested. She slid her feet into her shoes, thankful the patent black pumps hadn't been irrevocably damaged by the walk in the rain, and hitched up her bag from beside the bed.

In the sitting room of the suite Raffaele fought to bring his breathing back under control. When he'd insisted the boutique manager open the store at seven this morning so he could choose Lana some clothing he'd never imagined how stunning she'd look when she wore it. Imagined? No, that was the wrong word. He'd done nothing but imagine what she'd look like in the sexily soft lingerie he'd chosen for her, or what it would be like to undo each button down the front of her jacket to expose her creamy skin beneath.

He thrust his hands deep into his trouser pockets and closed his eyes for a moment, forcing the picture of his sister into his mind. No matter how beautiful and enticing Kyle Whittaker's widow and no matter his body's clamouring demands, the fact remained she had prevented his sister's happiness. Prevented his niece or nephew the joy of two loving parents. His hands clenched into tight fists as he remembered her denial of her legal name, a name Maria had wanted to bear as her own. Lana Whittaker was more craven than he had imagined.

He heard a small noise behind him as she left her room, and turned to face her, his face deliberately schooled in friendly lines he knew showed nothing of the grief that tore at him daily. For every minute he spent with her was another minute away from Maria's side.

"There are fruit and cereals or, if you prefer, a dish of smoked salmon and scrambled eggs. Please, help yourself." He gestured towards the white linen-draped catering trolley.

"Have you eaten?" She gracefully picked up a plate and lifted the lid on the chafing dish, her nostrils flaring ever so slightly as the aroma of smoked salmon in dill dressing wafted upwards.

"Not yet." He shouldn't be hungry. Food should be the last thing on his mind, yet from the minute he'd met Lana Whittaker two days ago, every sense in his body had heightened. His appetites stronger. All of them.

"Would you like me to dish up for you?"

Why not? Why not have her wait on him hand and foot if that's what she wanted? He noticed she barely made eye contact with him, it made him all the more determined to ensure she did. A slight blush stained her cheeks, the colour a complete giveaway that she was not quite as composed as she led him to believe.

"Yes, please do. I'll have some of the salmon and egg, thank you."

He watched as she served a generous portion onto one of the warmed plates, then a smaller one for herself and carried them over to the dining table. Almost as if it were she who was the hostess here—as if it were her right. He ground his teeth together firmly. He would let her dwell a little longer in her field of dreams, but only because it served no purpose to reveal his position just yet. He hadn't rebuilt his father's dying business into a name recognised on almost everyone's lips by acting in haste. No, he would bide his time—and when the time was right, he would strike to her heart.

Raffaele's driver pulled up outside Tom Munroe's office. Before he could come around to the passenger side Raffaele had alighted and whipped around the side of the car to open Lana's door and offer his arm. Slightly discomforted by his obvious intention to accompany her to the appointment, she tried to protest.

"I'm sure you have more important business to attend to. I'll be fine."

"No, I'll hear nothing of the sort. Yesterday was very trying for you, I am here for you today. Do not attempt to think otherwise."

Lana wasn't sure if it was the warmth of his hand on the small of her back as they entered the building or the absolute confidence of his voice, but she couldn't think of a single other reason to object—other than Tom's admonition yesterday to stay clear of Raffaele Rossellini. Back then, no less than twenty four hours ago, she had agreed thoroughly. But she couldn't have foreseen the situation she was now in nor the commanding, and strangely reassuring, presence of the man now at her side.

Tom Munroe's expression of surprise was swiftly masked as they were ushered into his office. He rushed forward, taking both Lana's hands in his.

"My dear, you should have called me yesterday."

"Oh, Tom." Sudden tears filled her eyes at his uninhibited concern. "I couldn't impose on you and Helen. You two have enough on your plate without my worries. Besides, Raffaele has been a mountain of support." She couldn't tell him about the reactions of the people she'd thought she could count among her friends. It would take her to a new low to have to admit that she'd been a trophy to them as much as to Kyle. A trophy that, once tarnished, was to be shoved in the trash and disposed of ignominiously.

"Raffaele." The name fell flatly from Tom's lips as he extended his hand to the younger man. A look passed between them, setting Lana's nerves on edge, challenge clear in Tom Munroe's eyes. Lana couldn't see Raffaele's face but she saw the determination on Tom's face soften ever so slightly. "Well, then, we'd best get to business." Tom settled himself behind his desk and picked up a sheaf of papers before putting them back down again. He leaned forward, his hands cupped in front of him on his desk, a worried frown creasing his forehead. "Lana, your situation is far more dire than I expected. Kyle had been in financial trouble for some time and had been approached several times by the bank and other creditors. Are you sure you had no idea this was going on?"

A sick sense of shame flooded through her, and left a bitter taste in her mouth. No, she'd had no idea. She'd blithely imagined the life she'd always wanted with a husband she believed had loved her was real. Was that so hard to comprehend? She'd trusted Kyle implicitly. Sure, if she looked back, there was the occasional strange message left on the message bank, or hiccup with their credit cards, but the problems had never been serious. Or at least they'd never appeared so. She shook her head slightly, not daring to speak.

"I thought as much. There is more, I'm sorry to say." Tom sighed deeply and picked up the papers again.

"More?" Lana clenched her fingers tightly together.

"The woman he was with at the time of the accident, you know she's on life support, don't you?"

Raffaele stiffened in the chair at her side.

"Yes, the police told me when they notified me about Kyle. But what does that have to do with me?"

"Mr Munroe, surely you don't need to distress Lana further with this information," Raffaele interrupted, an unexpected thread of anger in his voice.

"I'm afraid I must, Mr Rossellini. You see, the woman Kyle had been having an affair with is expecting his child. According to this information, she's thirty-two weeks along and the doctors are doing what they can to keep them both alive until the baby is a little stronger. It's not anticipated that she will live beyond the birth. It appears there is no record with any solicitors in the Wellington district, or even further afield, of her having made provision for guardianship in a will." Tom paused and took another deep breath before continuing. "Lana, under the terms of Kyle's will, *you* are the child's testamentary guardian."

Five

Expecting his child?

Kyle's mistress was pregnant? Lana froze in her seat, her eyes burned with unshed tears and a tight band squeezed excruciatingly tight about her chest as she tried to draw breath into her lungs. But nothing in her body functioned, nothing except her hearing and the awful, unbelievable echo of the words Tom had uttered.

She thought she'd borne the worst, knowing Kyle had cheated on their marriage and destroyed the vows they'd shared. Knowing Kyle had lied and deceived her in every way possible and left her without a roof over her head. But this. No, this was far, far worse. This pain sliced through her like a guillotine.

A baby?

After all the years of tests and infertility treatments, the discomfort, the indignity, the hopes that had blossomed only to be crushed when she'd failed to conceive once again. He'd reassured her, over and over, that it hadn't mattered that they couldn't have children. That they'd grow old and cranky together while living out every other dream they'd shared.

This final betrayal couldn't have cut more deeply.

Finally, Lana managed to drag a searing breath into her lungs, to find the strength to get to her feet, to find her voice and say the one word that repeatedly bounced around inside her head with the velocity of an accelerated atom.

"No!"

"Lana, please, I know this has come as a shock."

"No. No. No! I will *not* do this. I can't. I just can't!" She levelled a tear filled gaze at Tom. "You know why."

"My dear." The older man swallowed, clearly lost for words.

"I, however, do not." Raffaele's voice cut through the air like hail stones. "I fail to understand why you would ignore your own dead husband's direction in his will, a man you profess to have loved, or why you would ignore the desperate need of a helpless child."

"You don't understand." Lana swallowed against the pain in her throat.

"What is there to understand?" Raffaele's voice, usually only lightly accented, thickened with his anger. "You are denying a child a home. What kind of woman are you?"

"Now hold on a minute, Rossellini. You have no idea what Lana forfeited when she married Kyle, nor what she's borne since. You've no call to speak to her like that," Tom blustered.

"Have I not? I believe I have every right, sir. Maria is my sister."

"Maria?" Lana's voice wavered.

"Maria Rossellini. The woman your husband loved. It is no matter now to you. I will take the child. As its nearest blood relative I have the right."

"The right? And who had the right to take my husband from me?" She shot him an angry glare, watching his features settle into an implacable mask of determination. "There's more isn't there. How did you meet Kyle? How did Kyle meet *her?* Tell me!"

"Lana, my dear, this serves no purpose. Don't hurt yourself any more." Tom Munroe looked grey and worried.

"I deserve to know."

Raffaele stood and looked down at her. "Deserve to know? *Non c'è problema.* How I met Kyle—through business. Three years ago I started to look for an invest-ment project here in New Zealand to diversify my business interests, he had been assisting me in my endeavours. How Kyle met Maria—it is simple—I introduced them."

Lana flinched as if he'd struck her.

"You?"

"*Si*, and I've never regretted anything more."

Lana pressed her fingers to her temples. The nightmare that was now her life was spiralling out of control—it couldn't get any worse than this, surely. Raffaele Rossel-lini knew about the baby? He was the baby's uncle? As far as she was concerned he was welcome to Kyle's child. The irony that she was expected to be the unborn babe's guardian was altogether more than she could bear.

"It's yours," she managed between lips that didn't seem to want to move.

"What?"

"The baby. It's yours. I don't want it."

Tom raised a hand. "Now hold on a moment, Lana, Mr

Rossellini. We're not talking about a piece of land here. We're talking about a child—an as yet unborn child. Let's not be hasty."

"What is stopping me from having the child? It's clear she is unwilling to be its guardian," Raffaele argued.

"I will have to consult with a Family Law specialist. The situation itself is a difficult one. In general, under New Zealand Law, even as next of kin you would have to make application for a parenting order."

"Then do it."

Lana's skin chilled at the driven iciness in Raffaele's tone.

"I cannot take your instructions, sir. As Lana's counsel it would be a conflict of interests. I can however recommend you to one of my esteemed colleagues," Tom said evenly, his eyes severe in his face. "But you have to be aware, the legal process is slow. If Lana cannot—or will not—assume guardianship, the child will become a ward of the State until your parenting order is processed."

"My sister's child will not disappear in your State system. Not while I have breath in my body."

"And then there's another possibility." Tom steepled his fingers and fixed Raffaele with a challenging gaze even Lana had never seen him use before.

"Tell me of this other possibility."

"Lana could change her mind and contest the order. After some thought, she may choose to keep the child, raise it on her own."

"Why would she do that? She is not only unwilling to care for Maria's baby, she is unfit to do so. She has no means at her disposal."

"Stop talking about me like I'm not here. I've given you both my answer. That's the end of it." Clutching her bag to her aching chest, Lana rose unsteadily to her feet. She couldn't stand their debate a moment longer. Turning on her heel, she fled the room. She had to get out of there and as far away as she possibly could. She ignored Raffaele's driver as he moved to open the car door for her. She ignored the shout from behind.

Her feet ate up the distance on the pavement as she half ran, half stumbled along—oblivious to the curious stares of passersby. Finally she reached an oasis of grass and trees away from the prying eyes of stranger before her legs gave out beneath her. She slumped onto a park bench, uncaring of the moss that grew on the weathered wood and the rough edges of the seat that caught and snagged at her clothing.

A giant sob welled up in her chest and fought past the gasping constriction of her throat. Her eyes slid shut as hot tears scalded her cheeks and she gave into the overwhelming anguish that shredded every cell in her body with unrelenting talons. As hard as she had run, no distance in the world could save her from the unspeakable truth of Kyle's perfidy. Another sob rose, hard on the heels of the first, and tremors of shock ricocheted violently through her as she gave in to the irrevocable certainty her life had turned into a gaping hole so deep and so dark she had no idea how she'd ever climb out.

Through her grief she heard the fast clip of footsteps as they approached on the path behind her. It could only be one person. Lana swallowed hard, fighting back the urge to scream at him to be left alone, and forced the tremors to cease through sheer will. She raised a shaking hand to dash the moisture from her cheeks and opened her eyes, focussing on the imprint of the peaceful scene of the park in front of her and on the sounds of birds chattering—on the wind teasing through the leaves in the massive ancient puriri trees and the distant hum of traffic.

Raffaele slowed his approach, fighting to get his anger under control. How dare she reject Maria and Kyle's child the way she had. The news that she was the baby's guardian had come as an unexpected ripple in his plans—and had forced him to reveal his relationship to Maria far earlier than he had intended. It went without saying that further investigation was necessary to be certain the position Munroe had stated was indeed correct. What kind of woman abandoned a parentless child? She was everything he'd thought, and worse. But whatever he had discovered about her, Tom Munroe had one thing made painfully clear. She was the one person who could smooth the path to his goal. His fledgling plan to woo, destroy and discard Lana Whittaker would require revision.

His vow to his sister was a brand across his heart. One way or another, Lana Whittaker would agree to help him, then he would find a way to make her pay for the devastation she'd wrought on his family.

"Lana," he called softly, watching carefully as her body stiffened and her shoulders squared. "That is quite a run you managed."

"Please, don't. Don't try and make this funny." The words dripped like icicles in the chilly air. She stood slowly to face him.

"I agree. It is not a matter for joking. Why did you run away?"

"What else would you have me do? Stay in Tom's office and hear all about my duties as guardian to Kyle's baby? The baby he had with his *lover? Your sister!* You're no better than Kyle was. It's clear you condoned their affair and now you expect me to help you? Well it stops here. Now."

Unadulterated vitriol stained her words. Raffaele reached forward to grasp those firmly set shoulders of hers but restrained himself from giving them the shaking she so richly deserved.

"You would visit the sins of the father against the child?" He fought to keep his voice low and even.

"I cannot be that baby's guardian. Only a monster would expect such a thing of me."

"Of course you can. You're a strong woman, you can do anything you put your mind to. Look at how you've coped with the past few days. Any one else would have been destroyed by what you've faced."

"But this hasn't happened to just any one else, has it? It's happened to me."

"You will learn to cope with this also."

"Don't be ridiculous. How could I—even if I wanted to? As you so rightly pointed out back there, I have no home, no money. Even the clothes I'm wearing right now are what you bought for me. Everything, even my underwear!"

Beneath the line of her jacket he caught a glimpse of that very underwear she'd referred to. Underwear he'd personally chosen this morning. His body roused to life as he remembered the texture of the lace and imagined it caressing her skin. Imagined removing it and replacing it with his hands, his lips, his tongue.

Dio! She was a siren. Even he, with his agenda towards her, was not immune. How many other men had she ensnared this way?

"Lana, I can help you. If you accept interim guardianship of the child I will waive Kyle's debt and provide you with an income as well as meet all the expenses of care for the baby. Once guardianship is mine I will settle a cash sum upon you. You'll be free. Free to start over."

"Why? Why would you do that?"

"You would not understand."

"No. You're probably right. I don't understand your motives just as I'll never be able to understand how my husband could've lied to me for so long and how I never knew. Or how he could betray me with another woman the way he did. We were happy together!"

Raffaele firmed his lips. She lied so easily it roused an even deeper anger in him. Did she really think he didn't know the truth?

"I'm sorry, Lana, for your loss and for the pain you've been given."

Raffaele fixed his gaze on a statue in the centre of the park. Asking her forgiveness tasted like ashes in his mouth but he had to convince her to fulfil her duties. If she didn't, who knew what government agency would make decisions about Maria's baby until he could take care of it himself.

Her response was barely audible. "So am I. I'm sorry Kyle ever met you or your sister."

The wind picked up a little and Lana wrapped her arms about her, as if to ward off the cooling air. Overhead, fat dark grey clouds threatened to burst and drench them both. Big fat spots of rain started to fall. Lana shivered under their onslaught yet, if anything, seemed to be unaware of the escalating intensity of the rain.

"Lana?" She didn't acknowledge him.

Lana remained frozen in grief and shock. When would her husband's capacity to deceive stop flaying her inside? It hurt too much. Everything hurt too much.

"Lana!" His voice commanded, breaking through her reverie. "We must go."

He took her arm and together they marched briskly to where his driver hurried toward them, an unfurled umbrella in his hands. They completed their journey to the hotel in damp silence in the close confines of the vehicle, parting in the sitting room of Raffaele's suite to go to their rooms to dry off and get dressed. Lana was relieved to discover her other clothing had been returned, and hung—none the worse for yesterday's wear—in the wardrobe. She reached for them, then decided against it, choosing instead to wrap herself inside one of the hotels thick navy and silver monogrammed robes.

The phone rang in the other room and Raffaele's deep voice vibrated through the closed door as he answered. Lana sank onto the bed, she had no desire to eavesdrop on his call, nor any desire to be anywhere near him right now. Tomorrow she'd get up, get dressed and get out of here. Somehow she'd get some money.

About fifteen minutes later he knocked on her door.

"I must go away tonight, however I will be back by mid-morning tomorrow. I want you to stay here and consider my offer once more. When I get back tomorrow, we can discuss matters between us further, perhaps find some terms you will be agreeable to. Please feel free to charge whatever you need to the room—clothing, shoes, meals. Whatever you need."

"I'll be gone by the time you get back."

"I would like you to reconsider your position about the child."

"That won't be necessary."

"He or she deserves a home, as much as you do."

"Don't compare my position to the baby's. They're not the same. The State agency will ensure it's placed in a home. That's a lot more than I have right now." Her words hung in the air. Even to herself they sounded harsh and self-absorbed, but somehow she had to pull the frayed edges of her life together and that did not include bringing up her husband's illegitimate child.

"But you could have it all. Everything. I would see to that."

"No. I will not care for his bast—"

The cruel word she'd been about to say was lost in the sudden possession of his lips upon hers. Of the strength of his fingers as they raked through her hair, cupping the back of her head. His skin still smelled of fresh air and rain-drops—the scent intoxicating, natural, enticing. Desire blazed with wild demanding heat from deep inside her. She parted her lips against the pressure of his, tentatively stroking her tongue against his lower lip then scraping her teeth subtly against its slick surface and drawing the tender skin into her mouth to suckle it softly. A shudder racked his body and his fingers tightened in her hair. He groaned against her mouth and her body liquefied at the tug of his free hand on the tie of her robe, then the heated flare of his fingers across her hip pulling her hard against him.

He was rock hard and she flexed her hips against the ridge of his arousal that pressed between them. She gasped at the jolt of need that spiked between her thighs, letting go of his lip. Burning desire flared and pooled deep in her belly. His hand slid around to her bottom, cupping the warm globe of flesh and pulling her rhythmically against him. His lips played across her cheek, to the hollow at her neck behind her earlobe and a shiver of sheer want sent goose bumps over her skin as his tongue stroked against the sensitive spot.

"Is your need for revenge on your husband so great you would visit it on an orphaned child? Think about it, promise me. I will make it worth your while, that I promise *you*." His low, uneven demand shocked her back to awareness, to what she was doing and with whom.

She spun out of his grasp, grabbing the edges of her robe and drawing them about her tightly. Her heart pounded in her chest, her skin tingled where he'd touched. Through lips still swollen from his kiss she finally managed the words. "There's no point. I won't change my mind."

Raffaele flung her a searing look before reaching to collect a small overnight bag from the floor. "We will discuss this further tomorrow."

"I won't be here!"

But her words fell on deaf ears as he pulled the front door closed behind him, his control perhaps even more lethal than if he'd slammed it in his wake.

There wasn't enough money in the world to make her agree to what he suggested. She thought of the marriage she'd unequivocally lost. The money, the trappings of their luxurious life, they'd all been nothing to her in the face of the reality she and Kyle couldn't bear a child of their own. And nothing, apparently, to Kyle also.

She'd failed. Lana pressed her hand against her stomach, her barren womb, her fingers clenching into a tight fist. She couldn't do it. She just couldn't.

Early the next day Lana straightened the collar of her blouse in the reflection of the mirrored walls of the elevator speeding to the floor where she worked. She examined her features carefully. No one would guess by looking at her that she stood in all she possessed. If nothing else, she still had poise. A poise she'd allowed Raffaele Rossellini to shatter in his wake last night. Her hand rose to her face, her fingers to her lips.

He'd been angry both times he'd kissed her. And yet, despite the restrained power she'd felt in his body he hadn't hurt her. Instead, he'd enticed her, awakening her body. Making her feel things she knew she shouldn't be feeling and yet, conversely, felt she had every right to. She'd been scorned by her husband for another woman. Was it so wrong to want to rebuild her shattered confidence, her diminishing self-esteem, with a man who obviously found her attractive? Even a man who had his own agenda?

She pressed her fingers against the soft tissue of her lips, reliving the pressure of Raffaele's kiss. A charge of want spiralled through her body. Yes, he made her feel like a woman—alluring, feminine. With those kisses he'd begun to bridge the gaping chasm where her heart had been shattered, her trust destroyed.

It was too soon to feel this way for anyone, let alone a man like him. For goodness sake, her husband had been buried only a few days! What on earth was she thinking? And yet, she knew deep down that Kyle had been gone from her far longer than the month he'd been away before the accident that had stolen his life. She knew it, but was she ready to accept it?

The elevator door sprang open and like an automaton Lana stepped out onto the familiar floor where she'd worked for the past three years. All of yesterday afternoon she'd tried to get through to Frank Burnham, the chairman of the charity she'd worked with—he still hadn't returned her calls by this morning. Maybe he was simply being considerate of her bereavement. At least she hoped that was so. This job, with its small stipend, was the last financial bastion she had left.

"Mrs Whittaker? What are you doing here?" Katie, the receptionist, rose from her station, her hands fluttering like startled doves at her side.

"My job, Katie. I still need to work."

"Lana, what a surprise!" Frank Burnham's voice boomed down the corridor.

"Surprise, Frank? Surely not. I left you a message saying I'd be at work today."

"Now, you don't want to rush into these things. Why don't you take some more time?"

"I don't want anymore time. I need to get back into my work, to get busy again." *To make some money*, Lana prayed silently. The pay she'd received while on bereavement leave was frozen in her and Kyle's joint account.

"Perhaps you should step into my office."

A cold sense of foreboding swirled around her with ghostly fingers. While Frank's voice had been genial, there was something in his eyes that was anything but. In his office, Lana watched as he shuffled papers on his desk, clearing his throat several times.

"Cut to the chase, Frank. Why didn't you return my call?"

"Lana, I'm sorry. I hate to have to say this but you can't come back." He gingerly lowered himself into his chair, putting the width of his glass-topped desk between them.

"You can't be serious. Of course I do. I must have mountains of work waiting for me. What about the Charity Ball? The celebrity vintage car rally? I'll be up to my neck in things to take care of."

"You're not listening to me. It's not that there isn't the

work—and it's not that we don't appreciate all you've done over the years either."

"Then what is it?"

"We stand to lose sponsorship if you stay."

"So I'll drum up new sponsors. Give me a chance, Frank. It was Kyle who left such a darned mess, not me."

"I know, but mud sticks. His activities have raised too many questions, and by association you've been implicated, whether you like it or not. Every one of our sponsors has expressed concern about your being here. One has even requested an audit of our books. It's the kind of thing that takes us away from our purpose, Lana. It's competitive enough to win the charity dollar out there in the marketplace, you know that as well as I do. We can't afford the scandal."

"Let me speak to them." But Lana knew it was hopeless before the words even left her mouth. Many of her friends had been eager to support the children's charity—the same friends whose doors had metaphorically been slammed in her face only two days ago. Lord, it seemed like a lifetime.

"It's useless. I'm sorry."

"No more sorry than I am."

Without a backward glance, Lana left his office and left the building. She had one choice left. One she'd been avoiding at all costs. She had to call her father. Using a phone, however, presented a quandary. She didn't want to use the phone at the suite—she had no plans to return there anyway—which only left a public pay-phone; except she had no money. She had to sell something, but what?

The sun shone in wintry brilliance, its rays catching the diamond engagement and wedding rings she still wore. She'd become so accustomed to wearing them she barely even noticed their presence. She'd been a fool. Here she was, with thousands of dollars just sitting on her hand. Lana eased the rings off and curled her shaking fingers tightly around them. Suddenly her heart lifted. She had options; she just hadn't explored them yet.

Finding a dealer prepared to take the rings off her without ownership or valuation papers proved more difficult than she expected, but at close to four that afternoon she finally found a backstreet trader willing to pay her for them. Of course the money now in her purse didn't even come half way to the true value of the jewellery, but in its own way it had been liberating to sell the rings. She was her own woman, albeit of very limited means.

After purchasing an international calling card, Lana secured a telephone booth in a shopping mall that afforded her some privacy. With nervous fingers she punched in the string of numbers that would ring through to her father's private line. Although it would be just prior to six in the morning in Berlin, her father was an early bird. Her stomach lurched at the thought of having to beg him for help. They hadn't spoken since the day she'd told him of her plans to marry Kyle. His stinging words, denouncing her as his daughter, still hovered in her mind.

"Mr Logan's office, how may I help you?" The disembodied male voice at the other side of the world sounded sickeningly familiar. Was her father's aide still the same man he'd hoped she'd one day marry? Her skin crawled at the memory of what she'd been expected to do in the name of diplomatic relations.

"Mr Logan, please."

"Who's calling?"

"Malcolm, it's me. Lana."

"I'm sorry, Mr Logan is unavailable."

"Please, Malcolm. You know I wouldn't be calling if it wasn't important. I need to speak to my father."

"Your latest little scandal has reached even Berlin, Lana. He wondered how long it would take for you to call. I actually thought you'd hold out longer." The drawl in Malcolm's voice set her teeth on edge. He'd always had a cruel side, one he'd kept well hidden from her father's mentoring eye.

"Just put me through."

"It seems he knew you better than we both realised. He's left a message in case you should call."

"What message? Why can't he tell me himself?" Lana gripped the handset of the telephone so tightly the plastic squeaked in protest.

"He was quite explicit. The message reads, 'I have no daughter.'"

Lana slowly replaced the receiver as dwindling hope flickered and died.

Six

Raffaele paced the confines of the suite like a caged panther. Where the hell had she gone? After several calls he'd tracked her to her place of employment, although from what he'd learned she no longer worked there. Which begged the question, why had she resigned when she so desperately needed money? Was she considering taking him up on his offer to finance her as the guardian of Maria's child? Did she see him as an easy ticket?

Well, so much the better if she did. It would make what he had to do in the long run much easier. From the legal advice he'd received today via telephone, his case would be much stronger if he were based here in New Zealand. The news suited his business expansion plans perfectly. Bankrolling Lana Whittaker into agreeing to his demands would be a manageable risk if he could be assured it would pave the way for him to get full custody of Maria's baby.

He checked his cell again for missed calls. Nothing. It was heading for six o'clock and, according to the concierge, she'd been gone since nine this morning. Surely she wouldn't have done anything stupid. Maybe he'd pushed her too far yesterday. With some things, as with some people, it was far better to tread carefully, to take time to nurture their thinking around to your way.

He shouldn't have left her as he had last night. She was so emotionally vulnerable there was no knowing what she was capable of doing. But the doctor who'd rung last night had given him the news that Maria's body had begun having contractions, they would do what they could to halt them but felt it was timely for Raffaele to return. With his charter plane on standby at the airport he hadn't hesitated to make the journey to Wellington to be at his sister's side.

Maria had finally been stabilised at about three o'clock this morning and he'd remained at her side, holding her hand and speaking to her softly in Italian, hoping against hope that some measure of his love would reach through the depths and reassure her he would do everything he could for her unborn child.

While there, the doctors raised another more pressing concern. The special care unit for premature births at Wellington Hospital was full. If Maria went into labour again, and they were unable to halt its progression, the newborn would have to be flown to another centre. Raffaele and Maria's care team had debated several options, deciding eventually, provided Maria was stable enough to travel, that she would be transported to Auckland at the earliest opportunity, where the special care unit was under less pressure at present.

Raffaele had given his consent for his sister's move to

Auckland City Hospital, but only once he'd been convinced without doubt that this would be the best move for both Maria and the little girl the doctors told him she carried. He slipped the sonogram picture they'd taken this morning from his pocket and traced the tiny outline of his little niece.

Seeing the baby on the sonogram had suddenly made her more real, more defined—and had increased his determination to seek revenge on the woman who'd denied her two loving parents. But his revenge would have to wait.

Leaving his beloved sister again this morning had been difficult, but to honour his promise to her, he had to return to the one person who could have prevented the whole miserable situation. And now, unfortunately, the one person who held the immediate fate of his niece in her hands.

There was a click at the door as the lock disengaged. She was back. Relief swamped him but he composed his features and reached for the wine bottle he'd had cooling in an ice bucket and deftly poured two glasses of the golden Marlborough-grown chardonnay. He wouldn't show her how worried he'd been, nor how close he'd come to reporting her missing.

"*Buona sera*, Lana. You had a pleasant day I trust?" He turned and handed her a glass of wine as she came through the door.

She took the glass automatically, her slender fingers skimming across his and sending a buzz of electricity up his arm in a not so subtle reminder of the effect she had on him. A startled look crossed her pale face at his remark, almost as if she'd expected him to demand to know where she'd been. But that had never been his style. No, he preferred to lure his prey with gentle enticement, slowly but surely bringing them into his net.

"I wasn't going to come back, but it seems I have no other choice."

Although Lana's voice was composed she looked exhausted—totally tapped out. Clearly her day had not gone as well as she had expected. His instincts, honed through years of successful business endeavours, were never wrong. She was close to giving into his demands.

"Have you had anything to eat?"

"No." A cynical smile twisted her lips. "I haven't exactly had the time." She lifted a hand to brush a strand of hair from her face. Her left hand. "If you'll excuse me, I think I'd like to freshen up a bit."

It suddenly occurred to him her hand was bare. Gone were the trappings of marriage. What had she done? In one swift step he was at her side and he grabbed her wrist, twisting it gently so he could examine her hand. Her ring finger still bore the slight indentation of the wedding rings she'd worn, the paler band of skin mute evidence of their departure.

"Your rings. Where are they?"

"What does it matter? I don't need them anymore." She pulled away from his grasp.

Yes, that figured, Raffaele thought bitterly and reached for his glass of wine. Her marriage had meant so little to her of course she would shuck off its evidence as easily as one would change one's underwear.

"Where are they? They should be secured in the hotel safe if you are not going to wear them."

"Well, it seems they're not as valuable to some people as you might have thought." An acerbic note slid into her voice and a cynical half smile twisted her bare lips.

"What do you mean?" Not valuable to her, no doubt. She looked as if she was laughing at some private joke and the expression riled him far more than he wanted to admit. "Of course they had value, they were your wedding rings."

"I sold them. They didn't fetch much but I needed to make a call."

She sold her rings to make a call? She tossed off the words so casually. If he hadn't known better he'd have thought she was trying a little too hard to display such a flippant demeanour.

"A call you couldn't make from here?"

What was she hiding? A lover perhaps? That would make sense. She'd come to his arms easily enough. Jealousy flared with a vicious twist through his mind. The thought of her with another man made his mouth sour and his fingers curl tight around the delicate stem of his glass. Raffaele bit down hard, grinding his teeth firmly together to prevent himself from saying exactly what was on his mind.

"Yes. Something like that."

"Forgive me," he muttered the words beneath his breath, poor Maria—he should have acted sooner. This was all his fault and it had been completely preventable.

"Forgive you? For what? There's nothing to forgive. If anything I'm sorry. I shouldn't have come back here, but I had nowhere else. I couldn't bring myself to use a boarding house, not when I saw and smelled what it was like there. I'm sorry. I'm abusing your generosity."

He hadn't realised he'd said the words loud enough for her to hear. It was not her forgiveness he sought, but his sister's. How typical that Lana would think everything was about her. And what was this rubbish she was talking? A boarding house? He could no more see Lana Whittaker in a boarding house than he could see himself forgiving her for the damage she'd wreaked on his sister's happiness.

"So, what have you done today? Aside from examine boarding houses."

Lana put her untouched glass of wine down on the sideboard with a snap. "Walked, mostly, and tried to figure out what I'm going to do next."

Raffaele maintained a stony silence. He wished he could believe that somewhere through the passage of the day she'd spared a thought for his sister's child, for the request he'd made of her last night.

"And have you decided what you are doing next?" he prompted. "What of your charity work? Are you still not involved with that?"

A shadow crossed her face, her turquoise eyes darkened almost to green. "No, I'm not, I no longer work there."

"So your philanthropic works have come to an end. I assume then, that it was all for show?"

"Of course not!" Lana's cheeks flushed in anger. "What on earth makes you say such a thing?"

"Correct me if I'm wrong, but your charity work was for underprivileged children, *si*?"

"Yes."

"Then what is the difference between the strangers you raised funds for—to provide homes and clothes and food for—and a helpless baby?"

"The difference? The difference is…" Lana's voice trailed off as she clearly struggled for an answer.

"The difference is you are so filled with vindictiveness towards your dead husband you would take it out on his child. Perhaps you are right. It is time you found somewhere else to stay."

His hand shook slightly as he lifted his glass to his lips and took a generous swallow of wine. Had he gone too far?

It was hard to tell. Her face remained expressionless. The anger which flared so swiftly in her intriguingly coloured eyes had been as efficiently snuffed out as a candle's flame pinched between damp fingers. Then suddenly he noticed a subtle shift in her features, a softening of the set of her lips that only one who watched carefully, and who was beginning to learn the nuances of her moods, could pick up. It was time to swoop in for the kill.

"Perhaps I didn't make myself clear last night. I am prepared to forgive your husband's debt to me, to support you and to provide a home and all things necessary to keep you in the comfort you are accustomed to. You won't even need to attend to the day-to-day care of the baby; I can appoint a nanny to take care of that. Plus there is the allowance I mentioned, a generous one." He named a sum he thought would take her interest.

His words washed over her in a buzz of sound but she'd stopped listening as the truth of his earlier statement rocketed through her. He was right. Damn him. She'd been so focussed on her hurt, Kyle's betrayal and the shock of losing every last possession she'd thought her own she had lost sight of reality. Her father's continued rejection of her should have peeled the scales from her eyes. Her resemblance to her mother, who had never been mentally strong enough to withstand the rigors of the diplomatic life, had cast her in the same mould in his eyes. Even thought she was his blood, his flesh, still he denied her. She'd sworn years ago she'd never do the same thing to a child, and yet she had. By refusing to accept guardianship of Kyle's baby she'd turned the child into as much a victim as she herself—except she had the power to change that. The power to give the baby a stable start in life with a person who loved it unreservedly—who could love it as she would have loved her own.

Tears stung her eyes but she blinked them determinedly back.

"I'll do it." The words spilled from her mouth before she could think beyond her one greatest desire.

"You've changed your mind? Just like that?" Scepticism creased his brow, his grey eyes grew dark as slate as they bored into her. "How do I know that you will not change it back again as quickly?"

"I won't. Not about this. Not now." *Never about something as important as this.* As much as she still hated the circumstances that had brought her to this moment, a tiny spark of rightness sputtered to life inside, setting a trail of warmth coursing through her to beat back the numbness and desolation the day had wrought.

"Forgive me if I seem a little reluctant to accept your sudden change of mind. How do I know that once I set you up in a home you won't turn back on your decision?"

Lana was confused. It was as if he was playing a game of cat and mouse, lifting a paw to let her scamper just so far before trapping her again. One minute he was pressing her, demanding she accept the responsibility of guardianship, the next he was undermining her decision as if she was as fickle as the wind. She drew herself up straight, and met his gaze front on.

"Name your terms, draw up a contract. I'll do what I have to do."

"*You will do what you have to do?*" His lips curled in disgust. "You make your agreement sound like such hardship. I do not want to find that you have changed your mind and that my niece is relegated to Child Services while

I petition the courts. I want your vow not to walk away from your responsibilities to the baby until I have full custody."

"I said I'll do what I have to. I mean it." She did a double take. "Did I hear you right? Did you say 'niece'?"

"I found out this morning."

"That's where you went last night? To Wellington? To be with her?"

"Yes, Maria went into premature labour last night."

"And the baby, is she—"

"She is still safe within her Mamma."

Lana sagged deep into a chair. The weight of what she'd agreed to bore down heavily on her slender shoulders. The little girl, when born, would still require much care. Was she up to that? Could she follow through on her bold statement of just a few moments ago? As if Raffaele could see into the confusion that chased through her mind his next words made her sit up and take notice.

"I suggest that if you are truly serious about your intention, that you and the baby live with me. If I am supporting you at least the courts cannot deem you to be unsuitable to be the child's guardian, especially as you have no means to support yourself without my money."

Lana fought the urge to flat out argue with him that she wasn't about to change her mind about something as important as this. But then she realised, change her mind was exactly what she'd done. To his eyes she probably did look as fickle as the direction of the wind. She moistened her lips before answering, aware of his eyes tracking the movement of her tongue as it swept her lips and of the muscle that flexed in his jaw. "Live with you? Where?"

"On the outskirts of the city I think. Where you can ensure you will have the privacy you need until the media no longer wishes to pry into your life. Somewhere safe for the baby. I will set up appointments in the morning. We can look for appropriate accommodation together."

"But what about your business? How can you spend so much time away. Shouldn't you be back in Italy?"

"My brother is managing things capably at home. It is more important to me to be here now. Besides, I've been working to expand my interests in this country for some time; it was why I was already here when the accident happened. It will be no hardship to base myself here for however long is necessary."

"Then I agree. Get a contract drawn up. I'll sign whatever I have to."

She thought he was going to say something more but then he simply nodded and walked over to stand next to her at the sideboard. He picked up her glass and handed it back to her.

"A toast, I think. To new beginnings."

She raised her glass to his. "Yes. New beginnings."

Seven

Raffaele hired a car late the next morning and they headed south down the motorway, eventually taking the Manukau turnoff. After a short drive through the suburbs they hit rolling green countryside. For a few hours they meandered along the lazy country roads, getting a feel for the land and the district before stopping for lunch at a bustling café in the tiny township of Whitford.

While Raffaele waited at one of the outdoor tables for their coffees and lunch to arrive, Lana took the opportunity to browse in the gift shop next door. Clever groupings of colours caught her eye as she wandered between the shelves of artfully arranged gifts and the aroma of scented candles teased her nostrils.

A display of baby's clothing caught her eye, the tiny white cotton tops and booties eliciting a wistful sigh. For the first time since she and Kyle had given up hope of having a baby of their own, it didn't strike a painful blow to see the miniature items of clothing. She reached a tentative finger out to touch the fabric. So soft, so gentle. Without realising what she was doing, Lana lifted one of the cotton tops to her cheek, her eyelids fluttered closed as she indulged in the texture against her skin. For the first time in forever, it felt right to want something like this. She'd always wanted Kyle's baby, but hadn't ever imagined that it would happen like this.

Absently Lana selected a pastel coloured horse made out of a patchwork of fabrics, and a pair of socks so small only two of her fingers fit into the top. Mentally she tallied up the prices and her heart skipped as she remembered that she still had the proceeds from selling her rings in her purse. She could buy these if she wanted to. The simple pleasure in knowing she could do so sent her blood singing through her veins and she chose another toy, another T-shirt.

"Let me take those from you." Raffaele's voice rumbled behind her and she started, almost dropping her selections. Raffaele deftly scooped them from her arms before they could tumble to the shop floor. "Is there anything else you'd like?"

"I can get them myself. I have the money." Instantly her pleasure in her prospective purchases dimmed and it must have shown on her face.

"Keep your money. I know how hard won it was for you." Raffaele gave a tiny bow of his head and took her things over to the counter.

Inwardly, Lana seethed. Was this how it was going to be? Was he going to cut her out at every opportunity? She turned on her heel and stalked back to the table where she threw herself into the café chair and stared resolutely across the busy road to the shops on the other side. It was childish, she knew, but her disappointment had cut deep. A dark shadow fell across her as Raffaele returned, his purchases in a neatly packaged bundle.

They sat in stilted silence while they completed their al fresco meal. As Raffaele finished the last of his coffee and replaced his cup on its saucer he followed Lana's gaze to where she continued to stare fixedly across the road rather than make eye contact with him.

"Come," he said, rising from his seat and collecting the package. He gestured across the to estate agent's window across the street. "The agent should be ready to meet with us now. The area has a good feeling about it, don't you think?"

Lana followed Raffaele across the road and into the office that had caught his eye. The agent inside greeted them effusively and briefly outlined the properties he had to show them, offering to take them in his car.

"No. We will follow you." Raffaele insisted. "We need to be able to return to the city at a moment's notice."

The stark reminder that Raffaele might leave at any moment to attend the birth of his niece sent a chill down Lana's spine. Suddenly it was all too real. Could she really do this?

"Lana?" His voice penetrated her fear.

He stood in the doorway, holding open the door for her to precede him to the car. She swiftly gathered her thoughts and ducked past him. Even as she did so the intriguing aroma of his cologne tantalised her nostrils. She breathed in his scent, and tried desperately to ignore the tingle of awareness that crept through her body. She felt his presence beside her as if it was an imprint against her body. Even her heart seemed to beat in time with his stride as they crossed the road back to their parked car.

In the confines of the luxury sedan she tried to distract herself from the strength of his hands as he capably held the steering wheel, negotiating the car along the road and easing its speed up to the hundred kilometres an hour limit. His warmly tanned skin glowed against the crisp white cuff of his shirt. A smattering of fine dark hairs gave a raw masculine edge to the highly polished persona he presented. From the broad flat width of his wrists his hands tapered into long fingers.

She'd felt the brand of those fingers at her hips, her breast, and suddenly, desperately, she wanted to feel it again. A tremor shimmered through her body in response to her wayward thoughts.

"Cold? I will adjust the air-conditioning if you like."

"No, it's all right. Just a sensation, that's all."

"Sensation?" He shot a curious look in her direction before shifting his attention back to the road.

"Don't worry. It's nothing."

He nodded in acknowledgement then slowed the vehicle as the Realtor's car ahead of them slowed and turned left into a side road. The properties that intermittently showed along the road, some behind elaborate stone walls or thick hedges, were large and their infrequency allowed for a great deal of privacy. Lana wondered just what type of property the Realtor was leading them to and just how much Raffaele was prepared to spend. The land out this way was in high demand; the lifestyle spoke for itself in the verdant pastures, the glimpses of tennis courts and swimming pool fences and the sparkle of the ocean a short distance away.

They turned down another side road and travelled only a few minutes before slowing in front of a gated driveway. The Realtor leaned out the car window to punch in a series of numbers onto a security pad at the gate and the elaborate wrought iron fencing slowly slid away to one side. A pale terracotta coloured ribbon of driveway lay ahead, flanked with cypresses topiaried into military precision. He gestured for them to follow and they travelled in slow procession down the drive.

Stretching away to either side were groves of trees that Lana couldn't immediately identify, but as they pulled up in the large circular driveway, punctuated by an elaborate marble fountain, her pent up nerves released on an ecstatic sigh. The two-storied Tuscan styled villa sprawled with architectural elegance in front of them. If Lana hadn't known for a fact they were still in New Zealand she would have felt as though they'd been transported to the Italian countryside.

Inside the house they weren't disappointed. Formal rooms stretched with airy grace onto a huge cobbled patio at the rear where a long rectangular pool reflected the winter sun with dappled invitation and large terracotta pots planted with ornamental fruit trees stood sentinel at the base of each arch of the covered patio off the family room.

The Realtor watched them traverse the downstairs rooms with an indulgent smile.

"Mr Rossellini, when you mentioned you were interested in property where you could experiment with organically grown olive trees I couldn't believe my ears. This property has just come on the market in a deceased estate. The original owner was a powerful advocate for organic methods and the trees are mature and fruiting and there are several other growers in the area who supply fruit also." He rattled off yield figures and talked some more about the press and bottling facility that was also situated on the property. "The family are keen to sell as a going concern rather than parcel off the land."

Raffaele fired question after question at the Realtor while Lana continued her exploration of the ground floor rooms, then made her way upstairs. The master bedroom suite almost covered a third of the entire upper floor. She hurried through the bedroom, averting her eyes from the super king sized bed dominating the room and past the his-and-hers walk-in closets to the master bathroom. The bathroom was more ornate and well appointed than anything she'd ever seen outside of a lifestyle magazine. She drifted a hand across the edge of the large whirlpool tub mounted on a slight pedestal in front of glass-paned doors which opened onto a private balcony. It would be bliss to relax in here of a summer evening with the doors open to a sparkling night sky. The tub was more than large enough for two.

A sharp pang of longing tightened deep inside her and an all too vivid picture of Raffaele's tanned body, lying supine in heated rushing water, burned across her imagination. She shook her head slightly to clear it of the image. How did he do that to her? How did he invade her thoughts so she imagined him naked, imagined touching him, sliding her hands along the length of his legs and higher to his hips, his groin.

"No!" She spun away from the bath and moved swiftly through the master suite and across the upper level to the opposite wing where the other accommodations were.

She cursorily inspected the other three upstairs bedrooms, each with their own bathroom and view over the property in a different direction. Combined with the guest suite she'd seen downstairs the house boasted more than enough space for herself, Raffaele and one tiny baby.

She drifted back down the wide curved staircase and followed the sound of the men's voices as they stood outside on the patio. Raffaele turned to acknowledge her presence with one raised brow. His sharp grey eyes impaled her as he spoke and she almost felt as though he could see where her wayward thoughts had led in the master bathroom. Heat rose up her neck and bloomed in her cheeks.

"The property is suitable. I will take it."

Lana halted in her tracks. Just like that? She flicked a glance at the Realtor who looked like he'd suddenly died and gone to heaven. She could only begin to imagine the commission on a sale like this one.

"Are you certain?" She asked, a tiny waver in her voice. He had to be talking a couple of million dollars here, at the very least.

He stiffened. "There is something you don't like?"

"No—no, there's nothing. I just thought you might want to see the whole property before you made up your mind, that's all."

"I have seen enough to satisfy me. As it is a deceased estate I will take all the furnishings as well. I can replace anything not suitable."

The Realtor scurried out to his car to get the paperwork ready to be signed. It was obvious the guy could barely believe his luck. They completed the necessities in a modicum of time, the trustees for the estate having happily accepted Raffaele's offer over the telephone. It was agreed, until settlement could occur, Raffaele would lease the property and they could move in within the next week.

Lana looked around her. This would be her home for however long Raffaele's parenting order took to take precedence over her guardianship. As far as she could see in either direction the land would be Raffaele's. The olive grove was substantial and, if the figures the Realtor had been quoting were genuine, the property was self-sustaining with a growing market already well-established.

"It is beautiful, *si*?"

"Very beautiful. I can't believe you negotiated that so quickly."

"Negotiated? No. I do not negotiate. I made an offer that was more than fair. The family of the past owner wins, and I win too."

He swivelled around taking in the panoramic vista. If it were not for the different light in this part of the world he could almost fool himself that he was again back in the land of his birth. What he wouldn't give to be able to bring his mother and sister here. To make a fresh start for all of them.

Grief gripped his heart in a cold tight fist. Dreams such as those were self-destructive. One should never wish for what could never be; he reminded himself with the staunch practicality that had seen him rebuild his family's fortune after his father's poor decisions. It would have to be enough that he could provide this home for his niece. Already he could see her playing here amongst the trees as she grew up.

Between this property and his vast estate in Italy, Maria's daughter would want for nothing. She'd have freedom, security and everything his money could buy.

A movement on the periphery of his sight reminded him he was not alone. Lana. What did she think, he wondered. With the very obvious display of the power of his money in making this transaction happen so quickly did she think herself in line for some of it too? He fervently hoped so. The pittance he'd agreed to pay her to stay and act as guardian to the baby would not even scratch the surface of his wealth. She had no idea of what she was dealing with.

"Come, we will return in a few days. We must head back now to the city."

"Will you get an inventory of the furnishings and chattels?"

"Why do you ask?"

"We will need to order new sheets, towels—all sorts of things."

Raffaele fought to quell the surge of anger that rose within him—already she was spending his money, although, as much as it galled him to admit it, he had to concede that she was correct. The items she'd mentioned were necessary.

"You can get the lists she needs?" Raffaele asked the Realtor.

"Yes, certainly. I'll fax them through to you at your hotel in the morning."

"Thank you. That would be acceptable. If that is all, we should go now."

The soles of his shoes clicked on the tiled patio as he walked towards her and took her arm to lead her back through the house. They waited in the portico at the front entrance as the Realtor reset the alarm system and locked the front door. The man reached out a hand to Raffaele.

"Thank you, Mr Rossellini, it's been a pleasure doing business with you." He turned to Lana to also shake her hand. "Mrs Rossellini."

Raffaele's back went ramrod straight. "She is not my

wife," he corrected the Realtor in a voice that growled ominously in the semi-enclosed area.

"I do apologise."

Raffaele nodded his curt acceptance of the man's apology and opened the car door for Lana, ushering her inside. No, a woman like Lana Whittaker could never be his wife. He liked his women filled with warmth and passion. Not cold and calculating and driven by money. While Lana's response to him the other night showed she had passion buried deep within her, and physically she called to him on a base level, he could not forgive her for clinging to a marriage long dead and the resulting carnage that had caused.

Without another word he walked around to the driver's side of the car and slid in behind the steering wheel. As he reached to fasten his seat belt his cell phone vibrated in his pocket. His stomach dropped. The only people who knew to contact him on this number were the hospital staff and his younger brother in Italy. It would be the small hours of the morning for Vincenzo—it could not be him. Raffaele quickly flipped the phone open and recognised the number immediately—the hospital. He answered with growing dread.

As he closed the phone moments later and slid it into his pocket he leaned back in the car seat and rested his head against the head rest with a deep sigh. The news was better than he'd hoped for. Maria had stabilised sufficiently to be airlifted to Auckland hospital first thing tomorrow morning.

"Raffaele? Is… is everything okay?"

"Maria is being transferred to Auckland, tomorrow."

"Transferred? But why? Surely—"

"What? Surely she should remain in Wellington, where you can continue to ignore your responsibility? I don't think so."

"That wasn't what I meant at all." Lana's blue-green eyes sparked in indignation. "Is it safe to move her?"

"Do you think I would do anything to hasten my sister's death?"

"No, of course not. I'm sorry. I didn't think." Lana's hands fluttered helplessly in her lap before she knit her fingers together in a knot.

Raffaele took in another deep breath and rubbed wearily at his eyes. "I'm sorry, Lana. It has been a difficult few days. For all of us."

She shot him a look almost as if she didn't believe the sudden warmth in his voice. He felt her begin to relax when she realised he'd meant what he said. It *had* been a difficult few days—for everyone. And it didn't look as though it would become any simpler any time soon, he conceded. They would continue to live on a knife's edge until the child was born. Until Maria was dead. He clenched his jaw tight before continuing.

"It is better for the baby to be born here in Auckland. The services in Wellington are stretched to their limit. The doctors have recommended Maria be transferred to ensure the baby's safety."

"Do you…?" her voice trailed off uncertainly.

"Do I what?"

"Do you want me to come with you—to the hospital?"

Her offer surprised him. He examined her face carefully, trying to understand where her question had come from, but her features remained empty of emotion. Did she feel nothing about the impending arrival of his sister—the woman who'd supplanted her in her husband's affections—that she could ask such a question in such an unaffected way? If she did, she hid it well.

"No. That will not be necessary. While the doctors are certain that Maria's brain injury has left her in a condition where she cannot sense or understand what is happening around her, I do not wish to take the risk that she is aware of your presence."

Lana broke off eye contact with him and stared out the windscreen to the driveway ahead of them. "I understand," she murmured quietly.

Raffaele muttered a curse under his breath and started up the car to begin their journey back to the city. So, she thought she understood, did she? He gripped the steering wheel between tightened fingers. Her detachment was absolute proof that she had no idea of the damage she had wrought, nor of her acceptance of her guilt. A more rational man might feel sorry for her, that she could be so coldly unemotional. He did not feel very rational right now.

Eight

Rational or not he knew there were practicalities to be taken care of. The fact that Lana only had two outfits, and both of them more businesslike than casual, needed to be addressed.

"Where do you usually shop for clothing?"

In his peripheral vision he saw her head snap around and he felt her eyes boring into him.

"Why do you ask?"

"You cannot continue to only wear two outfits for the rest of the time we are together. We can gather some things for you now."

"Must we do that today?"

"I do not expect to have time to meet your needs once Maria is here in Auckland."

He felt her bristle at his comment but she held her tongue.

"So where do we need to stop?"

"Take the next turnoff and I'll direct you from there." Her

voice was stiff, as if she were fighting back words that were better left unsaid. He smiled inwardly, she was learning.

When they arrived back at the hotel Lana was happy to discover the inventory lists for the house had already been faxed through. Her experienced eye scanned them in detail, noting the sizes of the beds in the various rooms, and the tables in the dining areas, and she started to make lists for what new linen they'd need. She was oblivious to Raffaele as he looked over her shoulder as she methodically listed each area of the house and made notes, from memory, about the colours and style of each room. When she finally took a break to flex her cramped fingers she was surprised to see it had grown dark outside. Raffaele sat opposite her, dressed more casually than before in dark jeans and a charcoal grey long sleeved polo shirt, that reflected the colour of his eyes. Eyes which were riveted on her.

"I'm sorry, did you say something?" Lana gathered her sheaf of notes together and lined them up between her hands.

"No. I did not. I have merely been watching you. Are you finished?"

"For now. I think I have a good idea of what we need to buy and what we can keep from the existing inventory. If you'll agree, I'd like to start with replacing all the bed and bathroom linen. We can forward the previous owner's to the local shelters. They'll be glad of the donation, I'm sure."

A puzzled look crossed Raffaele's face.

"What's wrong?" Lana asked.

"Nothing is wrong. I merely expected you to dispense with the unwanted items, not to distribute them."

"But that would be a terrible waste."

"I agree." He surveyed her with a new expression on his face, one that made her feel like an insect under a microscope.

"What is it? Why are you looking at me like that?"

"You were upset that I didn't let you pay for the baby's things. Why?" He leaned forward and rested his forearms on his knees, bringing his face closer to hers, enveloping her personal space with the power of his presence.

"I just wanted to buy them myself, that's all." Lana leaned back into her chair. She wasn't going into her personal details now. Not with Raffaele. How would he ever understand?

"I think there is more to what you say. Tell me," he probed with a steady quiet voice.

"All right then, if you insist on knowing. When I take on a project I do it a hundred percent. I wanted to be able to give the baby something from me." Not something with money she'd been paid for agreeing to accept guardianship, money that was tainted by a brokered arrangement. She'd lost everything in the past week, her whole life as she knew it. Buying those simple items for Raffaele's niece was about as close as she was going to get to motherhood, and he'd taken that from her.

"She is a project to you?"

Lana thought about his question carefully before answering. He watched her intently, his eyes slightly narrowed. If Lana was going to be capable of walking away from this whole situation unscathed she had to depersonalise the baby as much as possible.

"For want of a better word, yes."

Raffaele sighed and leaned back in his chair again. "Thank you for being honest. If you'd told me you were doing it out of some misguided desire to have a child, when you quite clearly never wanted any, I would have known you for a liar."

Lana flinched as if he'd slapped her. Never wanted a baby? How on earth had he reached that conclusion? But no matter what, she wasn't about to disabuse him of his belief now. She didn't want to highlight her failures any more than the ten-foot high neons that publicised her failures in every newspaper that had hit the stands since Kyle's death.

She'd given her word she'd see this thing through. Today had been a perfect example of just how much it would cost her on an emotional level to do so. She needed to keep her distance—from the baby, and from Raffaele— as much as possible.

She pushed to her feet, that distance could start right now. As she stood one of her sheets slipped and fluttered to the floor. Raffaele reached down to pick it up, his brow furrowed as his eyes scanned the sheet.

"What is this?" he enquired, his voice a deep rumble.

Lana took the paper from him. "Exactly what it says. A list of nursery items we need to get."

"The list is extensive. How do you know we will need all of these things? This for example?" He poked a long neatly manicured finger at an item on the list.

"The apnoea monitor? It's a safeguard. Any baby can stop breathing during sleep, but premature babies are more prone to do so."

"Stop breathing?" His strong face blanched at the words.

"This monitor will sound an alarm and also has a tummy tickler, to stimulate the baby to breathe again." Lana had done her research thoroughly during their last round of IVF treatment. If she'd been so lucky as to have a baby she swore she'd do everything in her power to keep the child safe.

"How do you know about these things? You have no child of your own. Kyle said you never wanted any, so why would you have such knowledge?" Raffaele insisted, colour slowly returning to his face.

"Kyle said that?" Lana took a step back. It shouldn't still have the capacity to hurt her that he'd lied about this part of their lives too. How dare he have diminished what they went through? The pain of what they'd endured in the vain endeavours to have a child of their own, and the pain of knowing she could never bear a child, all came flooding back with heart-breaking intensity.

She chose her next words with careful deliberation. "Has it ever occurred to you that perhaps he lied?"

With as much dignity as she could muster, Lana turned and started to walk across the room. Her eyes glazed with tears, her heart aching anew with loss.

Raffaele watched her go, an uncomfortable niggle digging at his brain. No-one could have faked the soul-deep expression of sorrow that had crossed her face when he'd delivered his last words. A kernel of doubt opened. If Kyle had lied about something as important as having a family, what other truths had he been capable of twisting? While everything Lana had said and done since Raffaele had met her pointed to confirm her as the villain of the piece, it suddenly occurred to him that it was entirely possible he'd been thoroughly to reach such a conclusion. The thought brought anger rising to the surface. Had he been played for a fool?

As Lana quietly and firmly closed the bedroom door behind her Raffaele resolved to bide his time and see what he could discover about the marriage of Kyle and Lana Whittaker.

Over the next few days Lana busied herself with the necessary shopping for the move out to the house. Raffaele had authorised her to use one of his credit cards for the purchases and had also opened an account in her name, into which the allowance he'd agreed to pay her would be deposited each week. As much as it galled her to accept the money she consoled herself with the fact that she was doing a job, just like any other job. But that didn't explain the rawness that stung in the area of her heart every time Raffaele left the hotel to visit with his sister.

He spent hour after hour at the hospital, returning late each evening, uncommunicative and with his face grey and drawn. Several times while Lana had been out she'd had the uncomfortable feeling that she was being watched, but when she'd looked around nothing had prompted her as out of place or unfamiliar. Because Raffaele's visits to Maria were quite obviously taking their toll on him, she was reluctant to bring up her fears with him, convincing herself instead that she had become paranoid since Kyle's death.

They were almost ready for the move out to Whitford, a change in lifestyle that Lana found herself anticipating with an enthusiasm that caught her unawares. For the first time in what felt like a long while, she was looking forward, not back.

After finalising the delivery of supplies to the new property, Lana arrived back at the hotel suite late and was surprised to hear the sound of a loud, agitated male voice from inside. She pushed open the front door and dropped her purchases inside the vestibule, rushing inside to see what was wrong. Raffaele paced the length of the sitting room, a telephone clutched to his ear with one hand while the other gesticulated wildly in the air.

"What's wrong?" Lana mouthed as he turned and gave her a brief sharp nod of acknowledgement.

He gestured toward the tabloid paper sprawled on the coffee table. Lana straightened the sheets of newsprint as she looked to see what had upset him so much. Her blood turned to ice when she saw the front page headline emblazoned across the top.

Fraudster's love child!

Beneath the heading was a half-page colour photo of an unconscious pregnant woman in a hospital bed. While the picture was grainy, Lana immediately spotted the familial likeness to the angry male who stood silently, drumming the fingers of one hand against his hip, as he listened to the person on the other end of the telephone.

This was Maria Rossellini? Lana stared hard at the photo, waiting for the anger and hatred she'd expected to feel to come foaming to the surface of her emotions. This was the woman who had stolen her husband—the woman who now sustained the life of his baby daughter within her dying body. But instead of anger, all she could feel was an overwhelming and decimating sense of loss.

The unmistakeable proof of Kyle's infidelity distorted the smooth fall of the bed covering. Lana's fingers gripped the paper so tight it began to tear. Beneath the covers and within the woman lying unknowing on the hospital bed lived Kyle's child. The child Lana could never give him. She sank to her knees, her whole body shaking with reaction to the physical evidence of the death of her marriage—of her failure. After several shuddering breaths she dragged her eyes from the photo to scan the article.

Whoever had written it had done their homework only too well. It was all there—every detail about her marriage to Kyle together with statements from people who'd been their neighbours and their friends. People she'd *thought* were her friends. The sense of betrayal cut even deeper. And worse, they'd closed the article with a promise to next week's readers for more dirt on Lana's privileged upbringing and the shadow of her own family's hidden secrets including details of a mystery man she was reportedly living with since her husband's death.

Raffaele's angry voice penetrated the fog of shock that held her wrapped in disbelief.

"This is unacceptable. I want the person responsible for allowing that photo to be taken of my sister to be found. If your hospital cannot protect her sufficiently, I will provide my own security for her."

He fell silent as the person on the other end of the phone spoke.

"See that you do!" Raffaele enunciated with deadly precision. "Or I will hold *you* personally responsible."

He snapped his cell phone shut with an angry flick of his hand and thrust it back in the breast pocket of his jacket.

"*Maledizione!*" he uttered as he spun around to face Lana. A frown creased his brow as he saw her kneeling on the floor, her fingers white with the tight grip she had on the paper. No-one was that good an actress. What kind of fool was he to think that she wouldn't have such a shocked reaction to the news? He'd been thinking solely of Maria and her safety; he hadn't spared a thought for how Lana would feel. It was only a week since she'd heard news of the baby and now here she was, faced with the proof. As much as he'd schooled himself to distrust Lana Whittaker, his own sense of honour should have asserted itself and softened the blow from which she was obviously reeling.

"Lana?" he coaxed, reaching for the tabloid that had so raised his ire and left him insensible to anything but the most immediate of action. Prising the paper from her fingers was easier said that done. In the end he ripped it gently from her grasp then, supporting her by her elbows, coaxed her to her feet before settling her more comfortably on the sofa.

She felt cold to his touch, her face void of expression. He cursed under his breath and turned to the sideboard, splashing a measure of brandy from the crystal decanter into a tumbler and bringing it over to her. He pushed the glass into her hands and coaxed her to raise the glass to her lips and take a sip, then another.

Twin flashes of colour appeared on her alabaster pale cheeks, a sheen of moisture in her blue topaz coloured eyes. She dragged in a deep breath, and put the glass back on the table.

"Are you certain you don't wish to have more?"

"It won't cure what hurts inside, Raffaele. But thank you anyway."

The emptiness of her voice cut to his core. Over the past three days, on those occasions when they'd crossed paths, he'd seen a different side of her. She'd been animated and excited about her purchases and, at the end of each day when he'd returned from the hospital, had discussed with him all manner of items she'd bought. He'd found himself beginning to look forward to her presence here in the suite on his return—almost a homecoming in some bizarre way. But now, she was reduced to the same frozen, cold-natured female he'd met after Kyle's funeral. Withdrawn. Untouchable.

Suddenly he missed the warmth of her excitement. The pleasure in her voice. It was a sensation he did not feel comfortable with.

"I'm sorry, Lana. I should have kept the paper from you. It was insensitive of me to expose you to that."

"No, not insensitive. You don't need to wrap me in kid gloves. I can take it, honestly. It just came as a bit of a surprise—that's all."

She went through the motions, he noted, said all the right words, but he could tell there was far more going on inside her head than she was letting on. He felt her withdrawal from him as if it was physical. The damn picture reminded them both of their purpose, and of the end result.

She was right, he realised with damning accuracy. Nothing would heal what hurt inside. Nothing.

"I will deal with the paper, force an injunction on them—something, anything. They will print no more lies or conjecture about our families," he ground the words out like a vow. Lana fell under his protection now. He needed her and, whether she liked it or not, she needed him.

"Don't bother, they'll just find another way to spread the poison, to eat into my past and blow it all over the papers again." Lana placed a small slender hand on his coat sleeve. "It's nothing anyone hasn't tried to do to me before and I survived the last time. I'll survive now. Now, if you'll excuse me, I need to make sure everything is ready for tomorrow. Personally, I can't wait to get out of the city."

For once Raffaele heartily concurred. While he'd be further from the hospital and the commute to the city would take precious hours from his time with Maria, once the baby arrived and was strong enough to come home, she would be secure in the new home he'd purchased. After today, that security seemed more vital than ever before.

His gaze dropped from her earnest face to the fine tapered fingers that branded his arm. Her touch set off a jolt of electricity through his veins. Before he could think, or act, on it she withdrew her hand and rose to her feet.

"I think I'll take a bath and then turn in for the night. We have an early start tomorrow if we're going to beat the delivery truck out to the house."

"You wouldn't prefer to have a meal before you retire?" Food was the last thing on Raffaele's mind, but for some reason he was reluctant to let her go and lose her company. Before he could examine his reasons for coercing her to stay with him any longer, she shook her head and turned for her room.

Lana went through the motions of preparing for bed but her mind continued to race. By the time she'd soaked for half an hour in a foam-filled bath she was no more relaxed than she'd been when she'd first seen the newspaper. It was going to take far more than a long soak in a bath to rebuild her self-esteem.

She stroked a washcloth over her body, removing the last of the grime of the day. If only it could be as simple to wash away the pain of rejection and failure. Her hand stilled over her flat lower belly and the picture of Maria Rossellini's belly, swollen with the life of the unborn child Lana would have given anything to have borne, imprinted itself on her mind. Would any man ever want her knowing she couldn't bear his children? Kyle had told her it didn't matter, but quite obviously the evidence proved his conciliatory words to be the pathetic lie they were.

With a frustrated sigh of resignation she rose from the bath and reached for one of the hotel's thick fluffy towels. The texture of the warmed towelling on her skin sent a wave of heat through her body, and awoke a deep-seated want in her she hated to acknowledge. She needed to feel like a woman again—needed the affirmation she was still attractive, that life wasn't measured in how fertile or otherwise a woman was, but instead in the other things she could bring to a relationship. The things that apparently hadn't been enough for Kyle. Hot tears stained her cheeks as, later, she lay unmoving on the bed, waiting for sleep to claim her and give her surcease from the painful truth.

Nine

The night sounds from the city outside did little to soothe Lana's tumbling thoughts. Eventually she gave up her attempt at sleep, and decided to see if she could find something to read in the main lounge. She dragged on the matching sea foam coloured peignoir to her sheer nightgown more out of habit than out of any practical need to cover herself. Raffaele would be long since in bed. The toll his time with his sister was taking on him was visible in every line on his face and the emptiness in his eyes when he returned each evening. Tonight's fiasco with the paper had struck an even deeper cast of weariness about his features.

Lana tied the belt of her wrap tight at her waist and opened her bedroom door. A light still burned in the sitting room and she stilled in the doorway to her room when she recognised that the object of her thoughts was still very much awake. Dressed only in navy pyjama bottoms

Raffaele looked up at her, a frown creasing his brow. Lana's eyes were riveted on the expanse of muscular tanned shoulders and his broad chest, which was dusted with a light coating of dark hair that fined and trailed to the centre of his flat abdomen, and below.

"Is there a problem?" His voice sounded thick.

Lana stilled in shock. Surely he hadn't been crying? Not the indomitable Raffaele Rossellini. Throughout this whole ordeal he'd shown cool calculating control or individually targeted anger—never sorrow, never weakness.

"I—I didn't mean to disturb you. I'm sorry."

"You do not disturb me. I cannot sleep." He lifted a hand to wipe his eyes and turned his head from her, away from the light.

He *had* been crying. Lana didn't know what to do. Her instincts wanted to drive her into the room, to stroke her hands over his cheeks and remove the silver tracing of moisture she'd glimpsed there. But she remained where she was. Raffaele would never accept comfort from her. Clearly he wanted to be alone.

"I should go back to bed." She turned to go back to her room.

"No. Please. Sit with me a while. It is obvious you cannot sleep either."

On legs that suddenly felt as weak as water, Lana crossed the room and sat where he indicated. Next to him on the wide sofa.

"What troubles you now, Lana? Why do you not sleep?"

"I don't know," she answered, knowing it was a lie. The discomfort that had slowly ignited in her earlier tonight had reached the stage where it could no longer be ignored. Her self-esteem had taken one battering straight after another over the past week and a half. She needed—her heart began to race—she needed to reaffirm herself as a woman. As a desirable woman.

She started as Raffaele's hand lifted and he trailed a long warm finger down her cheek to her jaw line.

"I think you know what troubles you." His voice dropped an octave. "I also think you do not wish to talk."

She nodded in silence, her eyes linked with his. His long thick lashes, still slightly damp, framed dark grey eyes—eyes that held her enthralled with the sudden flare of desire that grew within them. A shiver of anticipation ran the length of her spine, making her body straighten, her breasts thrust out ever so slightly.

His finger traced the edge of her jaw before following the corded line of her throat and lower until it reached the edge of her wrap.

"I do not want to talk either." Raffaele leaned closer until she could feel his breath against her skin.

The air in her lungs dried. Every nerve in her body focussed on the trail of heat his finger left in its wake as he slowly eased aside the edge of the flimsy fabric and exposed the spaghetti strap of her nightgown. A tight curl of need spiralled low and deep in her belly. A tiny sigh escaped her lips only to be caught against the heat of his mouth, his tongue. She felt the tremor that spread through him as his hand slid across her skin and under the bodice of her gown to cup her breast. Her nipple beaded tight, the sensation bordering on the pleasure-pain of intense desire.

She felt the sash at her waist loosen and fall away, the peignoir followed, dropping off her shoulders and down, imprisoning her arms at her sides in its silken folds. Raffaele brushed his thumb over her taut aureole, circling the rigid point and sending darts of pleasure deep inside to her core, then lifted both his hands to her shoulders. Slowly he eased the thin ribbons of fabric over the soft curve of her shoulder. The bodice of her nightgown fell away with the merest brush of his hand.

Raffaele tore his lips from hers and murmured in Italian, something soft and low that Lana couldn't understand. His eyes darkened as he looked at her—a long slow appraisal of her face, her throat, her breasts. For a moment she felt self-conscious, and started to move—to gather up the fabric to hide herself again. Kyle had been her first and only lover. This was frightening new territory for her. But the look, the appreciation, in Raffaele's eyes made her hesitate.

"*Ti desidero*. I want you, Lana. Be very certain of your reply because I will only ask this once. Will you make love with me tonight? Just tonight. I need you."

The plea in his voice was her undoing and her strength at the same time. This strong influential man wanted her. *Her*. In itself it was a powerful aphrodisiac, but the sensations he aroused in her were her affirmation. In answer she leaned forward, feathering light kisses across his forehead, his cheekbone, until she reached the corner of his mouth. The taste of him was on her lips and she wanted more. Much more.

She pressed her lips to his, and whispered, "Yes."

It was all he needed to hear. Raffaele stood in one fluid motion and scooped Lana's delectable willing body into his arms. He was not prepared to sate the clawing overwhelming need to be with another person, to do what he wanted with her, on a couch in the sitting room. No, he wanted the comfort and expanse of his bed, the privacy of his room.

The gentle golden light of the lamp in the sitting room

cast long deep shadows in his bedroom as he laid Lana against the covers of his bed. She pulled her arms free of the sleeves of her wrap and raised them to him. For an instant he questioned the wisdom of his decision but the instant was fleeting, overwhelmed instead by the inferno of want that now drove him to seek comfort and diversion in her body.

Her gentle hands caressed the width of his forearms and slid upwards as she rose to her knees letting her clothing fall to her waist and beyond. Her long blonde hair flowed over her shoulders, the tips caressing her breasts, enticing him to do the same. He bent his head and buried his face between her breasts, cupping them with his hands as he inhaled the intoxicating fragrance of her skin. His tongue darted out to trace the line of one breast, to caress the underside. Her gasp of pleasure was his reward as he continued his journey, laving her skin with strokes of his tongue until he worked his way to the tight nub of her nipple. Her fingers tangled in his hair as he suckled at the tiny button of flesh, coaxing a moan of delight from deep within her throat. Then he afforded the same attention to its partner, taking every care to bestow the same concentration as he had before.

His hands skimmed down the length of her body, to her slender waist, to the curve of her hips. She was so soft, so warm, so giving as her hands followed an identical path. He knelt on the bed with her, curving his arm around her waist and drawing her against his bare torso, against the straining flesh confined in his pyjama bottoms. The sensation of skin against skin was almost his undoing as they cleaved together. With his free hand he swept away the silken swathe of hair at her neck then bent to nip gently at the graceful curve of her throat and at the tender skin behind her ear.

He felt her hands at the drawstring of his pants, felt the fabric give. It was too soon. She'd drive him over the edge with her touch he knew, and then—*ah, si*—it was too late to stop her as she gloved him with a firm stroke of her hand. A groan tore from his throat, her name on his lips. Her fingertips caressed the tip of him, spreading the moisture she found there before she stroked him again in a long caress that made everything inside him tighten and bunch with longing, craving release.

"Protection," he growled even as he strained against her hand, his hips already fighting to assume the rhythm that would bring swift release.

"I'm safe, Raffaele. I won't get pregnant."

"You are certain? Because I cannot wait. I want you now."

"Then take me now." A secret smile curved her lips, in the semi-lit room she was beautiful. It was all he could do not to throw her against the covers and take her in one deep thrust.

Instead, he watched as she swung one leg off the bed, then the other and stood slowly before him. The last scraps of her nightwear cascading off her hips and exposing the golden triangle of curls at the apex of her thighs, her long slender legs. Legs he wanted wrapped around him this instant.

He reached for her, taking her lips in a punishing kiss, parting them with a sweep of his tongue and probing deep inside the moist heat of her mouth with a promise his body cried out to deliver. He guided her back to the bed without breaking his kiss and spread her beneath him. A push of one hand dispensed with his pyjama bottoms, exposing his hungry flesh. Then, at last, he was nestled at her entrance.

He could feel the welcoming heat that emanated from her body and could hold himself back no longer.

Her eyes glistened in the near dark. He watched intently as her pupils all but consumed her irises as he guided the head of his penis inside her. Every muscle in his body locked rigidly in place as he forced himself to stop, to savour the sensation of her slick heat as it pulled gently against him. Enticing him further. He withdrew slightly then surged forward again and felt her inner muscles bunch and tighten along his length. He could control himself no longer, nor would he want to even if he was still capable of such control. A sheen of moisture broke out on his skin as he hesitated one precious second longer before giving in to the instinctive need that drove him to sink himself to the hilt, to lift her legs to his hips. She wrapped herself around him, tight. Barely allowing him any room to withdraw and sink himself within her again, but it didn't matter, nothing mattered as the rhythmic pull of her drew him ever deeper.

Time disappeared, the world around them receded to a shadowed purgatory that could no longer touch him, could no longer hurt. He gave himself over to the moment, to the heat, to the passion. His climax built with overwhelming speed, taking him to a place where pain and suffering no longer existed, where only pleasure reigned. Lana's legs tightened around him, he felt her thighs quiver, heard her cry of release and he hurtled over the edge and into the realms of pure unadulterated satiation.

Lana lay, wrapped in the band of Raffaele's arms, and listened carefully as his ragged breathing slowed to a steady pace once again. Her heart still hammered in her chest, her nerves still tingled with the aftermath of their lovemaking. She hadn't believed her body was capable of such dizzying heights of pleasure. Lovemaking with Kyle had always been good, better than good. But this? This was off the scale.

Her mind quickly sobered. What had she done? She'd been widowed only eleven days and she was already finding comfort in another man's arms. And not just any man—Raffaele Rossellini, the person responsible for Kyle and Maria getting together all along. Raffaele's arms tightened around her waist, one hand starting a lazy circle across her belly.

"This is no time for second thoughts, Lana," he whispered against her neck before pressing his lips at her nape then licking gently at her skin.

"I'm not," she protested, as a new enticing spiral of desire wound within her.

"Do not lie. Not to me, not to yourself. It is only natural you should feel…uneasy." His hand slid up to caress her breast, his palm lightly skimming across the surface.

"It's so soon. I shouldn't have—" Her voice broke and his ministrations ceased, and she felt the mattress shift as he raised above her. His fingers gripped her chin, forcing her to look at him, eye to eye.

"Lana, Kyle left you a long time ago. If not physically, then at least mentally. Take tonight. You deserve it. We both do. You enjoyed what we have shared together, yes?"

"Yes," she sighed. She couldn't deny it.

"We have the rest of tonight. Let's not waste it."

She could feel his growing arousal against her hip and her insides clenched in feminine anticipation. He wanted her again so soon? This was the salve she needed, this was the dressing to her wounded heart, her self-esteem.

"No, let's not."

She pulled his head down to her and kissed him with all the invitation she was capable of and felt the shudder run through his body, felt his arousal firm and harden, felt the hammering of his heart beat as she stroked her fingertips across his chest. He was addictive. Already she craved more of him, his touch, his taste. The pleasure she knew he could bring her. The escape from the reality of her world.

She traced the outline of his lips with her tongue, then delved inside the dark velvet of his mouth, relishing the taste and texture of him. He returned the pleasure, stroking his hands over her body, leaving incendiary traces in his wake. She moaned as he stroked the indentation at the top of her thighs with a feather light touch. His gentleness drove her crazy. She tilted her pelvis, pushing her hips against his hands, silently begging for more. She felt his smile against her lips, felt the pressure of his fingers increase as they stroked ever closer to the bundle of nerve endings that craved his touch.

She bucked as he grazed across the hooded nub, once, twice, a third time, before circling the tiny bead of flesh with increasing pressure. Her orgasm burst out of nowhere. One second she was relishing the sensation of his lips against hers, his touch at her most private parts, the next she was catapulted into paroxysms of pleasure that left her gasping and trembling in their wake.

Before she could gather her scattered thoughts he was inside her again, filling and stretching her, rocking her with an ever increasing beat that satisfied every primitive instinct known to man. She felt his body stiffen, his back arch. Felt the hot spurt of his seed as he came apart inside her body.

He collapsed against her, his body slick with perspiration.

"I am glad you are on the Pill, for I think it will take all night for me to finish with you," he whispered in the shell of her ear.

Lana stiffened. On the Pill? Where did he get that idea? She forced her mind back to when she'd told him that she was safe. Clearly he'd misunderstood. She stroked her hand down the length of his spine, then back up again.

"I'm not on the Pill, Raffaele, but I am safe."

He pulled away from her slightly, his eyes dark and full of questions. "You are on some other form of contraception?"

"No. I'm not."

He started to withdraw, a look of shock on his face. She gripped him and held him to her.

"Don't. Don't worry. It isn't a problem. Truly. I told you I'm safe."

"How can you be safe when you take no contraception?" The shock in his voice illustrated his growing fear and alienation from her.

Lana hesitated, she needed to tell him the truth but she could barely enunciate the words. She wanted to be feminine in his arms, not a failure. If she told him, would he think any less of her, as Kyle so obviously had? Even if this was only for tonight, she deserved the whole night, surely.

"Why do you not answer? Have you lied to me?" His voice grew hard. "I will not be tricked."

"There is no trick. I can't have a baby. I'm infertile. It's why Kyle—"

Raffaele placed a finger across her lips. "Shh, do not bring him into the bed with us again tonight. Say no more of this. I'm sorry I grew so angry. I did not understand. Now I do. Tonight we forget everything, everyone. Tonight we are alone."

Lana nodded, her eyes bright with tears. She could hold on to tonight. There was no need for why; no need to make it harder than it had to be. After a lifetime of planning and shattered dreams she knew better than anyone else now how important it was to take the moment. So she did.

Ten

Lana woke the next morning in a tangle of sheets and masculine limbs. Gently she eased herself from Raffaele's sleeping clasp and stood at the edge of the bed looking down at him. What now, she wondered. Would they go back to how they'd been before? Polite strangers?

A strong dark arm snaked out and grabbed her by the hand, pulling her off balance and back onto the rumpled bed and into his arms, against the heat of his chest.

"*Buon giorno.*" He didn't smile, but the flame in his eyes left her in no doubt that 'polite strangers' was the furthest thing from his mind right now. "I want you again, Lana, but first, we shower."

He rose from the bed and scooped her in his arms. She felt deliciously fragile in his grasp. She reached up to kiss him and they didn't so much as break apart as he strode into the bathroom and set her feet on the floor. His erection pressed against her belly as he reached beyond her to switch on the dual shower jets in the stall.

Lana took the lead, and stepped inside the shower, relishing the cascade of warm water down her back. She reached for the soap and lathered her hands.

"Let me wash you," she said, almost shyly as Raffaele stepped inside with her. It was different being with him like this in the cold light of morning. Under the cloak of last night's darkness, they had been anonymous to each other. Now, she felt as if she was bare to the world.

"Do with me what you will," he rumbled in reply.

Lana took him at his word, and turned him around to lather soap across the back of his shoulders and down his back to his buttocks and further down his legs. Then, slowly, she worked her way back up his legs, until she reached his inner thighs. Gently she reached between and massaged his balls. They were tight and firm and she smiled as she withdrew only to hear Raffaele's groan at her abandonment of her attention to that part of his anatomy.

"Turn around again," she commanded softly.

He did as he was bade and Lana's mouth dried as he faced her and stared at her with a hunger in his eyes that built her confidence to a higher threshold than she'd believed she could possess. She reached for the soap, without breaking eye contact, and slowly lathered her hands up again, letting her fingers entangle with one another in enticing promise. His breathing quickened as she reached forward and began anew at his shoulders, tracing tiny whorls in the soap as she caressed his chest, and grazed her nails across his dark flat nipples. This time her path down his body was punctuated with tiny suckling kisses as the water sluiced away the suds.

She worked her way lower, and lower still, until she knelt before him and carefully washed his straining erection, stroking the velvet length of him, allowing the water to rinse away the remainder of the foam. She held him firmly at his base, then gently closed her lips around his swollen head, swirling her tongue around and around before taking him deeper into her mouth. Again and again, she repeated the motion, reaching with her other hand to cup his balls and gently squeeze them as she suckled his tip.

"Stop!" His voice was rough as gravel.

"Am I hurting you?" Lana looked up at him.

"No. I just can't take anymore. I want to be inside you. Let me be inside you."

His plea spoke to her on a level she'd never known before. She let him help her to her feet.

"But first," he continued, "let me wash you. Let me torment you as you torment me."

He wasted no time spreading soap over her body, circling her breasts until she was nearly screaming at him to touch her nipples, to pull at them, kiss them, anything to release the tension that wound ever tighter within her. He directed the shower spray to rinse away the bubbles and closed his mouth over one distended nipple, his teeth pulling gently at the tender flesh while his tongue flicked against its surface. With one hand his fingers reached to roll its twin, squeezing firmly but gently so that her knees threatened to buckle as sensation poured through her. With his other hand he gently washed between her legs until she lost perception of where the powerful electric arcs radiating through her body came from.

He straightened, and kissed her, their heads under the cascading jets of the shower, the freshness of the water mingling with their own flavour. He cupped her buttocks with strong hands, kneading her flesh before lifting her to him.

Instinctively Lana wrapped her legs around his waist, her arms about his shoulders as he lowered her onto his erection, sliding within her with deliberate control. He leaned her against the shower wall, directing the shower spray between them at the apex where they joined, and thrust deeper, his hips pumping faster and faster until she screamed in release. With one final thrust he reached his climax and through her own haze of pleasure, Lana watched as he gave himself over to fulfilment.

Raffaele rested his forehead against her, his body still trembling from the force of his climax. He pulled himself from within her and supported her as she released her legs from around his waist and slid them to the base of the shower. Making love with Lana had brought him to greater heights of pleasure than he thought his body could sustain and still remain conscious. In a desperate attempt to soothe his mind of the worry and responsibility that beset him he'd made a plea to her. He'd asked for the night, she'd given him so much more than that with her generous body.

Now, the night was well and truly over. They had to face the day. He reached out to switch off the shower and then grabbed a heated towel from the rail to dry her thoroughly. She seemed incapable of speech. He felt much the same. As he painstakingly stroked every inch of her body dry he saw the flush of heat that infused a rosy glow on her skin, saw her nipples tighten, felt the heat and moisture that gathered again at her centre. His own body began to tighten in anticipation, but Raffaele drew a tight rein on his instincts. All he'd wanted was the night. A few hours of mindless surcease. He'd had that and now he needed to move on.

In his bedroom, the phone started to ring.

"I'll get that, you go and get ready for the move out to the house." He wrapped the towel around Lana's body tight, more to prevent himself from reaching out to touch her one more time than to provide her with privacy. After what they'd shared there was no room for embarrassment between them. Even though he knew he could not repeat their actions again. Last night had been an aberration for him. It would not happen again.

"Okay, I'll order breakfast when I'm dressed, then we'd best be on our way," Lana agreed.

The call was the transport company confirming the delivery time of the new items Lana had ordered. Between them they were ready, finished packing, checked out of the hotel and on the road back out to Whitford within the hour.

By evening, Raffaele was surprised to find how much like a home it already felt. Lana had organised a cleaning crew to spring clean the property the day before and she put fresh cut flowers in many of the rooms. It was time for a celebratory drink. He uncorked a bottle of Australian red wine, poured two glasses and went in search of Lana. He hadn't seen her now for about an hour, although he knew that while he'd unpacked his cases and hung his clothes in one of the large dressing rooms in the master suite she supervised the setting up of the baby's nursery. He'd stepped in to look at one point and was surprised to see her ordering the delivery crew about with the precision of a drill sergeant on parade.

He ascended the stairs a glass in each hand and covered the distance to the nursery with a silent tread on the thick woollen carpet. A noise from the nursery alerted him to her presence, a noise he couldn't quite identify. Not quite knowing what to expect, he pushed open the door. At one glance he could see she'd transformed the room from a guest bedroom into a fully equipped nursery. Each item from one of those lists of hers had a place here in the room, but what stopped him in his tracks was the sight of her seated in the rocking chair, an oversized brown bear with a pink ribbon at its neck clutched tightly to her chest and a look of grief on her face so raw, so deep, it cut him to the quick.

He quickly placed the wine glasses on the top of the tall chest of drawers to one side of the room, and dropped to his knees in front of her. She barely acknowledged him as he took one of her hands in his.

"Lana, tell me. What is it?"

"It's too hard, Raffaele. I can't do it. It just hurts too much."

"What are you talking about? You've done marvellous work here today."

She lifted her head to face him, the flat emptiness in her eyes shocking him to his core.

"I mean it. You have no idea of what you're asking of me, of what it's doing to me inside."

"So tell me. Make me understand." She couldn't renege on her promise now. A part of him wanted to give vent to the instinctive and reactive anger her words fuelled deep inside, but reason told him to stop and listen. Reason and a sudden desire to know more, understand more.

"I've done all this before. Created a nursery, chosen every last piece of equipment, clothing, bedding, towels— and had to give it all away when I couldn't have a child of my own. This has brought it all back to me again. The wanting, and not having. Do you have any idea of what its like to be told you can't have a child? To be told you're im- perfect, not completely whole? You take so much for granted your whole life and then out of the blue, one day you're told you can't be what you want to be, you can't do what you want to do.

"Kyle and I went through every possible procedure you can imagine to conceive, but it was all futile. All along I was the one who was flawed, I was the one who failed us both. I'd forced myself to forget what it felt like, to forget how much I'd wanted a baby."

"You did not try adoption?" Raffaele asked quietly, his fingers stroking the back of her hand.

"Kyle wouldn't hear of it. He said we didn't need to have a baby to be a family. That we were enough. That I was enough for him. But I wasn't, was I? I wasn't enough. If he'd been telling me the truth he wouldn't have fallen in love with your sister. He wouldn't have fathered a child with her."

She pulled her hand free and pushed out of the rocking chair to walk over to a shelving unit filled with soft toys. Into the final space she inserted the teddy she'd been hugging to her body as if it could heal the emptiness Raffaele knew scored her inside. The words she'd painted of Kyle showed a different side to the smooth and urbane businessman he'd introduced to Maria. Had he inadvertently set the chain of events in motion that had led to Lana's devastation, both financially and emotionally?

He could not doubt the veracity of her words. The truth spoke in every syllable that fell from her lips. The extent of what she had gone through today showed in every line of her body. He could sympathise with what she was going through, he'd be inhuman not to acknowledge her pain. But one thing and one thing drove him and, from her, he had to know.

"You are not withdrawing from our arrangement?" His voice was colder than he'd intended, more direct.

She took in a deep breath and faced him. "You would let me pull out?"

"Of course not." Not in a million years would he fail to fulfil his promise to his sister.

"Then no, I'm not withdrawing. But don't expect too much of me, please."

"I have already contacted a nanny service to ensure the physical needs of my niece are met. As we stated before, your contribution is purely legal. I do not expect any emotional involvement from you."

A bitter smile twisted her lips. "That's it then. I know exactly where I stand. Just one thing, though, Raffaele. What about us? Where do I stand with you?"

"I do not expect any emotional involvement from you either."

The smile froze on her face and slowly faded away completely. As she turned and left the room Raffaele couldn't help but wonder if he'd said the right thing. The words had tasted bitter in his mouth, like a lie. But he couldn't afford to second guess himself. Not anymore. During his visit to the hospital yesterday Maria's condition had begun to deteriorate.

He collected the wine glasses from the dresser and went back downstairs. There would be no celebration tonight.

Raffaele listened to the grandfather clock at the foot of the staircase chime the hour and cursed his inability to sleep. The evening had been peaceful enough. Lana had prepared a simple meal for them which they'd eaten together in the informal dining area off the large family room. She'd retired early and, after completing some work on his laptop, he'd done the same. Sleep had seemed so close, as he slid naked between the Egyptian cotton bed sheets. But now his senses were assailed with the hint of Lana's fragrance, leaving an indelible imprint of her presence in the room from when she'd made up the bed.

Without realising he'd made a conscious decision to do so he was out of the bed and had pulled on a pair of pyjama bottoms. His bare feet were soundless as they traversed the stairs and the distance to the downstairs guest suite she'd chosen as her room. No doubt believing herself as far removed from Raffaele and the nursery as possible.

It wasn't far enough, he thought, that he couldn't give into the hunger she'd aroused in him. A hunger he'd tried to quench with what he'd believed was their final encounter this morning. But all it had done was kindle his appetite for more. She was in his blood and his only hope was to purge this hunger by satiating himself in her body until the desire burned itself out.

At the door to her rooms he hesitated and listened. There was only silence on the other side. For a moment he wondered if he was doing the right thing to be seeking to lose himself in her arms, her body, her heat. It was the total opposite of what he'd set out to do with Lana Whittaker. But for some reason, it was only with her that he could retreat from the weight of his responsibilities, from the growing burden of knowledge that Maria would not be alive for much longer.

Raffaele reached out to turn the doorknob and pushed her door open, then stepped inside her room. He was only human. He sought relief of far more than a physical nature, and sought also to give it. What he'd said to Lana before hadn't entirely been the truth.

He was beginning to be far from uninvolved on an emotional level. Where Lana Whittaker was concerned he felt nothing but the height of emotion. She'd brought everything within him to screaming point—in anger, and in sorrow. She was exactly what he needed right now and, hopefully, so could he be for her.

Eleven

For the second morning in a row, Lana woke beside Raffaele Rossellini. She turned her head on the pillow so she could watch in him the early morning light. Even in sleep he looked determined, his face barely relaxed. When he'd come to her last night she'd been surprised, but not so surprised that she wanted to spurn his attention. Every touch, every kiss, every sigh had been an affirmation for her. Proof that she was desirable, proof that she could satisfy a man—even a man as driven as Raffaele.

Making love with him had been deeply satisfying on many levels, but most importantly she felt as if he'd given her a gift of self. Both herself, and his. Even though he still held himself aloof by day, by night he had proven to be hers and hers alone. While she didn't understand his murmurings in Italian in the throes of passion, he spoke to her with such gentleness, touched her with such care, she could feel her heart begin to warm toward him in such a way that shocked her with its intensity.

She had never felt this way with Kyle. He'd swept her off her feet and out from under her father's watchful gaze while he was travelling on a European tour. With her father's pressure to welcome Malcolm's advances, Kyle had been an escape route she'd accepted readily. Their elopement had caused a major furore, culminating in her father cutting her off from his life completely when she'd refused to have the marriage annulled.

Lana hadn't thought her life could become any more isolated after that, but in the aftermath of Kyle's death and the truth of how their marriage had fallen apart around her when she thought everything was still okay had taught her a whole new meaning to isolation.

Raffaele stirred and stroked his hand over her hip before settling back into sleep. Instantly desire licked hungry flames across her skin and she snuggled in closer to him. She certainly didn't feel isolated right now.

A small smile caressed her lips. His sexual appetite had been voracious during the night, but now it was her turn to stir him awake and pleasure him with her touch. He had given her so much, on so many levels, and she already was growing to know his body almost as well as she knew her own. She slid down the sheets to expose him to her, he was already half aroused. Her loose hair brushed against his stomach, and she felt his skin tauten in reaction under the moist stroke of her tongue as she followed the shadowed line of his hip. As she took his hardening length into her mouth and stroked her tongue around his swollen head she decided this time there'd be no stopping her. This was her gift to give him.

It was some time later, as they both lay sated by their activities, that Raffaele spoke.

"You will move into the master suite today."

Lana stiffened at his side, her body still pulsing with the aftermath of the orgasm he'd given her. Move into the master suite?

"I have no desire to come searching for you in the dark of night." He rolled over to face her. "Let us be honest with one another, Lana. This thing we have between us, it is not something that will burn out swiftly, nor is it something to be ignored. We are consenting adults. Let's behave as such."

She could think of nothing to say, certainly no argument. In Raffaele's arms she'd enjoyed mind shattering intense pleasure such as she'd only briefly touched the surface of during her marriage. To be able to wake like this morning, every morning, would be wonderful. A light of hope glimmered in her chest. Could it even, perhaps, become permanent? They'd had the rockiest of starts together, but look at them now. Her eyes traced his features hungrily before returning to meet his grey stare as he awaited her answer—the tiny frown between his dark brows his only indication that his patience was running out.

"If you're certain?" she answered softly.

"I would not have suggested it were I not."

"Then, yes. Yes, I will move my things in with yours today."

A slow lazy smile transformed his face. *"Excellente."* He started to say something else but was interrupted by the sound of the phone ringing in the passageway. He took a moment to drop a swift hard kiss on Lana's lips before striding, in glorious nakedness, to take the call.

Lana stretched back against the sheets but straightened

abruptly as Raffaele came back into the room, his face
pale and strained.

"What is it? Maria?" she asked.

"She is worsening. The doctors have decided to delay
no longer. They operate to take the baby this morning. I will
leave for the hospital as soon as possible."

"I'm coming with you." Lana pushed off the bed and
rummaged through her things to find some clothing.

"No!" he protested.

Lana stopped what she was doing and went over to him,
raising her hand to lightly cup his cheek so he could not
look away from her. "Raffaele, you need someone with you
today. Whatever happens. I want to be with you."

Raffaele looked into her eyes, and in them, to his
ultimate surprise, began to find solace. As much as it ag-
gravated him to admit it, he wanted her there too. No, he
needed her there. Somewhere, from deep inside, he acknowledged she would be the strong silent support he
suddenly so desperately needed. He tried to pinpoint the
moment when he stopped viewing her as his enemy and
started to see her as something else, something more than
a means for revenge on his family's sorrow. But the
moment evaded him.

He turned his face to press a kiss into her palm. "*Grazie*.
Be ready in ten minutes."

She was ready in eight and waiting for him in the vestibule as he tore back down the stairs. The journey to the
hospital passed in a blur, as did much of the next few days.

Baby Bella was a fighter and every tiny inch of her as
beautiful as her mother. Maria continued to hold onto life
with a tenacity that stunned even the doctors. Her life
support had been withdrawn a day after the baby's birth

and Raffaele had spent every possible waking moment at his sister's side. It had been four days since Bella's birth and still Maria drew breath. A scan had revealed that any hope of recovery was futile, Maria's brain activity was nil, but something continued to keep her alive and, for however long that happened, he would stay with her.

Raffaele fought to keep his eyes open. He'd virtually lived at the hospital, while Lana travelled back and forth to the house—each day bringing him a change of attire and silently taking his old clothing away with her again. He would not allow her in the room with Maria and he could see she felt the rejection like a blow, but he knew she spent time in the special care unit with the baby each day.

They'd been warned that the newborn might not want too much handling; that it could stress her fragile body as technically she should still be cocooned within her mother, but the nurses said that Lana would come and simply watch the wee girl for hours on end. Never offering a word, acknowledging the nurses when spoken to, then silently leaving, only to return and repeat the process the next day.

She looked shattered. He knew he looked little better. Today he would suggest that she stay away for a few days. In fact he would do it right now. She did not need to run herself ragged. He could visit with both Bella and Maria. Raffaele leaned across the bed and placed a kiss on his sister's smooth cheek.

"*Ti amo,* Maria," he whispered into her ear, his breath catching in his throat as he did so. He was almost too frightened to leave her side, fearful for any sudden deterioration, but he had to go to Lana, to get her to see sense and stay away until she'd had a decent amount of rest.

The sound of machinery, interspersed with the mewls

of fractious premature infants in the special care unit always took him aback. His eyes scanned the room and he nodded to the duty nurses. Lana was nowhere to be seen but a movement from further down the hall caught his eye.

He watched as she walked back towards the unit, oblivious to his scrutiny. Every line of her body bespoke an intense weariness, every step she took told the toll that was taken on her.

Unbidden, a fierce sense of protectiveness welled inside of him. She had to go home, to rest. He stepped forward and noticed the exact moment she became aware of his presence. A light filled her eyes, lifting her exhausted features. His heart beat in double time as he recognised that he could have such an effect on her.

She closed the gap between them and his heart swelled with something he didn't want to define. Not on top of everything else—not on top of the life of the infant in the unit behind him, not on top of his sister who he'd left just a few short minutes ago.

"I want you to go home and rest," he said as she drew near.

"Raffaele, I do that every evening."

"I know you go home, but you do not rest enough. Look at you. You are so tired you have dark circles under your eyes." He stroked her skin gently with his thumb, brushing gently against the evidence of her exhaustion. "You need to stay away from the hospital for a few days. Really rest."

"I'm no more tired than you," she protested quietly. "I will go home tonight, but I'll be back again in the morning."

"Lana, I insist."

"You can't make me stay away. I couldn't anyway. I want to be here. To be with Bella. To be with you when you'll let me."

Raffaele sighed. She was stubborn this fragile looking woman. Her appearance had deceived him from the beginning. He'd never imagined that beneath that slender feminine body beat a heart with a capacity for giving as wide as an ocean, or a backbone as strong as steel.

"Raffaele?" She interrupted his thoughts.

"What is it?"

"Will you come home with me tonight? You need rest, too, and I know you've hardly slept in the past four days."

"I cannot."

"Raffaele, you're no good to Maria if you're dead on your feet. Come home with me. Just for one night. Please?"

He looked at her as she pleaded with him and lifted his hand to her cheek, much as she had a few short days ago. In similar fashion, she turned her face towards the warmth of his palm, her lips pressing against his skin and sending a jolt of need through his body with the force of a thunderbolt.

He needed her as much as she needed him.

In that instant he knew they would both be going home tonight for a break in their vigils.

"Come then, we shall return home together." He drew Lana into his arms, his body leaping to hungry life at the impression of her form against his. Inside he battled over his need to stay at Maria's side. Her condition had remained static since the birth of the baby, but right now he craved to give in to the yawning hollowness inside of him and spend some time alone with Lana.

Later, stepping into the vestibule at the house Raffaele was stunned by how welcoming it felt. Lana had woven a web of homecoming. Somehow she'd still managed to retain that sense of a lived-in home, despite the length of time she spent at the hospital. Raffaele turned to lock the front door then followed Lana up the stairs.

It struck him anew, how much had changed since Bella's birth. Back then Lana was still a resident on the ground floor. Obviously she had moved her things upstairs as he'd bidden. His body tightened in anticipation, his skin ultra sensitive to the texture of the cotton shirt he wore. He couldn't wait to be rid of the trappings of sensible behaviour and to indulge, for however long, in pure sensation.

He jogged lightly up the stairs and towards the warm glow of light from the master suite. Lana wasn't in the bedroom, but he could hear her moving about the bathroom over the sound of water gushing from the taps over the bath. He shed his clothing with a swiftness that underlined his need of her and stalked through to the en suite.

She'd obviously disrobed with the same speed as he. She stood, dressed only in a silky aqua coloured robe. With a graceful hand she sprinkled some lightly spice-scented bath salts in the bath, and bent to swirl them through the water.

"I thought you might like to unwind a bit first."

Raffaele growled a response, neither in confirmation nor denial.

"Step in," she instructed.

"Do you plan to join me?" He asked as he stepped into the swirling fragrant water.

"Of course. How else will I be able to massage out the tension in your shoulders?" She smiled, gently and placed a bottle of oil on the edge of the bath pedestal. "Is that okay?"

"Yes, that is more than okay." He stepped into the bath and lowered himself in the soothing water. A ragged sigh shuddered from him as he relished the relaxing rhythm of the jets of water as they massaged against his lower back.

Lana untied the sash of her robe and tilted her shoulders, letting the fabric slither in a waterfall over her body, pooling at her feet. His eyes drank in the sight of her, the slender length of her legs, the gentle curve of her hips, the narrowness of her waist and above to the compact shape of her breasts. Her nipples tightened before his gaze, the buds peaking enticingly. Blood pooled low in his groin as he hardened even more. Since he'd met Lana he'd remained in a constant state of physical awareness. No other woman had ever tempted him this much.

"Move forward a little, let me sit behind you," she whispered in his ear, her breath a warm fan of air against his skin.

He did as she bade and held back a groan of anticipation as he felt her body slide in behind him, and her legs press against the outside of his thighs. He heard her slick her hands with massage oil then felt their glorious strength as she began to massage his back in sweeping circular strokes. Her fingers kneaded the knotted muscle at his neck, his shoulders, and lower down his spine. Inch by slow inch the tension in his body dissipated and he began to relax.

Then her hands slipped around to his waist and he felt the pressure of her breasts against his back as she hugged him to her and massaged across his belly, then up to circle his chest and to pluck at his nipples before soothing them again with a flat palmed stroke that worked its way steadily down his body, to his waist, then lower to his straining erection.

Her fingers slid around him, stroking gently, and he felt the warm press of her lips against his back.

Raffaele reached down and stilled her hand. He swivelled slightly in the large bath and reached for her slender form, gripping her by her waist and sliding her around in the water until she straddled his groin. The heat of her body enticed him to lift her, to sink her slowly over his body and assuage the demanding need that pumped through him, almost overruling rational thought. But he wanted to wait, to extend the anticipation of that glorious moment for as long as he could bear it.

He grabbed he bottle of massage oil and squeezed a small amount into his hands.

"Now, it is my turn to relax you."

He slicked the oil over her shoulders and down her arms, her slenderness striking him anew. Had she lost more weight in the past week? A pang of guilt lanced through him that he hadn't taken more notice of how she was coping, or whether she'd been looking after herself.

He stroked back up her arms and across her prominent collar bone before caressing her breasts, coating them with oil then massaging their firm roundness, rubbing his thumbs across their tight peaks. Her hips rocked forward against his erection, driving a moan of want from her lips. He leaned forward to capture the sound in his mouth, sliding his tongue against her lips in a possessive sweep. She shuddered against him, her hips rocking again.

He deepened the kiss, tangling his tongue with hers, suckling at her lips as if she were his sole nourishment. He slid one hand down past the curve of her waist and traced the line of her pelvis, then deeper into the neatly trimmed nest of curls that hid her inner core. He brushed against her clitoris with one finger and smiled as she jerked against his touch.

"More, please, Raffaele, more!" she implored against his lips.

In answer he circled the hooded bundle of nerves with a slow gentle motion, increasing the pressure and frequency until a pink flush started to spread across her chest and her eyes glazed with passion.

Her entire body bunched on the point of release and in the precise moment he felt her begin to shatter against him he lifted her and slid inside the welcoming sheath of her body. Sensation poured through him in a forceful wave of desire then focussed on that one point of where their bodies joined. In that one simple thrust he climaxed, pushing deep inside her, feeling every pull of her inner muscles as a command to pleasure.

Lana collapsed against Raffaele's chest. This was supposed to have been about him, about giving him release and comfort. Not about bringing her to mindless pleasure. She tried to lift her head from his shoulder but she felt as weak as a kitten, and instead she melded into his body, into the water lapping around them.

There was a distinct chill to the water when, some time later, she felt him shift beneath her and, too tired to protest, allowed him to withdraw from her body.

"*Cara,* we must get out of the bath or we will turn into frozen fish." There was a humour to his voice that Lana had never heard before. It energised her enough to lift her head from the curve of his shoulder and to nuzzle against his neck.

"If you insist," she agreed.

She extricated her limbs from about his body, and reluctantly stepped from the bath, a tiny shiver of cold racking her body. Raffaele reached past her and grabbed a large thick bath towel and wrapped it about her before getting another for himself. Once they were dry they went together to the bedroom and slid between the sheets, their bodies spooning together as though they'd been together for years instead of only a matter of weeks.

Dawn broke with watery sunshine pushing through the tall bedroom windows. Lana lay in Raffaele's arms and relished the comfort she found there. Reluctant to move and disturb what was the first decent sleep he'd had in almost a week, she simply allowed herself to savour the warmth of his body as it sheltered her. A bubble of pleasure grew deep inside of her. She'd felt so empty in the harrowing days after Kyle's death. She would never have imagined in all the world that she'd have the chance to rebuild this deep sense of belonging ever again, let alone so soon.

Raffaele's hand spread across her belly and pulled her tight against him, her buttocks pressing against his hips and the firm evidence that he was awake and wanting her again. His hand slid down between her legs, playing with her there until liquid heat seared her senses. He parted her folds with gentle fingers, and slid inside her, his body stilling once they were joined.

They lay like that for several minutes, Lana clenching against his hardened length—wanting more yet, unexpectedly, afraid to ask. The truth of her feelings for Raffaele bore down upon her with frightening speed. She was falling in love with him and suddenly the prospect of not being able to wake with him each new day filled her with fear. Could she begin to hope that his feelings towards her might have changed? That they might be able to have a future together, as a family?

Her breath caught as Raffaele began to move, at first slowly, allowing her body to expand and stretch as he pressed deep against the entrance to her womb, then with increasing speed as the fever of need overtook him. His fingers continued to caress her and her orgasm hit hard, making her buck against him as wave after increasing wave of blissful satisfaction radiated through her body.

He cried out in his release—a harsh sound of pure surrender that filled her heart with the hope that he wanted her so much, that she could give him so much pleasure.

Twelve

As the perspiration dried on their bodies and their heart rates returned to a normal rhythm Lana formulated her words carefully. Her whole future hinged on Raffaele's response. If his hunger for her was any indication, she hoped she could begin to believe that his feelings for her may in fact mirror that hunger. But she'd never know if she didn't ask. Suddenly, it was imperative that she know.

"Raffaele?"

"Mmm." He nuzzled against the back of her neck and she could feel the smile on his lips against her skin.

"I've been thinking."

"Si?"

He pulled away slightly and Lana felt a frisson of foreboding. Dismissing the sensation as being fanciful, she carried on. "Yes. About the guardianship of Bella."

She rolled over in the bed to face him, to try to gauge from his expression how well he'd receive her suggestion.

"Continue." His voice was pitched low, with a note of wariness that underlined his suspicion.

Lana took a deep breath and forged on. "I never realised just how much I would fall in love with her. She's stolen my heart. I know there's so little that I can do for her right now, but I want to be a part of her future. I want to be there for her."

Raffaele pushed up from the bed and stood next to it, oblivious to the picture he made—his form as strong and well-defined as if it had been carved from marble by Michelangelo himself. His dark brows drew together in a formidable straight line, his grey eyes were colour of flint.

"You are saying you've changed your mind?"

Lana pushed up to sit and face him. There was something in the tone of his voice that made her gather the tangled sheets from about her waist and to lift them to cover her breasts, to shield her from his angry stare. What had she said that was so wrong? Surely he wanted what was best for Bella.

"I know it looks that way, but think about it, Raffaele. Bella needs two parents. She's had a hard enough start in life without the objective care she'll get from a nanny, or even a succession of nannies. She needs people around her who will love her and be there for her—always."

"Be there for her like her parents would have?" Raffaele sliced through the air with a hand. "Enough! Bella would have had two loving parents there for her every day of her life if Kyle hadn't been coming back to you the day of the accident. If you were a real wife, you would have known something was wrong with your marriage. You should have let him divorce you when your marriage started to falter."

"How can you say that? I didn't know anything was wrong—I thought he loved me!" And it was true. Lana had offered him the chance to walk away from their marriage when they'd learned the truth about her infertility. He'd refused, emphatically. "I always believed he was working when he was away. If I'm responsible for anything, it's that I didn't recognise when we started to drift apart when we couldn't have a child of our own. I couldn't see it then, I was too lost in trying to live through my own grief." So lost in her grief that she hadn't been able to see her husband's and had effectively closed him out of her life altogether. She'd never seen it before now, never acknowledged it, but now it was painfully clear. The truth was a searing brand on her heart.

"And you feel he owes it to you? His child? In death he has given to you the one thing you couldn't have while he was living?" His voice seethed with steaming accusation.

This wasn't going how she'd planned at all. Raffaele had twisted her words, had put a spin on them that she couldn't refute. Yes, it was true. In death Kyle had given her the one thing above everything she'd ever wanted. The one thing she'd never be able to have herself. A child. Spending time with Bella in the special care unit over the past few days had forced her to face anew her grief at not being able to bear a child of her own. But at the same time, the tiny babe's fight for life had given Lana renewed hope. And as each hour Bella grew stronger, she also took a stronger hold on Lana's heart.

"You don't understand me, Raffaele. I love Bella. I want to be a part of her life. Together with you. By your side, if you'll let me."

"And if I choose not to let you? What then? Will you

fight the parental order? Will you assert your right to guardianship?"

"You're not listening to me, Raffaele. I don't want to have to do it that way."

"To have to do it that way?" His voice began to rise, giving way to the anger that flamed in his eyes and held his body in rigid check. "So you're saying that you will if you don't get what you want?"

From his jacket pocket Raffaele's cell phone started to ring.

"I'm saying nothing of the kind. I want to be with Bella. I want to be with you!"

"Do not bother to speak of this any more. You have shown your true colours to me. And to think I had begun to believe in your sincerity, begun to have feelings for you!"

His last words hung on the air as Raffaele strode across the room and pulled the phone from his breast pocket. "Rossellini!" he answered.

Lana watched in horror as the colour drained from his face, leaving it a sickly grey. In a voice she barely recognised as his, he thanked the caller and let the phone drop to the floor.

"What is it? Was it the hospital?" Lana scrambled from the bed, the sheets still wrapped around her.

Raffaele lifted his head, his eyes swimming with tears. "She is gone. My beautiful baby sister is gone." He rose to his feet, his face a frozen mask of pain. "And instead of being by her side as she let go of our world, I was with you! You! The wife of the man she loved. Through you, I have betrayed my sister, my whole family."

"It wasn't like that. You didn't betray Maria. You needed rest, you needed to come home, and maybe she needed you to leave her so she could let go." Lana reached a hand to touch him, to attempt to offer him some form of comfort, but he shook her off.

"Do not touch me. Because of you, I was not there for my sister when she died. I can never forgive myself for that. I want you gone. From this house, from my life."

He strode to his wardrobe and Lana heard the screech of hangers as he dragged clothing from the wardrobe and went through to the bathroom. On numb legs she staggered after him.

"Surely you don't mean that. You're not thinking straight. You've just had terrible news. Please, Raffaele, don't be hasty."

"Hasty? I am not hasty. I wanted to wait until I had the parenting order, to make certain that I had every legal right to Bella before seeing the back of you. I see no need now to wait. When I first met you, all I wanted was to bring you some measure of the pain you inflicted on my family when you would not give Kyle a divorce. Instead, I foolishly handed you a weapon to inflict more pain. I will not give you any further power. You can be certain of that."

"More pain? You're calling our lovemaking more pain?"

"Call it what you will. It is over now."

He stepped into the shower stall and flicked on the taps, through the glass she saw him flinch as the cold spray hit his body. The reality of his words hit home, slamming into her heart, her mind, with the full weight of a wrecking ball.

"You planned this?" she whispered in disbelief. Ice ran in her veins. Had she been a complete dreamer to believe he'd been falling in love with her, as she had with him? She couldn't have been so mistaken. By his own confession a few minutes ago, he'd admitted having feelings for her.

Could he quell them so easily? She made it back to the bed before her legs gave out beneath her. Once again she'd been a fool for love—a failure. She was too shocked to cry, too full of pain to move so much as a muscle. Lost as she was in her thoughts she didn't hear Raffaele finish in the en suite and she jumped as he re-entered the bedroom, shrugging into his jacket and straightening his tie. He flicked a glance at her as if she was nothing more than a stranger as if the intimacies they'd shared had been nothing—meant nothing. Her passionate lover was gone, instead a coldly lethal businessman stood in his place.

"I am going to the hospital to make arrangements for Maria's body." Raffaele crossed over to a dresser and withdrew a cheque book. A few quick strokes of his pen and he ripped the sheet from the book. "I believe this was the sum we agreed upon. Make sure you are gone before I return."

"Raffaele, please, don't be like this. You're in shock, let me help you. I love you and I think, if you'll only let yourself admit it, you're falling in love with me, too. Can't we try to work through this?"

"Love? Do not confuse sentiment with reality. How could I ever love the woman who destroyed the light in our family?"

He dropped the cheque on the bed beside her, then, he was gone. With that parting action he'd turned her into little more than a whore. Lana stared at the cheque, at the figure carved in thick black ink, and finally gave way to the tears that had built with increasing pressure behind her lids.

Lana eventually forced herself to move off the bed and to shower and gather her things together. She was back where she started. With nothing but the clothing on her back. She neatly folded and packaged the items Raffaele had bought her into plastic sacks, labelling them carefully on the outside. He could see to their disposal wherever he chose. Her fingers lingered over the negligee and the under- wear he'd selected. She'd been stupid not to see he had a hidden agenda. A crazy quixotic fool to think for a minute that he could ever contemplate thoughts of a future with her.

When she was satisfied she'd removed every last trace of her presence from the house she knew she had only one thing left to do. She took a box of matches from the kitchen and stepped outside to the poolside patio. The cool breeze sent a chill through her and dark clouds gathered threaten- ingly in the sky overhead. Lana looked around at the sur- rounding olive grove, the loggia at the end of the patio, where she'd envisaged hosting summer barbecues, and the long rectangular pool. She squeezed her eyes shut against the image that sprang vividly to mind of Raffaele and herself playing in the water with Bella. Of watching the dark haired fragile babe growing into a healthy, chubby toddler. That future would never be hers.

She opened her eyes again and struck a match, holding it to the edge of the cheque Raffaele had given her and watched the flames lick over the coloured paper, consum- ing the ink, consuming the end of her dreams. The light breeze kept the flame alive, as the cheque turned to flakes of ash, then bore the remnants in the air. The flames snapped at her fingers where she held the last remaining corner of the cheque, forcing her to let go and leave the scrap to fall unheeded to the floor.

Without a backward glance, Lana turned toward the house. She shut and secured the patio doors behind her and, collecting her hand bag on the way, went outside to await the taxi she'd called to take her into Manukau. She hesi- tated over closing the front door, reluctant to cut herself off completely from the house, and by association from Raffaele. It would be time enough when her ride got here.

Where she would go to next she had no idea. But somehow she'd find the courage to start again. In the depths of her bag she'd found the money she had left from selling her rings. If she was careful she'd get through the next few days and hopefully find a job, anything, before she ran out of money completely. Tears washed her eyes anew and, as if in sympathy, the heavy skies opened—the downpour sudden and ferocious.

Would it never stop raining in her life?

The sound of a car engine coming down the driveway alerted her and, expecting to see her taxi, she lifted her head only to identify the rural post delivery van. Puzzled she waited on the edge of the portico as the postie dashed from the vehicle, getting drenched in the process even in the short distance. At his request she signed for the registered mail delivery. He hastily thrust the envelope in her hands before sprinting back to the still running van.

Her fingers already numb from the cold, Lana didn't quite grasp the envelope fully before he'd let it go and it fell into the growing puddle of water the postie had left at his feet. With a cry of dismay she bent to pick it up. The water had already damaged the envelope and, if it wasn't to continue to damage the contents, she'd have to remove it completely. She went back into the house and peeled away the ruined paper from the letter inside. A glimpse of the High Court insignia on the letter made her heart stop in her chest.

So soon?

She quickly skimmed the contents of the letter before deliberately placing it onto the hall table where Raffaele would be sure to see it on his return home. The parental order had been hurried through due to the extenuating circumstances surrounding Bella's birth. Now he had everything he wanted.

A car pulled up outside the house and tooted its horn. Lana left her key on the hall table next to the letter and went back outside the house, pulling the front door closed with a finality that underlined just how impossibly alone she was now in her life.

The house was in complete darkness as Raffaele returned home. His very soul ached with the loss he'd endured today. Finally, Maria was at peace. The undertaker he'd met with had promised to ensure that all the necessary requirements would be met to see to her body's burial in the plot beside Kyle Whittaker. Raffaele had expected some difficulty in being able to acquire the plot, but surprisingly it had still been available. It had been important to him that Maria be able to forever lie beside the man she'd loved. It didn't make up for what they'd missed out on together, but it would have been her wish. It had been up to Raffaele to respect that, even if his blinkers had been finally removed from his eyes about the man he'd thought would one day be his brother-in-law.

The fact that he could even see how elaborate Kyle Whittaker's web truly was, bore mute testament to the cracks Lana had made in his belief. Cracks that had slowly widened until he could no longer deny the reality. But despite all that he could understand what had driven the man to maintain what was in reality two wives in two cities. He'd wanted it all. The support and prestige of a consummate society wife, for it was clear that Lana had fulfilled that role for Kyle in abundance, and conversely the comfort of the mother of his child.

Because Maria had loved Kyle with every last breath in her body, Raffaele owed it to his sister to do what was right for her, no matter how much it shredded his soul to know he was saying goodbye to her for the last time.

His brother would arrive late tomorrow afternoon. Raffaele drew in a deep breath. He could cope until then. His grief could wait until it was shared with the only other person left in his world who would understand how he felt.

He wondered what Vincenzo would think of Bella. Raffaele was already eager to show their niece off to him, although the baby had been fractious and unsettled today. One of the nurses had suggested that perhaps she'd been missing Lana, but he'd wasted no time in letting the nurse know that Lana would not be returning.

He drew on the remnants of anger that lingered after her threat this morning, staving off his grief and allowing the anger to rise above it, to gain shape and form. He had all but been lulled into a false sense of security with Lana. He'd seen for himself how vulnerable she was, how wounded by her husband's actions. That very vulnerability had drawn out his protective instincts. The instincts he'd honed after his father had died and when his entire family had depended solely on him for their next meal. It was only natural that he'd done the same again. It was what he excelled at, after all.

And then she'd shown her true colours. Her intention to keep the baby all along. For as long as he drew breath in his body he would fight that intention, he silently vowed. She would no longer come between his family and happiness.

Weariness assailed him. Too tired to bother to garage the

car he parked at the front door and let himself inside. As he flipped the light switch he was immediately struck by the hollow emptiness of the house. She was gone. He'd briefly wondered today if she would obey his command, or if she'd force a confrontation. It was with a measure of relief he noted she'd chosen the former. He felt so raw right now he couldn't have promised his reaction to her would have been civil, and yet something pricked at his conscience at the way he'd lashed out at her. He forced the sensation aside. He had no wish to examine his feelings now. It was best to focus only on the future. On what needed to be done.

His eye caught on the opened letter on the table and he stepped forward to pick it up, his eyes quickly scanning its contents. Relief bloomed in his chest at the message therein. His promise to Maria had been fulfilled. Bella was his.

The next morning, as dawn streaked the sky with pink fingers, Raffaele woke and reached across the bed, seeking the welcoming warmth he'd grown accustomed to. He shot to alertness as his fingers encountered nothing but the wide cool and vacant expanse of high-thread-count cotton. How could he have forgotten so easily?

He flopped back over onto his back, cupping his hands behind his head as he stared at the darkened ceiling above him. He would get over this emptiness inside of him, it was merely a matter of adjusting, he tried to convince himself as grey light filtered into the room, in fact it probably had nothing to do with the emptiness in his bed at all, but instead everything to do with Maria.

Raffaele pressed his eyelids shut tight against the wave of anguish that swelled within him. Resolutely he pushed it aside. He would cope with this as he had with every other heartache in his life—with hard work and single minded determination and focus. That focus now belonged to Bella absolutely.

He settled back deeper, his elbow brushing against the pillow where Lana had so recently laid her head. A ghostly waft of her fragrance teased the air around him, sending his body into full alert. There was no mistaking her effect on him, he acknowledged with a stoicism he was far from feeling, but it took more than physical need to make or sustain a relationship.

Relationship? Ha! Who was he kidding. He'd never had any intention of forming a relationship with Lana aside from whatever it took to avenge what he'd believed she'd done to his family. Even though he could now acknowledge that his words to her yesterday morning had been wrought from the pain of hearing of Maria's passing, of the guilt that he'd failed to be at her side to see her across the gulf between life and death, he still stood by his decision.

And what of his own needs? a tiny voice slid through his mind. Needs? The physical could be easily assuaged, he argued back. *And the emotional?*

Raffaele tried to ignore the piercing pain of emptiness in his chest. He rolled to his side and inhaled, drawing the lingering remnants of Lana's scent deep within him. The pain deepened. She was gone from his life, it was what he'd wanted—what he'd planned from the moment he'd first heard of the accident—yet he missed her with an ache that went beyond unfulfilled desire.

Somewhere in the past few days he'd lost the edge of his need for retribution. Even as hard as he'd tried to fan the flame of reprisal, Lana's innate honesty had inveigled its way past his defences. At what point, he finally acknowledged, had he gone from hating her with every breath in his body to wanting her with every beat of his heart? The reality of his actions sluiced over his body in waves.

He'd driven her away. He'd spurned her as viciously and effectively as had her husband. He thought back on every thing Lana had said to him, and every thing she had done. She was as much a victim as his sister had been, as Bella was now.

Raffaele shot from the bed and tried once more to push aside the reality of his thoughts. He went automatically through the motions, showering, dressing, eating breakfast. Finally, he gave up pushing his cereal around the bowl with disinterest and drawn by the growing light of the sunlight caressing the pool, he went outside.

As far as his eye reached, he was master of this domain. It would be a fine place for Bella to grow up during the time his work didn't keep them home in Italy.

Home. How long had it been since he'd thought of Italy as home? It shocked him to realise that since he'd bought this property the idea of living and working in Italy had been further from his mind than exporting olive oil to Mars. Yet what sort of home would it be without Lana inside it?

What the hell had he done? With his single minded bull headedness he'd driven away the one person he should have done everything in his power to nurture. He'd blindly ignored the facts, choosing instead to believe the version of events engineered by a man who'd been proven a fraudster. It had never occurred to Raffaele to wonder why Kyle hadn't simply walked away from Lana or what his ulterior motives had been in staying with her—maintaining two households, two lives.

Raffaele had allowed himself to be spun instead into the

web of lies Kyle had woven with such consummate skill. And then, when the accident had happened, it had been easier to apportion blame to Lana than to admit to himself he'd been wrong. Wrong to have introduced Maria to Kyle, wrong to have encouraged the relationship.

Wrong to have treated Lana so cruelly.

The fault was his, and his alone. As was the responsibility of rectification.

Thirteen

Raffaele faced off against Tom Munroe who looked none too pleased to see him waiting for him in his office.

"What have you done to her? She was beside herself when she rang me, insisted on doing everything on her own," Tom growled fiercely.

Raffaele instinctively bristled. "I left her well compensated. It was what we had agreed on together."

"Well compensated. Bah! You used her abominably. Worse even than Kyle. Do you have any idea of what she gave up to be with him? Any idea at all?"

"I cannot begin to imagine." Raffaele sank into the red leather button back chair that faced Tom's desk feeling little more than a guilty party facing a hanging judge. "Mr Munroe, I was wrong about Lana. It is not something I accept easily or willingly, but I am at least man enough to own up to my transgression. I want to put things right."

"Man enough? Kyle thought he was man enough when he wooed her out from underneath her father's watchful eye. The foolish man never believed that Trevor Logan would cut off his only child if she acted against his wishes. Little did he know." Tom leaned forward on his desk. "Can you begin to imagine what it felt like for Lana—a girl who'd lost her mother when she was only six, a girl whose father was the axis of her world—to suddenly be cut off from the only support line she'd known in her entire life?

"And then you waltz in and do exactly the same. Give her false hope, a false sense of security. Frankly, I couldn't be happier if I never saw you again."

Raffaele drew in a deep breath, accepting each word as his due. He couldn't fault the man for wanting to protect Lana. Given the chance, he would ensure she'd never need such protection again.

"Where is she?" he asked, his voice as neutral as he could make it given the frustration rising within him.

"Even if I knew, Rossellini, I wouldn't tell you. You went too far."

Raffaele stood. It was clear the older man neither could nor would give him any further information today. He extracted a business card from his slim card holder and placed it deliberately on the desk blotter in front of Tom Munroe.

"Please, call me if she gets in contact with you."

"And give me one good reason why I should do that, Rossellini. You've been nothing but trouble from the first day we laid eyes on you."

The older man met his non-verbal challenge with a steadfastness that made him grateful that Lana had a champion on her side. It was little enough in her world right now.

"A reason? I'll give you the reason you demand. It is

quite simple, Mr Munroe. You will tell me because I love her, and because I believe she loves me. I only need a chance to tell her."

"And you think your declaration of love will be enough?" The man's voice shook with incredulity.

"Enough? No. But it is a start, and we need a new start. One without Kyle Whittaker's shadow or his influence colouring what we do."

Tom reached out and picked up the card, reading it carefully before sliding it into the inner breast pocket of his jacket.

"I will think about it, Rossellini. But don't hold your breath. Even if she does contact me again I cannot guarantee that she will want to see you."

"I need to know where she is. To know she is safe," Raffaele answered. "As for the rest, that will be Lana's choice."

Two weeks later, Raffaele was no closer to finding her than he'd been the day he'd seen Tom Munroe. Worse, as he'd discovered from the bank today, she'd never presented the cheque nor had she touched a cent of the funds he'd deposited in the bank account he'd set up for her.

He fought the bitter taste of anger that flooded his mouth. What on earth was she thinking? She'd needed that money to get back on her feet again. From his enquiries this week, he knew that her old associates, still smarting from the loss of their investments, had had nothing whatsoever to do with her since the day of the funeral. A few had the grace to look shamefaced when he'd called upon them to ask if they'd seen anything of her recently, but most had been quite explicit in their condemnation.

Lana was on her own, and it was all his fault.

The only light glimmering on his horizon at present

was Bella's slow and steady improvement. Fifteen days after her birth, she'd come out of the intensive care unit and her feeding tube had been removed. While she still struggled a little with her suck-swallow-breathe coordination her medical team were confident she'd be home in another week or so.

He was enraptured with her and held her every moment he could. His heart swelled with an indefinable sense of love and pride to feel her tiny form in his arms. To know Maria lived on in the tiny scrap of tenacious humanity.

Lana would be so proud to see how far Bella had come. Raffaele had admitted to himself that the nurses' suggestion earlier on that Bella had been missing Lana had been correct. For several days the little girl had stagnated, before showing steady improvement once again.

Only one thing was left now to make his life perfect and that was to have Lana back by his side, in his bed, in his life.

Lana let herself into the tiny sleep-out accommodation she'd secured. Lord but her feet ached. She'd never known such exhaustion as she'd endured in the past month waiting tables in one of Orewa's popular restaurants. The ocean front town, north of Auckland, thrived on both tourist and local visitors and there was no such thing as a quiet night. It was thanks to that very busyness that she'd been able to secure a position almost as quickly as she'd stepped off the bus.

Resolutely she pushed the memory aside. She'd promised herself she would only look forward. There was no point in looking back any longer. She was on her own. It was up to her to make things work. She'd been lucky that her new employer's aunt had this cheap accommodation available. The amenities were very basic. One large bedroom–sitting room area, a postage stamp of a bathroom, a jug, a microwave and refrigerator. It was all she needed. She had one good meal a night at the restaurant and had learned to make do with little else.

It had been gratifying to get her first wages, supplemented by some healthy tips, even if paying her rent did eat into the money in a large chunk.

She worked hard from early evening through to whatever time the kitchen closed, sometimes not until the small hours of the morning, and she relished the tiredness that saw her fall into a dreamless sleep each night. Mornings saw her walking the few blocks to the length of the surf beach where she tossed stale bread to the seagulls before taking a leisurely jog along the shore line.

Yes, she had her routine. And even if she couldn't categorically state she was happy, she was making her own way. What she'd do next she had no idea. With time at her disposal during the day she'd begun to think of possibly doing some kind of course and gaining a more useful qualification than society hostess and charity fundraiser. Whatever came next, it really didn't matter. Each day as it comes, was her new motto.

Tonight there'd been quite a crowd, a lot of cameras flashing off all through the evening as people celebrated various functions. The activity had made her nervous and obviously it had shown in her performance. She counted her tips as she eased off her shoes and sat down on the edge of her bed, not as much as previous nights. She needed to learn to relax a bit more. Not everyone was out to get her. She'd all but faded into obscurity. The latest scandal was plastered over the society pages, which was exactly what she'd wanted.

Lana dropped her head back and rotated her shoulders. It was so tempting to just flop backwards onto the bed and fall asleep in her clothes, but she forced herself upwards. She slid out of the black trousers and peeled off the white short sleeve T-shirt, with the restaurant logo printed on the front, that was her uniform. It had eaten into her reserves of cash to buy the pants, but thankfully there'd been a recycled clothing store not far from the restaurant and she'd found the pants in a clearance bin. By making sure she gently hand-washed the items each night she hadn't needed to invest in any other items for work just yet. For a second she allowed herself to think ruefully of the bags of clothing she'd left behind at Raffaele's house. She shook her head against the memory, her pride wouldn't let her take any of it. No. He'd bought her lock stock and barrel and she'd let him.

As frightening as being solely responsible for herself was, it was empowering too. And she was managing very well so far.

She went through her routine, arranging the wet T-shirt on a coat hanger and putting it on the shower curtain rail so it would dry. The damp trousers she put into the cupboard that housed the hot water cylinder and which doubled as an airing cupboard.

As Lana pulled on the soft and well-washed man's shirt she'd also found at the recycled clothing store and used as her nightgown, she thought she saw a flash and heard a noise outside.

There was one thing that living on her own like this had taught her, even in such a short time, and that was self-preservation. She hit the light switch, plunging the sleep-out into darkness, then carefully manoeuvred the vertical window blinds until she could see out the front of the sleep-out.

The small building was at the back of the main house and the security lights she'd tripped as she'd come down the path at the side of the house should long since have switched off. Her eyes scanned the shadows in the garden. Nothing.

She swivelled the blinds closed again and stepped back, reluctant to switch the light back on again. There! There was that flash again. She clapped a hand to her mouth to hold back the scream that bubbled up her throat. Although it had been raining when she'd come in tonight, there'd been no hint of thunder in the air. Surely it couldn't have been lightning. She waited, counting to ten. A shiver racked her body as the cold air set in around her. For the first time she regretted not asking her landlady to reconnect the telephone, but it was an expense she'd decided she could well do without. And even if it had been connected, who would she call? Her landlady was away at the moment, visiting family in Australia. Aside from her, there was no one else.

Twenty minutes later her feet were frozen and her teeth were beginning to chatter. The massive adrenalin surge that had roared through her body, sending her senses on full alert, had long since dissipated, leaving her tired and feeling strung out. This was ridiculous, she reasoned. There was no-one outside. She needed to get to bed and to get warm. But even though she'd reassured herself, sleep was elusive.

A few days later the morning skies were bright and clear, the antithesis of how Lana still felt. The episode the other night had left her feeling rattled, vulnerable, and always she had the sensation of being watched. She'd tried to kid herself she was being unreasonable and forced herself from the bed and to her feet, flicking on the electric kettle to boil water for a coffee on her way through to the bathroom. One of Lana's luxuries, with her landlady away, was to clear her mail box and read her morning paper before a walk to the beach and, after quickly changing into a faded tracksuit, also courtesy of the recycled clothing shop, she went up to the letter box to retrieve the paper.

Back in her tiny unit, Lana spread the paper on the bed, before spooning some instant granules in her cup and pouring on the hot water. She grimaced as she took a sip of the bitter brew. She'd almost managed to get used to doing without milk, but not using freshly ground coffee was proving more of a hardship than she expected. She shook her head sharply. She couldn't afford to be a princess about her life now.

She'd had it all, twice in her life. Three times if she counted the time she'd spent with Raffaele. But each and every time, she'd been reliant on a man for her position. First her father, then Kyle, followed by Raffaele. No. As tough as this was, it was good. She missed a lot of the luxuries she'd taken for granted, but one day she'd be able to spoil herself again. Until then, she'd just keep taking one day at a time.

Taking another sip of the coffee she leisurely turned the pages, until she hit the gossip column. With a shaking hand she put her cup down on the rickety bedside table.

Her voice shook as she read the headline out loud. *"How the Mighty Have Fallen"*.

Lana's eyes were riveted on a collection of photos, one obviously taken of her at the restaurant and placed side by side with the publicity photo the charity had used when she was acting as its spokesperson. The "before" and "after" shots also included a photo, taken from a glossy magazine spread done soon after she and Kyle had furnished the apartment, as well as one of Raffaele's Whitford property, to a poorer quality one of the sleep-out she now called home.

The article itself was pure conjecture, and delivered in the kind of gossipy style that alluded to "sources close to" her on more than one occasion. Her blood chilled in her veins. What would her boss think if he saw this? Would she lose her job? She imagined there would be quite a few people who'd come to the restaurant just to see with their own eyes what she'd been reduced to.

She felt physically ill. It was one thing to be cut off from everyone but quite another to be the object of their conversation while serving them. Still, she had little other choice than to suck it up and see what happened.

Walking to work that night Lana felt extremely anxious. She'd debated whether or not to find a pay phone and call her boss to discuss the article with him, but in the end had decided that face-to-face was best.

As she let herself in through the front door she began to wonder if a phone call mightn't have been a better idea after all. The restaurant was eerily empty, with the exception of her boss, Calvin, who was waiting with a strained expression on his face.

"I was hoping you'd still come in tonight," he greeted her as she came in.

Lana looked around. "What happened? Did we lose all our bookings?"

"On the contrary, the restaurant is booked out for tonight. A private function."

"Oh? That wasn't in the book though, was it?" She leaned forward to check the bookings schedule but Calvin's hand obscured the details on the page.

"No, it wasn't. This was... unexpected." A flush of colour lit his cheeks.

"Is it to do with that article? Look, I'm sorry, Calvin. I

don't want your restaurant to become a freak show. I'll leave if you want me to. Find somewhere else."

"No! It's not that. If anything, bookings have never been stronger. Look, why don't you take a seat over here for a bit."

"I should start getting ready," Lana protested, still uneasy with the emptiness of the dining room, but Calvin shook his head and with his hand at her elbow guided her to a small table, romantically set for two, in an alcove at the back of the restaurant.

It felt odd to be sitting here. What on earth was he playing at?

"Calvin? What's going on?" She asked after his retreating back, but he didn't answer.

This was too weird for words. Calvin's attitude, the empty restaurant—even the silence from the kitchen. She should just get up and go. The sound of the kitchen door swinging open caught her attention and she turned her head to see who was coming.

She should have trusted her instinct to get up and leave, Lana realised as she fought to swallow against the lump that rose in her throat. Bittersweet recognition plunged all the way to her core as her whole body recognised Raffaele's tall dark form walking toward her.

Fourteen

Raffaele carried a bottle of her favourite wine, something she hadn't enjoyed in some time. With a flourish, he poured two glasses of the elegant sauvignon blanc and took a seat opposite her.

Lana's eyes hungrily raked over his face, noting instantly the tired expression in his grey eyes, the fatigue etched on his features and the increased prominence of his cheekbones. Darkness shadowed his jaw, as if he hadn't taken the time to shave today. His appearance shocked her. He, who'd been the epitome of sartorial elegance at all times. But she couldn't afford to care. Look where it had left her. Lana stiffened her spine.

"What do you want?"

"It is simple. You." His voice was rough as he answered, his words sending a shocking shaft of longing through her. She watched as he lifted her wine glass and handed it to her. His fingers deliberately brushed against hers as she took it. She almost heard the sizzle of awareness that electrified her at his casual touch.

Without breaking eye contact with him, Lana deliberately replaced her glass on the table and pushed her chair back. She couldn't take another second of this.

"Don't go. Please."

Lana froze at the longing his tone imbued. If she had any sense at all she'd get up from her seat and walk steadily to the door and keep going until he was back in her past where all her mistakes belonged. But there was something in his plea that struck straight to her soul.

"Why?" It was just one word but at the bottom of it lay her heart, shattered into tiny pieces.

"I was wrong. Very wrong. I didn't understand how much you mean to me."

"How much I mean to you?" Lana finally acknowledged the pain she'd kept at bay for the past month, allowing it life and words as it expanded in her heart and mind with razor sharp precision. Her voice shook as she gave vent to her anguish. "You mean as the constant reminder that your sister couldn't marry her baby's father? That because of me Bella doesn't have a living mother or father?"

"Stop! That's not it. I was a blinkered fool when I said those things. Yes, I meant them at the time. I would be lying to you if I said I didn't, but all I wanted to do was lash out, to hurt as I hurt. To destroy as I felt destroyed. It doesn't make what I did right, nothing will. I was cruel and wrong and I have done irreparable damage."

Lana's response hovered unsaid on her lips as Calvin came out of the kitchen towards them and placed entrees at their place settings. The aroma instantly assaulted Lana's nostrils, dragging her eyes to the delicately poached scallops in front of her. Her favourite entrée on the menu, one she'd served to customers who, like she herself had in the past, ordered it without a thought to the cost or to making every dollar last to the end of each week. Her mouth salivated in anticipation of the flavour hitting her tongue, but she stayed her hand. Did he expect to buy her back with her favourite wine and food, with the lifestyle to which she'd been born? Nothing was worth that. Not ever again.

His touch on her hand made her flinch and she pulled away to avoid the contact.

"Don't touch me." She wasn't that strong that she could bear his touch again—the reminder of the pleasure he'd wrought from her body; or the surcease from the grief of betrayal at Kyle's hand. She'd given him a weapon when she'd given him her heart. She wouldn't be that careless again.

"*Scusami.*" Raffaele gave a curt nod. "But please, eat. You look as if you haven't eaten properly in weeks."

"Whether I have or haven't isn't your concern."

He shot her look that left her in no doubt he wanted to argue that point, but it said a lot for his control that he held his words in check. Reluctantly Lana lifted her fork to spear one of the scallops, and brought it to her mouth. Her tastebuds exploded with delight at the flavour and a tiny groan of pleasure fled her lips. Raffaele's eyes darkened, his pupils widening in appreciation of her unabashed pleasure in the food. The heat of embarrassment stained her cheeks and throat as she identified the look in his eyes.

After Calvin had cleared the dishes away, Lana took a sip of her wine, she may as well enjoy it anyway, she decided. Who knew how long it would be before she could afford to do so again.

"What do you want from me, Raffaele? Why have you done this?"

"What I want? It is simple. I want—no, I *need*—your forgiveness. I need the chance to make up to you the wrong I have done, to make things right between us again."

"Raffaele, we cannot make right what never was right. There's too much between us, separating us. It will always be there."

She heard his muffled curse as Calvin came through with their main course, and watched as his long fingers tapped impatiently on the table as the plates with phyllo-wrapped parcels of snapper were laid out, the vegetables served, the wine topped up. When Calvin finally left them again, Raffaele leaned forward.

"We can build a bridge over that, Lana. If you'll let us. If you'll let me."

"No. It's not possible." She couldn't bear to be hurt again. Three times in her life she'd been spurned by the men she'd loved—from her father through to Raffaele. It was more than any woman could bear to do again and survive with her senses intact. Desperate to change the subject, she asked after Bella, her heart twisting at the look of absolute love that crossed Raffaele's face at the mention of her name.

"She is thriving, and is home now. We have three nannies around the clock. Between us, we are managing well."

"That's good. I really am glad to hear that, Raffaele." Lana pushed her food around her plate, all appetite suddenly diminished at the reminder that she would never be a part of the infant's life.

"She needs you too, Lana. We both need you."

Tears sprang into Lana's eyes and she blinked them back. Oh, he knew how to strike where it hurt most. "Don't," she begged. "Don't use her to get at me."

"I'm sorry, *cara mia*. I do not want to cause you pain."

"It's too late for that. Just being with you like this hurts." She turned her face away from him, barely believing what she'd just said, of what she'd admitted.

Across the table she heard him sigh deeply.

"So you are certain there is no hope for us. No chance you can still love me as I love you."

He loved her? Or was it just more lies?

"I don't believe you," she answered in a voice as flattened and colourless as her spirits.

"If you let me, I will prove it to you, Lana. Please. Let me love you. Let me make things right between us again. I did a terrible thing, but only you can give me permission to make amends for what I did. Only say the word and I will do everything in my power to restore your love for me."

She couldn't speak, could only shake her head. Her throat was too choked up, her heart too sore. She closed her eyes against the tears that spilled down her cheeks. Tears she thought she'd spent weeks ago.

The sound of Raffaele pushing back his seat and standing forced her eyes open. He slipped his hand into his trouser pocket and withdrew a small box, placing it on the table in front of her with a look on his face that spoke volumes as to the truth of his words, of the genuineness of his declaration of love.

"This is yours, whatever you decide. Keep it, sell it. Do what you will. But if you cannot return my love, I do not need it either."

Tall and dignified, he turned and walked away. Lana watched until he was gone then reached out to open the box. Inside, nestled in white satin, was a spectacular three stone diamond and platinum engagement ring. The central emerald-cut diamond refracted even the subdued lighting of the restaurant, it's slightly smaller partners nestled on each side. A small piece of paper was lodged through the ring and she slid it from inside the loop.

Unravelling the paper she instantly recognised the writing as Raffaele's. She read the words he'd written.

> *L, if there had been enough room I would have had engraved the following:* Ti amerò per sempre. *It means "I will love you forever" but as there was not enough room on the band it is instead engraved forever upon my heart.—R.*

He loved her. He really loved her. And come what may, she still loved him in return. Lana rose to her feet, the paper fell unheeded to the table. She couldn't move fast enough and stumbled slightly as she made towards the door. *Please, oh please, don't let me be too late to stop him.* She flew through the front door, her eyes scanning the street for his figure, her heart stuttering to a halt in her chest when she couldn't see him. And then, yes, there he was at the end of the street facing the beach, dejection apparent in every line of his body.

"Raffaele! Wait!" She launched herself in his direction, her heart bursting with relief as he turned to face her. Even from this short distance she could see the strain on his face instantly chased away with the pure joy of seeing her.

She flew into his arms, her body colliding with his rock

solid strength, and relished the taste of his lips as he bent his head to kiss her with a hunger she mirrored with her response.

She tore her lips from his and framed his face with her hands. To her horror tears, streaked his cheeks, tears she was responsible for. The realisation that he'd been prepared to walk away from her, rather than try to force her into listening to him, shook her anew. This domineering powerful man had left the choice to her. Had walked away from her in the belief that he couldn't guarantee her happiness. Had left their future in her hands.

"No more tears, Raffaele. Not for me, or for you. I love you too much to ever want to hurt you."

"So you forgive me? Please, *cara mia*, put me out of my misery. Say you forgive me, say you want me."

"Yes, and yes. Nothing would make me happier."

He held her to him, his head bowed against the curve of her neck, his breath hot on her skin.

"Thank you. I do not deserve you, but I will spend the rest of my life trying to. I promise you."

"Raffaele, we haven't had the best of starts, but what's important is that we love each other. Now we can make the best of futures, together."

"Yes, we will. Now where is your ring? I want the whole world to know you are mine."

Lana laughed, a joyful sound that bubbled from her attracting glances from the handful of passers by. "I left it in the restaurant!"

Together they walked back to the restaurant where Raffaele gently pushed her back on her seat.

"Now, I will do this properly."

He sank to one knee in front of her, holding the ring box in one hand, her left hand in his other.

"Lana, will you do me the honour of becoming my wife?"

"The honour will be mine, forever," her voice caught in her throat as she answered, her heart swollen with the love she felt for him.

Raffaele eased the ring onto her finger and rose to pull her to her feet and to wrap her in his embrace, where she belonged, forever.

* * * * *

Turn the page for a sneak preview of

The Texan's Contested Claim

by

Peggy Moreland

An exciting new story available from
Mills & Boon® Desire™ in January 2009

The Texan's Contested Claim

by

Peggy Moreland

To Garrett Miller, timing was everything, both in business and in life.

And the timing on his trip to Austin, Texas, couldn't be more perfect.

His number one goal in making the trip was to reunite his stepmother with Ali Moran, the daughter she'd given up for adoption thirty years prior. If that failed, he intended to persuade—or coerce, if necessary—Ali to give him the missing portion of the deed she held, which would enable his stepmother and her new husband to fulfill the requirements to claim a ranch they had been given.

As fate would have it, he also needed to locate

property for an expansion he was planning for his company. Since Austin was quickly establishing itself as the Silicon Valley of the Southwest, it seemed the natural choice and gave him the perfect excuse to make the trip.

The kick was, he had to accomplish it all without anyone discovering he was in Austin.

Scowling, he punched in the code for the electronic gate of Vista Bed and Breakfast, given to his secretary when she booked his reservation. If he'd known success would make him so damn popular with the media, he would've remained a geek for the rest of his life and never started Future Concepts. Who would've thought the public would care about a businessman's every move?

Or that success would make him a target for some crazy who wanted him dead?

He shoved the disturbing thought from his mind as he drove through the open gates. As far as the rest of the world was concerned, he reminded himself, Garrett Miller was currently attending a technology seminar in Switzerland, a lie his public relations department had fed the media at his request. All Garrett had to do was keep his presence in Austin under wraps, and his stalker would follow the bait to Switzerland and hopefully fall right into the trap being set for him there.

Pulling up in front of the two-story home, he

parked the rental car he'd picked up at the airport, then leaned across the seat to peer up at the house. He studied the structure a long moment, thinking of the woman inside, as well as his chances of gaining her cooperation. He'd given himself a month to find a way to convince her to reunite with his stepmother, though he doubted it would take anywhere near that long. Everyone had a price—or a weakness. It was just a matter of discovering Ali's.

He smiled smugly as he climbed from the car. He didn't doubt for a minute he'd succeed. Knowledge was power and, thanks to the P.I. he'd hired and the research he'd done on his own, he knew all there was to know about Ali Moran.

And she knew virtually nothing about him.

MILLS & BOON
Desire 2-in-1

On sale 19th December 2008

The Texan's Contested Claim by *Peggy Moreland*

Garrett Miller was Texas's wealthiest, most eligible bachelor –
and he was about to uncover the past Ali kept hidden!

The Greek Tycoon's Secret Heir by *Katherine Garbera*

To carry out his father's dying wish, Christos must marry the woman
who betrayed him. But she has a secret more powerful even
than his passion for her…

❧

Vows and a Vengeful Groom by *Bronwyn Jameson*

When scandal overwhelms the opening of his latest diamond
boutique, Sydney's sexiest bachelor proposes that Kim Blackstone,
his lover, be by his side – as his wife!

Pride and a Pregnancy Secret by *Tessa Radley*

Ryan Blackstone is a confirmed bachelor, but Jessica wants to
be more than his secret mistress, especially now that she's
pregnant with his heir…

Series – Diamonds Down Under

❧

Shattered by the CEO by *Emilie Rose*

To fulfil his father's will, tycoon Rand Kincaid must convince his
former love to work for his company – but all she wants is
a second chance…

The Boss's Demand by *Jennifer Lewis*

Overcome by desire one night in the desert, this powerful oil baron
struggled to keep his distance from the woman he swore
he'd never touch…

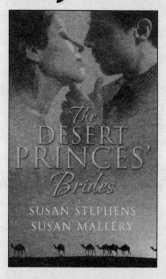

Newborn babies will bring three couples together

...in the most surprising circumstances!

Stranded with a gorgeous stranger…
Rescued by a rich man…
Snowed in with her billionaire boss…

Available 2nd January 2009

www.millsandboon.co.uk

FREE!

2 Books
and a surprise gift!

We would like to take this opportunity to thank you for reading this Mills & Boon® book by offering you the chance to take TWO more specially selected titles from the Desire™ series absolutely FREE! We're also making this offer to introduce you to the benefits of the Mills & Boon® Book Club™—

- ★ **FREE home delivery**
- ★ **FREE gifts and competitions**
- ★ **FREE monthly Newsletter**
- ★ **Exclusive Mills & Boon Book Club offers**
- ★ **Books available before they're in the shops**

Accepting these FREE books and gift places you under no obligation to buy, you may cancel at any time, even after receiving your free shipment. Simply complete your details below and return the entire page to the address below. You don't even need a stamp!

YES! Please send me 2 free Desire books and a surprise gift. I understand that unless you hear from me, I will receive 3 superb new titles every month for just £5.25 each, postage and packing free. I am under no obligation to purchase any books and may cancel my subscription at any time. The free books and gift will be mine to keep in any case.

D8ZEF

Ms/Mrs/Miss/Mr ....Initials ....

BLOCK CAPITALS PLEASE

Surname ....

Address ....

....

....Postcode ....

Send this whole page to:
UK: FREEPOST CN81, Croydon, CR9 3WZ